WHEN THE LIGHTS GO OUT

RUSSELL L. ESTES

Created with Vellum

CHAPTER 1

THE DECISION TO WIN

THE STADIUM LIGHTS SHINED THROUGH THE MISTING RAIN AS THE WIND picked up. It was cool in the October night, but the fans remained. Oak Creek High was undefeated, but for the first time all season, they found themselves trailing. Hampton High, their cross-county rivals, had come to town.

The home band echoed across the field; Oak Creek neared a score that would put them ahead! Like a heartbeat, drums kept rhythm with the intensity of the game. The sky looked like God had popped peepholes in it so He and the angels could watch the game, allowing the moon to peek through at times. Lights shined down upon the field as if all the lights on Broadway were centered on the two teams at that very moment. The field was wet and soggy, and after three and half quarters of football in the rain, it was more mud than grass.

"I can beat my man. He's cheating inside every play. Come on, Andy! Let me take him down the sideline," Mike said as he came back to the huddle after a play.

Mike Talley was a wide receiver for Oak Creek. He was a team captain and one of the stars of the squad. He was as energetic and vocal as they came, always pepping up his team.

Andy Higgins, the team's starting quarterback, reached inside his facemask and wiped the mixture of rain and sweat from his face. "Are you sure?" he replied, squinting at Mike.

"Dude! Just put the ball in the air. I'll go get it," Mike insisted.

"Coach said to keep it on the ground until he said otherwise," a lineman reminded them.

Andy glanced around the huddle and felt his lips pull into a thin line. He shook his head. "Split right, forty-five shift, orbit left. And Mike?! Don't make me get pulled. Toby, you stay in on this one and watch my blindside. That end has been kicking Dale's ass tonight. Keep him off me until I can get the pass off. On two. Let's do this!"

They broke the huddle and trudged up to the line of scrimmage.

The clock read 1:03 remaining in the game. Forty-seven yards separated Oak Creek from their destination. There was excitement and anticipation in the air as hundreds of fans stood and chanted for their teams, the noise growing louder and louder. Light beaming from the gigantic floodlights above was blinding. It shone down on the field, and the glare from the wet helmets made everything bright and dazzling.

The ball was snapped and Andy stepped back, looking for his intended target. Just as expected, the left defensive end came streaking toward Andy. Toby moved into his path, stood the rusher up, and drove him away, giving Andy just enough time to let Mike get open. Mike made a move inside, and his defender took the bait. He then cut back outside, and as he'd predicted, he beat his man.

Andy had already let the ball fly, and slow motion seemed to take over for everyone watching. The ball sailed down the field like a wingless plane, like a rocket searching for its destination, over the defender's head and right into Mike's outstretched arms, who caught it mid-stride and continued into the end zone for the score that put them ahead.

The crowd roared, and the band struck up the fight song! Players rushed to the end zone to meet Mike in a celebratory fashion. With only thirty-one seconds remaining in the game, Oak Creek had just taken the lead.

The offense came running off the field as the field goal unit took their place, anticipating the extra point that would extend their lead. Andy was almost to the sideline, still receiving high-fives and congratulatory pats on the helmet when Coach Woods stepped in front of him.

"What the hell was that, Higgins?" he barked, arms crossed over his wide chest and his brow raised.

Andy smiled enthusiastically. "That was a touchdown, Coach! We got this now!"

Coach Woods stood firm and stared directly into Andy's eyes. "I *said* to keep the ball on the ground."

Without saying anything else, Coach Woods turned and stomped away. Andy remained in place. His smile vanished as he bit his bottom lip, and he wondered why his coach was upset with him for possibly winning the game.

Coach Cecil Woods had been Oak Creek's head football coach for twenty-one years and had developed a program that demanded respect. In a town of roughly two thousand residents, Coach Woods might as well have been the mayor. His way of molding young men into great leaders wasn't held to the boundaries of the football field. He insisted his players volunteered in the community and made a difference in their town. In over two decades with him at the helm, they had only brought home one state championship, but he was a staple, and they loved him.

Toby walked up to Andy with a puzzled frown. "What was that about?"

"Guess Coach didn't like me changing the play. I'm sure I haven't heard the last of this," he said as he removed his helmet and stormed toward the bench.

"Great pass, Andy!" came a voice from the other side of the fence. It was Maribeth, Andy's on-and-off girlfriend of three years. It had recently been more off than on, but the two remained friends even in the "off" times.

Andy's smile reappeared, and he gave her a wink.

Oak Creek kicked off to give Hampton High one last chance at victory. Only six points separated the two teams. A touchdown followed by the extra point would steal the victory from Oak Creek. The kick was short, fielded by a returner at the twenty-five-yard line and returned to midfield, making it possible for a heroic pass to the end zone.

The clock showed 0:21—only twenty-one seconds to victory for one of the two opponents. A nervous tension fell over the entire stadium. Even the band laid down their horns and drumsticks and became fans, standing and watching anxiously.

On first down, Hampton High threw a short pass near the sideline. Their receiver turned upfield as a would-be tackler from Oak Creek slipped in the mud. The receiver tip-toed down the sideline a few more yards before his momentum caused him to lose balance; he fell out of bounds, stopping the clock at nine seconds. Hampton High was only thirty-one yards away from victory.

Coach Woods was screaming from the sideline. Defense looked to the sideline for instructions as Hampton High hurried to the line and snapped the ball, catching Oak Creek off guard. Another pass to a streaking player across the middle sailed just above his outstretched hands and through the back of the end zone. Had the pass been on target, it would have spelled defeat for Oak Creek. But instead, the clock stopped at 0:02.

The last play was coming up, the play that would send someone into celebratory mode while the other hung their heads and retreated into the locker room. The ball was snapped, and the quarterback rolled out to his right, giving his receivers just enough time to reach the distance to victory. He let the ball fly!

Everyone watched as silence fell on the stadium. The ball seemed to take twice as long as normal to reach its target. It was right on the mark as a Hampton High player leaped high into the air to bring it down. The velocity of the throw was too much, and the ball went straight through the hands of the receiver and fell harmlessly in the end zone as the clock read 0:00.

The Tigers had done it! Oak Creek remained undefeated!

THEIR FIGHT SONG HAD PLAYED, celebratory high-fives ended, and the team made their way into the locker room. Everyone was upbeat, and the atmosphere was as it should have been after winning a big game. The noise was nearly too loud to make out the jubilant conversations taking place just a few feet away.

Coach Woods sauntered into the locker room without saying a word, and the sounds grew fainter as each member of the team noticed his presence. He held a football—the game ball. It was a tradition that it went to a member that Coach Woods thought was a key factor in each game, even in the games they'd lost. His motto was, "We never really lose; we learn."

In the center of the room, holding the ball in the air above his head, he said, "Okay, boys. Who deserves this? Andy, you threw that winning pass. You want it?" Andy smiled but didn't respond before Coach Woods continued. "Mike, you caught it. Fine catch, too! Do you deserve it?"

Mike nervously glanced around the room. Players began anxiously shifting on the benches where they sat or fidgeting with their pads and helmets as they stood.

Coach turned and gawked at the other members of the squad. "Nobody wants this? We just won, and nobody wants the game ball? Well, that's hard to believe! Hell, last week we didn't make it out of the locker room before Toby announced to everyone on social media that he got it."

A tense chuckle from a few members of the team floated through the small space as someone threw a towel at Toby. Coach Woods plodded over to one side of the room and peered down at an underclassman.

"Caleb, who do you think deserves it?" Caleb Jones, a skinny tenth grader, shrugged. "You don't know? You don't think anyone here deserves this? Is that what you're saying?"

Caleb looked up at Coach Woods from the bench he sat on. "Yes, sir. I believe someone deserves it. I believe a few deserve it. I'm just not sure which one. Maybe Andy?"

"Andy? You want to give it to Andy?" Coach Woods walked a few feet away, back to one side of the room before stopping. He turned and focused on Caleb again. "Caleb, I think you deserve it," he declared as he pitched the ball to him.

Caleb caught the ball, and his eyes widened. "But...but, Coach, I didn't even—"

"Didn't what?" he interrupted. "Didn't even play a down?"

Caleb sheepishly replied, "Yes, sir. I didn't go in at all. I don't think I deserve it."

Coach Woods turned his back to Caleb and returned to the center of the room. "You're right, Caleb. You didn't. Know what else you didn't do, son? You didn't become selfish. You did everything I asked you to do tonight and nothing more."

Andy lowered his head and whispered to Mike, who was sitting beside him, "I know where this is going."

Coach spun on his heel and rushed to tower over Andy, roaring, "Son, is there something you need to add? You want that ball?" He turned toward Caleb again. "Caleb, bring that ball to Andy. I think he said he deserves it more than you do."

Wide-eyed, Andy said, "No, sir. I didn't say that!"

"Well, what *did* you say, son?" Coach asked.

Andy glanced up at Coach Woods from under an embarrassed frown but said nothing.

Returning to the center of the locker room once again, Coach Woods looked around at everyone and continued. "Caleb is a tenth-grader. This is his first year as a Tiger. Y'all have pushed him around at practice, laughed at him, and drove him into the dirt on almost every play. But he keeps coming back. He knows he has some good players in front of him, knows he most likely won't see playing time. But all night, wherever I went, he was no more than five feet away from me—his helmet on, ready! Hell, I don't think he ever spit out his mouthpiece. He was ready to do whatever I told him, whenever I told him. *That's* what makes a good team player. Being ready!"

Coach started pacing, glaring at everyone. It was silent, except for the sound of Coach's rough breathing from getting worked up. "Andy is out there calling his own plays. Guess y'all don't need Coach Smith anymore, huh? After you shower, go tell him you're relieving him of his duties." The players hung their heads as Coach continued around the room.

"Mike, was that your call? Toby? Jake? Anyone else? Did that play just fall out of the damn sky? I know I didn't call it. Last I heard was to keep running the ball. Y'all don't think I hadn't seen Mike beat his man all night? I knew that if we kept running the ball, the cornerback would get comfortable out there, and we could hit that pass whenever we wanted. Hell, Mike can beat half the cornerbacks that play down at the college. I knew we had that play in our pocket! I wasn't giving them another opportunity. I was running the clock, waiting for the right time. Those extra few seconds we gave them almost cost us the game."

He pointed to a quote on a dry erase board mounted on the wall where his pacing feet had brought him.

DON'T TRY TO BE THE BEST ON THE TEAM,
TRY TO BE THE BEST FOR THE TEAM.

Coach read it aloud, and then slammed the palm of his hand against it, knocking one side off the wall.

Suddenly, he turned and shouted at the team, "Hotshots!" and took a few steps. "Superstars!" he screamed and continued pacing. "VIPs!" He pointed at the board again, hanging slanted on the wall. "We got a few that want to be the best *on* the team, but not *for* the team!"

Coach Woods grabbed a folding chair from a corner and dragged it to the center of the room, the metal screeching loudly throughout the still concrete room. He sat on it and took a few seconds to let his words sink in before he went on.

Lowering his voice and speaking more calmly, he said, "Guys, I'm proud of the win, but I'd give it back if I could. I'd much rather build teamwork than a trophy case. You guys worked your asses off tonight.

It didn't go unnoticed. But we need to all agree right now—before we leave this room—that we are a team, I am the coach, and we will do as I say. *All* of us. We have something special here. You guys are talented. And I don't think I've ever had boys work as hard as y'all. Now, I want it to be understood that I call the plays. Is that clear?"

A rumbling sound of acknowledgment echoed in the room. Coach sat silently for a moment, looking at everyone. He took off his cap and rubbed his head, letting a deep sigh escape him.

"Okay, I'm glad to hear that. What we talked about tonight doesn't need to go anywhere. As far as anyone outside this room is concerned, Coach Smith called that play, and I was okay with it. Caleb, son, you're the player of the game. Anyone object to that?"

Another round of approval rebounded through the room. Coach Woods stood and walked toward the door, then stopped and turned.

"One more thing. Come Monday, we have no starters. Everyone will earn their spot again. Caleb, next week you're getting your uniform dirty. I'm starting you on special teams. Be ready, son. I expect nothing less from you than what I do a senior."

A few minutes later, the team emerged from the locker room and walked out to the parking lot where friends and family waited. Pictures were taken, and talks of where everyone was headed to celebrate were discussed. Many former players were there. Some business owners and even elected town officials had waited for the team. The whole town, the entire community, was proud of the team's success.

Like every year, football season was important to them. The sport was more than a game. It was one of the things that hundreds of other small towns across the south listed on their city limits welcoming signs, and they were found all over: *Braxton High, 1A State Champs 1988 ... Spring Hill, 1A State Champs 1991 ... Bankhead High, 2A State Champs 2005.*

Little towns put up signs proclaiming their victories faster than they did stop signs fallen victim to errant drivers. It was bragging rights; something they were a part of, their dads had been a part of, and their granddads, and on down the line. Most communities weren't any more than a dot on a map. Some had names that others snickered at, like Cow Pen and Tickle Hill, but nonetheless, they were called by their mascots: Tigers, Bears, Raiders, and so many others that were printed across jerseys proudly worn by the girlfriends of every map-dot school football player.

Oak Creek was proud. It was one of those small towns that seemed to have gotten lost in time. The way the town was now was the way it was twenty years ago, and folks that called it home wouldn't have it any other way.

Back in the forties and fifties, their claim to fame had been the rich coal deposits that came from the area. Some boasted that it was the richest coal in the South. But after the mining company stripped all the black gold they could from the large vein, they moved out and took the vast amount of revenue the town relied on with them. But that didn't break the spirit of the community. Instead, they found new things to be proud of. For instance, Jud Franklin.

Jud fought in Vietnam and was the most decorated soldier in the state in 1972. Rumor had it that he single-handedly carried nine wounded soldiers, one at a time, almost three miles to safety. Jud was awarded a bronze star and a presidential award when he returned to the states, along with enough other awards to give him back issues when he wore them all.

He eventually retired from the military and settled down just outside of Oak Creek, where he remained until he succumbed to a self-inflicted accidental gunshot while hunting. Many speculated that it was no accident; Jud battled horrible memories of Vietnam and woke at night with trembles, recalling what he had seen while serving. He was alive when they found him, and he stood by the claim that he'd tripped. But Jud was an infantryman, trained in gun safety, and there was no way he would have been walking with the safety off.

The town recognized him with a full military memorial service, and a plaque was placed in City Hall. The state also had his name, along with other war heroes, engraved on a statue at the capitol building.

Other prideful subjects within Oak Creek's radius were Harold Jenkins's hot sauce, and Craig Lipton, who played two seasons with the Dallas Cowboys before getting cut and taking an assistant coaching position at a small college in Texas. Lipton seemed to have forgotten his roots and hadn't returned to Oak Creek for several years, not even during the successful state playoff runs, but Harold's success in the sauce business hadn't changed him. He still lived in the same little wood-framed house he grew up in.

Harold's hot sauce started as a side business until he won a contest at the Natchez Trace BBQ Festival, one of the state's most prestigious events for such. From there, he took it to a bottler, who mass-produced it and sold it as Harold's Southern Heat Sauce. It was sold in stores everywhere.

In Oak Creek, folks still referred to it as "Harold's hot sauce," and when someone asked for it by that name, local store and restaurant owners knew exactly what they wanted. It was said that one drop would make a person sit up straight, but two drops put them on their knees. For kids, the bottle became the source of many dares and even more drinks from a water hose.

That, in a nutshell, was Oak Creek—a prideful little town that would much rather keep it that way than let the worries of the big city infiltrate their way of life. They were proud of everything the town had to offer, from the summer festival to the award-winning vegetables grown in the rich soil of an old mining community.

And then, of course, there was football.

Football shut down the town on Friday nights. Folks joked that if someone wanted to rob the town, they'd best do it on a Friday night in the fall when everyone was at the stadium. There wasn't much exaggeration to that claim, as everyone knew somebody on the team and most likely cheered for them as if they were one of their own kids. To be an Oak Creek Tiger meant having something meaningful —something that would never leave.

And like many other map-dot schools across the state, come fall, it was the most important thing in town.

CHAPTER 2

SEARCHING FOR ANDY

THE SATURDAY AFTER A GAME WAS SPENT DIFFERENTLY FOR MANY OF the guys on the team.

For some, it meant hunting with their old man, and just another workday for others. Some found themselves getting ready for a full day of watching college football on TV while fitting in a few games of backyard football between college games. The contrast between teammates' schedules was often the result of their parents' schedules, but for a few, like Toby, it was the result of his job at the lumberyard. However, Toby Chandler had little choice in his decision.

His dad, Eric, was a mechanic at the county bus shop. It didn't pay much, but the county school system had decent insurance and that was more important in helping take care of his youngest son, Alec, who had Down syndrome. With his dad doing all he could to help keep the family afloat, if Toby wanted to keep gas in his car and have a little spending money, Dodson's Sawmill was his only answer.

Toby stepped onto the front porch of their modest three-bedroom house. Ferns hung from the hooks his mom, Julia, had placed along the edges of the porch ceiling. He leaped, clearing the last two steps, as he made his way toward his car parked on the side of the street.

"Hey, Toby! Going to the Tiger Den to grab some breakfast.

Wanna come?" Andy yelled from his pickup window as he stopped in the street next to Toby's house.

Toby pitched a jacket into the backseat of his car. He turned and walked over to Andy's truck, leaning over and resting his arms on the window sill. "Dude, I'd love to, but I'm late getting down to the sawmill. Mr. Dodson is already on me because I broke the belt on the conveyor last week. Cost us two hours' downtime."

Andy chuckled. "Man, get real. Ol' man Dodson loves you. He's at every game cheering for you. Come on, let's grab a bite. It won't take long."

"Raincheck, man," Toby said as he straightened his posture, taking his weight off the truck door. "I gotta run. I'll give you a call after work and see what you're doing. May swing by for a few minutes on the way home."

"That reminds me. Party at Nick's tonight. His folks are out of town for the weekend. Want me to pick you up?"

Toby sat in his car and tried starting the engine. "Don't know, man. I told Alec I would go night fishing with him."

"Dude! Your little bro will be there any day. Nick's parents won't be gone again any time soon."

Toby pumped the gas on his 1980 Camaro, which was still rejecting his attempts at turning the engine over.

"Come on!" he huffed, banging the steering wheel with his open hands. He pumped the gas again as he turned the ignition. Finally, the engine came to life and puffed out a large plume of smoke, as if a dragon had just roared. He glanced over at Andy. "We'll see. I gotta run before this scrap metal of a car decides it doesn't want to go."

Toby pulled away from the curb and eased down the street, his thoughts on his brother.

Alec was in the special needs program at Oak Creek. He was two years younger than Toby and his biggest fan. He was also the Oak Creek Tigers' biggest fan. Alec paced the sidelines at every game as an honorary team manager.

Although Down syndrome slowed him down some things, his knowledge of football wasn't one of them. He could tell anyone what every player was supposed to do on each play, and he was quick to call out players that failed to execute their assignment correctly. More importantly, Toby was Alec's biggest fan. They shared an amazing bond.

Only a few miles down the road and just outside the city limits, Toby pulled into a dirt parking lot and jumped from his car, the dust around him still settling.

"Well, at least I know what to get you for your next birthday. An alarm clock," teased Frank, one of the labor hands at the sawmill.

"Sorry, Mr. Chapman," Toby said, hurrying through the lumberyard. "Rough morning."

Frank climbed inside the cab of a forklift. Shifting in his seat, he yelled down at Toby, "I bet. 'Bout got y'all's tails handed to ya last night. Good game, though. Y'all boys may take it all this year."

"Thanks, Mr. Chapman," Toby replied as he continued toward the spot he was supposed to have been an hour earlier.

"There he is!" Toby heard as he arrived at the debarker machine. He rounded the machine to find Tom Dodson, the owner.

"Sorry, Mr. Dodson. I couldn't get going this morning."

Mr. Dodson shut down the machine, pulling his leather gloves off and placing them on the control box. "Just glad you're here, son. I got Henry catching on the other end. Run this end for a while, and then swap out with him. He's got a hell of a hangover."

"Yes, sir," Toby replied while slipping on his gloves.

The hours passed quickly, but Toby's mind wandered all day. The radio had been playing the Alabama versus Tennessee game, and he imagined what it would be like to play in front of thousands of people. Football was as much of a part of his life as anything.

Being an older brother, he knew his role in Alec's life was a busy one. But he didn't complain. He enjoyed the time they spent together. Alec had already outlived what doctors expected, and Toby felt every moment together was a gift. But football was his escape. Not from Alec, but the world.

He often felt as if he carried a tremendous weight on his shoulders. Toby grew up quickly. When Alec came along, all the attention went to him, leaving Toby to fend for himself many days. He had seen the stress his parents endured, witnessed them weep many nights, holding each other.

The life of a low-income family with a special needs child carried many burdens. But when he strapped on that helmet, everything went away. He put all his efforts into what he was supposed to be doing at that moment. Toby sometimes got lost in his mind as he found himself battling long after the play ended. Stress seemed to leave his body with every bead of sweat that dripped from it.

"Toby! Toby!" someone shouted from the other end of the machine.

He quickly jerked, blinking his eyes, as if snapping out of a delusional state.

"Toby!" Henry shouted again. "Boy, are you going deaf? The buzzer sounded two logs ago. Shift's over!"

"Sorry, Henry," Toby said as he shut off the machine. "A lot on my mind, I guess."

He walked by a pile of logs, grabbing the flannel shirt he'd shed earlier in the day as the heat became more intense. Walking to his car, he pulled his cell phone from his pocket. He opened a text message from his girlfriend, Ruby:

Hey babe. Call me when you get off work. Love you MORE!

A smile spread across his face just as another message popped up from Andy. He opened it before calling Ruby.

Call me when you can. Want to see if you'll ride with me to the county line. Picking up beer for Nick's party.

Brigdon County was a dry county, which meant no alcohol sales, but the neighboring Gallatin County wasn't, and if a booze-thirsty teen caught the right person at the County Line Store, they didn't get their ID checked.

Toby put the call returns in order of importance and dialed Ruby's number first. After only one ring, she picked up.

"Hey, baby. How was work?"

Smiling, Toby spoke back, holding his phone between his

shoulder and ear as he fought to pull his car keys from his pocket. "Woulda been better if you were here."

"Aww," Ruby gushed. "I love you, baby. Hey, I know you and Alec are spending time together tonight. I thought about stopping by and seeing you before y'all leave if that's okay?"

Ruby knew how close the bond between Toby and Alec was and never tried to infringe on their time. Toby's compassion for Alec was one thing that drew Ruby to him, to begin with. She enjoyed watching from afar how their love was shown.

"Sure, baby," he replied. "Was gonna ask if you wanted to have dinner with us at the house before we go fishing, anyway."

Suddenly, his phone beeped, signaling an incoming call. As he sat in his seat, he pulled the phone from his ear to see who was calling. He rolled his eyes and let out a sigh, one loud enough for Ruby to hear on the other end.

"What is it, Toby?" she asked.

"It's just Andy calling. I'll call him back in a few," he continued as he started his car. "He's wanting me to go to a party at Nick's tonight."

"Oh, yeah. Kinsley said something to me about that, too."

"Go if you want, baby. No telling how long Alec will keep me out tonight. I promise; it's no big deal."

Toby could hear Ruby breathing, almost huffing, as if thinking about her answer.

"I may, but I'm not sure yet. If I do, I'll let you know, and if you and Alec get home early, maybe you can come by."

"Sure, hun. Hey, let me call Andy back; he's calling me again. I'll see you at the house. Around five okay with you?"

"Perfect," she replied. "Love you."

"Love you more," Toby responded as he hit the "end call" button.

Toby started dialing Andy's number, but Andy beat him to it, calling again before Toby could hit "send."

Toby answered, his irritation apparent. "Dude! Give me a freaking minute. I was trying to call you back."

"My man! No worries," Andy said with a chuckle. "Hey, I'm headed to the county line. Wanna ride? Leaving now, though."

Toby sighed. "Can't, bro. I'm taking Alec fishing, remember? I already had to break off one trip with him because of the ACTs last weekend. Not doing it again."

"Come on, dude," Andy whined. "This party is gonna be off the chain!"

"No chance. Besides, man, how many times have I told you that nothing good comes back from that store? That junk is just trouble in a can. You need to leave it there. Holler at me tomorrow, though. May go shoot pool after church."

Andy huffed with disappointment. "All right. But, if you change your mind, you've got my number."

Toby ended the call and drove out of the sawmill parking lot. He thought about the party and many others like it he'd missed. It crossed his mind to make the fishing trip short and head to the party anyway, but he knew Alec loved nighttime adventures with him and had been planning for it all day.

As soon as he got home, Alec would greet him—dressed as if he were going on a weeklong hiking trip—and ask when they were leaving. Toby knew his thoughts of cutting the trip short meant cutting into his brother's enjoyment. His love for Alec helped make the decision an easy one. They would stay out all night if it's what Alec wanted.

A few hours later, the fishing trip became reality. Ruby, who joined them for dinner, was making their goodbye last a little longer. She playfully kept Toby from loading the lights and fishing gear into the trunk of his car. Alec ran to her, grabbing her with one of his trademark bearhugs.

"I love you, Ruby Sue! I'm gonna catch the biggest fish and bring it back for you to see."

"Aww, Alec!" She blushed, returning the hug and gently rocking as they embraced. "I could just hug you to pieces. I can't wait to see your big fish."

"Hey, Alec! Get your own girl. You always try to steal mine," Toby exclaimed, smiling at Alec and placing his hand on his ball cap, gently shaking his head. Alec returned the grin with his bigger-than-life smile.

After a few more minutes, they were off and on their way. The weather was perfect for the outing. The rain that came the day before was gone, and warmer air had moved into the area. They couldn't have planned for a better adventure.

Five hours into the trip, everything was going as planned. Toby spent most of the time either baiting Alec's hook or untangling his line from trees. For anyone else, it might not have sounded like a good time, but Toby didn't mind. He saw the joy that every catch brought to Alec. He thought Alec would be ready to get home, but the success of the trip kept his interest up.

Toby had just reeled in his tenth sun perch, a small but feisty fish that loved the big nightcrawlers they were using. Toby placed the fish on his stringer and baited the hook when he saw his phone light up. It was Ruby.

"Hey, babe. What's up?" he answered.

"Is that Ruby Sue? Tell her about my fishes," Alec yelled.

"Have you heard from Andy?" she replied frantically. "He was supposed to be back hours ago, but he's not. He's not answering his phone either."

Toby stood and paced a few steps away from the water's edge. "No, and I haven't talked to him since after work today. He wanted me to ride to the county line with him to get beer."

"Yeah, he went alone. I came over to Nick's with Katelyn for a little while, and he never made it here. We're worried something happened. He was supposed to be back by seven. That was like four hours ago. It's not like him not to call or anything."

"Let me try to call him. Call you right back."

"Did you tell her?" Alec yelled.

He scrolled through his recent calls to find Andy's number, telling Alec, "Yeah, she's excited, buddy."

Toby tried his number, waiting for Andy to pick up.

"Hey, this is Andy. I'm probably being awesome somewhere and can't answer the phone. I'll put you on the list and hit ya later."

Dang. Voicemail, Andy thought to himself.

He dialed Ruby, and she answered on the first ring. "Did you get him?"

"No. Straight to voicemail. Has anyone called his parents?"

Ruby seemed more frantic, a slight quiver in her voice. "No. We didn't want to get him in trouble if he's just goofing off somewhere, but now—Toby, what do we do? Call them?"

Toby began gathering their gear. "Hang tight. I'll be there in a few."

Alec stood as Toby grabbed his rod and started reeling it in. Confused, he shouted, "Hey, I was getting a bite! What are you doing? I'm not done fishing."

Toby picked up the battery-powered lantern and looked over at his brother. "Sorry, Alec. Andy is missing, and I've gotta help find him. But, hey, man. Look at all these fish!" He pulled the stringer out of the water and held it up to be illuminated by the moonlight and lantern's glow. "Dude, you killed it tonight. Straight up master fisherman!"

Alec smiled, but his eyes quickly narrowed and he tilted his head. "Toby, where's Andy?"

Toby returned the worried look and moved to pack their gear in his car. "I don't know, buddy. I don't know. But I'm going to look for him."

"I wanna go, too," Alec replied as he hurried his steps to catch up to Toby.

Throwing stuff in the car, he turned to Alec. "I'm gonna take you home. It may be a long night—"

Alec plopped down on the ground and crossed his legs. "No! I wanna go find Andy!"

Toby sighed, tightened his lips, and raised his brow. "Come on, buddy. We don't have time for this."

Narrowing his eyes, Alec said, "I wanna go find Andy, too. Andy is my friend!"

Toby knew how things would go. Alec was stubborn enough to sit in one spot until he got his way. Without much of a choice, he gave in to his brother's pleas with a sigh.

"Okay, okay! Get in the car."

Toby sped to Nick Adam's house, where several of their friends were gathered. He jumped from the car, instructing Alec to stay in the vehicle. Ruby met him halfway, and the look on her face told him that they still hadn't heard from Andy.

He also knew that Andy sometimes went rogue, prone to venture off without letting others know. They had once planned a trip to go hunting, but Andy ran into an old friend from his junior high days and spent the day running back roads with him, leaving Toby wondering where he was. He reminded Ruby it was probably another one of those cases. Nonetheless, he was still worried Andy wasn't answering his phone.

Toby had to think about the situation. He knew he should call Andy's parents, but what would he tell them? That Andy went to get beer and hadn't come back? If he told them he hadn't shown up without telling them where he had been, they'd still ask if he knew where he was supposed to be so they could look for him. Either way, it didn't look good.

He grabbed Ruby's hand. "Okay, come on. We're going to look for him. I know the roads he takes when he goes to the county line— always the back roads."

Ruby stopped and suggested, "Let's take my car. Dad just filled it up." She knew Toby's car wasn't reliable, and taking that trip was "iffy" at best. She added, "But what if he went a different way? Being by himself and all. Would he have stayed on the highway?"

Toby nodded. "We can take yours, but I've got Alec with me. I guess we can go the backroads there and if we don't find him, we can come back on the highway."

Billy Wright, a member of the football team, was standing nearby and overheard the conversation. "I can go, too. Me and Doug will take the highway to the county line while y'all go the backroads. We'll meet at the store."

"Sounds good. Call if you see him or hear anything." Toby glanced at the others gathered outside. "If he shows up, call us."

He and Ruby hurried toward her car and he called out, "Alec, come on, bro. We're gonna ride with Ruby."

Alec jumped out, excited to ride in Ruby's car. "I love Ruby Sue's car. It goes fast. Hey! Did Toby tell you about all my fish?"

Toby stopped in his tracks, reminded of the fish that Alec just had to bring home. "Crap! Those fish are gonna stink up the car. Let me grab the bucket and at least set them outside."

He hurried and was back in Ruby's car in no time. As they pulled out of Nick's driveway, Alec busied himself by telling Ruby about his catch. He was excited and going nonstop, hardly pausing to take a breath. Toby was trying to tell Ruby which roads to take, but Alec kept getting louder and louder.

"Alec! Stop for one minute," Toby snapped.

Alec gasped, leaned back, and sank into his seat. Ruby glared at Toby, her lips pouted and her brow raised. Andy sensed her shooting daggers at him with her eyes and knew he deserved them. He turned to her, sighing, and then turned to look over the seat at Alec, whose eyes had tears in them.

"Hey, buddy. I didn't mean to yell at you. I'm just worried about Andy. I know it's not an excuse, but I'm so sorry, buddy. Forgive me?"

Alec peeked up, wiping a tear from his eye. "Yeah, I forgive you." Toby smiled as Alec nervously asked, "Toby, can I talk again?"

"Sure, buddy. Tell Ruby Sue all about your fish."

Still pressed down into his seat, he sniffled. "Not that. I just wanted to say that you don't hafta ask me to forgive you."

"I know, buddy, but I feel like I need to."

Alec wiped another tear. "Toby, you don't, though. I forgave you before you asked me to. I love you. You're my brother."

Ruby glanced over at Toby as she swallowed hard, fighting back her tears. Toby felt his eyes start to well up. Suddenly Alec sat up, his eyes wide with concern.

"Is Andy okay, Toby?"

Toby sniffled and turned again to stare out of the window, searching for signs of Andy's car. "I hope so, buddy. I hope so."

———

AFTER SEVERAL TURNS and long straightaways, Ruby came to a stop at an intersection that brought them out to the main highway.

"What now?" she asked.

Toby sighed and took off his cap. "Take a left. The County Line Store is just a mile or so that way. Billy's probably already there."

She turned onto the main road and continued until they arrived at the store. As expected, they spotted Billy's truck. They parked and exited.

Alec spotted Billy and took off toward him. "Billy! Hey, friend!" He gave Billy a hug, which was returned. He turned and looked at Ruby. "Ruby Sue, me and Billy are bros! Ain't that right, Billy? Best buds!"

Billy grinned. "We sure are, A-man. You're the man!"

Doug Mann, another member of the team, smiled. "What about me, dude? Thought I was your bro?"

Alec stepped to him and offered the same hug. "You are, Dougie-Doo. I got a lot of bros!"

Toby gave Billy a hand-clasped greeting and half-hug. "I'm guessing you got the same results we did?"

Billy shook his head. "Nothing."

Ruby let out a nervous sigh. "Guys, I know you don't want to, but we have to call his parents. What if he's hurt somewhere?"

Billy looked at Toby while wiping his face, stopping his hand on his chin. "She's right. You wanna call?"

Toby took a deep breath. "Not really, but I will."

Ruby put her arm around him. "You got their number, babe?"

"Yeah, I got Mr. Higgins's cell number," he said as he took his phone out and scrolled through numbers until he found the one he was looking for. He hit "send" and placed the phone to his ear. After a few rings, Andy's dad, Kyle, answered.

"Umm, Mr. Higgins—umm, this is Toby. Toby Chandler. Sorry to call so late, but I was wondering if Andy was there?" He paused to listen to Andy's father on the other end. "Oh, okay. Yes. Okay. Yes, sir. I am."

Ruby anxiously watched with the others, wondering what was being said on the other end of the conversation.

"I understand. Okay. Sorry to bother," Toby continued. He paced a few steps away, holding his hand up as Ruby followed. "Yes, sir. You, too."

Finally, Toby ended the call and turned to the others.

"Well?" Ruby asked.

Toby shook his head and took several deep breaths. They could tell something was wrong by his blank stare, but Toby seemed to be lost for words.

Billy took a few steps toward Toby. "Bro! Is he okay?"

Toby looked up, his eyes wide and the color drained from his face. "He—he's in jail!"

"What?!" Ruby and Billy responded.

Alec related jail to things he saw on TV shows, and his rational thinking always seemed to go back to the last show he watched.

"What did Andy do? Rob a bank?" he asked.

Toby placed his arm around Alec's shoulders. "No, bro. He was in a wreck, and he—"

"Is he okay?!" Ruby loudly interrupted, her breathing also heavy.

"Yeah, he's fine, but the girl he hit, she's not. She may not make it," he continued.

Doug stepped over and placed his hand on Toby's shoulder. "Bro, why is he in jail?"

Toby shook his head, letting out a sigh. "He was drinking, and—"

Billy snatched his cap off his head and slammed it against the ground. "Damn it, Andy!" He stomped off without picking it up. "Shit!" he screamed. Finally, he turned back toward them, and said, "Dude, if that girl dies—"

Toby cut him off. "She won't! You gotta believe that. We aren't gonna think about that! We're gonna pray it away, and—"

Crying, Alec grabbed Toby and hugged him. "If she forgives him, will he get out of jail?"

Toby returned the hug. "I wish, little bro. I wish."

Ruby stepped away and leaned against her car, sobbing. Toby noticed and walked over to her, putting his arms around her. She screamed, "Why the hell did he do that!? He knew better! He *knew* better!"

She sank her head into Toby's chest, sobbing uncontrollably. He held her but didn't have any words to comfort her.

Doug picked up Billy's cap. "Come on, guys. Let's go home. Nothing we can do about it here."

WORD SPREAD LIKE WILDFIRE, and by the next morning, Andy's wreck was the talk across social media and text messages.

Churches all over town sent up prayers for the young girl involved, and everyone learned that another girl was also in the car. She was checked and released from the hospital, but the driver wasn't so lucky. The young lady, Lacy, took the brunt of the impact when Andy swerved into her lane. She remained in critical condition in the I.C.U. unit with multiple injuries. Both girls were high school students from the neighboring county.

Lacy was seventeen and in her senior year. She recently signed a scholarship offer to play softball at Coastal Community College, but all that seemed irrelevant. With her head injuries, brain swelling, broken bones, and several internal injuries, the fight had moved from the ball field to the hospital. Points scored weren't as important as breaths taken.

Andy was being held for twenty-four hours in the county jail for his mandatory D.U.I. charge before bail would be determined. He was also hit with another charge—causing bodily harm, the results of a felony D.U.I. If Lacy didn't survive the accident, the charge could be changed to manslaughter or murder, and he would be arrested for those charges as well. So much hung on the next few hours as Andy sat in his cell and thought about his decision to drink and drive.

Finally, his father, Kyle, was able to see him. He was led by an officer to a dark room where Andy was waiting, sitting at a table in a cold, dingy interrogation room. Kyle entered, and Andy sprang to his feet, grabbing his dad as an emotional tidal wave was released from him.

"I'm so sorry, Dad," he sobbed uncontrollably. "Dad, please forgive me. I'm sorry."

The officer grabbed a chair from nearby and slid it over to Kyle. "I'll be outside. Take as long as you need."

"Thank you, officer," Kyle replied as the officer exited. He looked at Andy, who was disheveled and bruised, but otherwise okay. "Son, what happened? They said you were drinking. And—"

"It was an accident, Dad! I didn't mean to. Are they okay? Are those girls okay?"

Kyle pulled the other chair around the table so they weren't separated. "Andy, son, sit down. We need to talk."

"No! Dad! No," he cried. "Please tell me they're alive. Please, Dad!"

Kyle sat in one chair and directed Andy to sit in the other. They faced one another, only a few feet apart. "Son, were you drinking? I need to know the truth. I've already seen the breathalyzer report, but I need to hear it from you."

Andy peered up at his dad as tears streamed down his face. "Yes, Dad, but I—"

"Damn it, Andy!" Kyle jumped up and clasped his hands behind his head as he stomped away from Andy. "What the hell were you thinking?"

"Dad, I'm sorry," Andy continued through sobs.

"Tell me what happened," Kyle said as he sat again.

"Dad, this ain't me. I don't do this all the time," Andy cried as he looked for support from his dad.

None came. Kyle sat in silence, waiting for his son to continue. He leaned forward, looking into Andy's eyes.

"What happened?"

Andy sat up straight and took a deep breath. "I went to the store to buy beer for Nick's party, and I was—"

"How the hell did you get it? Fake ID? Know somebody there? You're seventeen years old. Hell, you ain't even old enough to vote, let alone buy alcohol. They just sell it to you like that?"

Andy whispered, "Yeah, sometimes."

Kyle slammed his hands on his knees. "Jesus freaking Christ! What the hell do we even have laws for? Keep going. You bought the beer, then what?"

Andy continued. "I left the store and was driving back. I bought this new drink, watermelon flavor. It was moonshine, but the store kind. I decided I wanted to try it, so I opened it in the truck before I left and took a swig. I left the lid off and put it in my cup holder. I knew nobody would be at the party yet, so I drove around for a while. Before I knew it, I'd drunk over half. But, Dad, you could hardly taste the alcohol in it. It was—"

Kyle interrupted. "Could hardly taste it, huh? So, you've drunk enough before to know what it should taste like?"

Andy nervously got louder. "No, Dad. I mean that it was good, and, well, it didn't taste much different than a fruit drink, like a Gatorade or something."

Kyle crossed his arms. "Go on. I'm listening."

Andy leaned back, resting his elbows on his knees. "Well, I was on the backroads heading back, on, what is it? County Road 54, I think. I drank a lot. But, Dad, I felt fine. Like, it had no effect on me. But I wanted a drink of water, and I had a water bottle in the backseat. I reached back there and turned really quick; just a second, Dad, that's all. When I turned around, they were there! I couldn't get back in my lane in time. Dad, I saw her face when I hit them! She was so scared, Dad. She was so scared!" Andy began weeping again.

Kyle sat up and let out a deep breath. "Well, son, I guess we need to start praying hard for that girl."

Andy straightened quickly. "Is she alive, Dad? Did she make it? The cop told me when they were handcuffing me that she was barely hanging on. Dad, is she alive?"

Kyle nodded. "For now, but she's pretty banged up, son. The other girl has some bumps and bruises, but she's going to be fine. The driver wasn't so lucky. She is in the I.C.U. down at Memorial Hospital. Son, if she doesn't make it, they'll go after you as an adult."

"What do we do, Dad?" Andy asked.

Kyle stared at his son, tears in his eyes as well. "Like I said, we pray."

CHAPTER 3

I QUIT

THE MOOD AT SCHOOL ON MONDAY MORNING WAS SOMBER. OF COURSE, the talk was all about Andy and his arrest. The topic was the same regardless of the student group.

Toby walked into the school from the senior parking lot. Ruby was with him. They heard many of the conversations, and it seemed like everyone had added their twist to them.

"I heard he was going over a hundred miles per hour," one girl stated.

"Did you hear that he had drunk half a case of beer?" another asked.

Toby was nearing a group of teammates he normally hung out with. He stalled nearby and listened.

Ruby looked up at him. "What is it, baby?"

Toby shook his head and didn't say anything, but kept listening.

"Man, I can't believe it," Scott Stiles, a junior player, said. "But he had it coming. He drinks every weekend. Almost hit me a few weeks ago. He's gonna stop now, especially behind those cage doors."

Toby had heard enough. He dropped his backpack and busted into the middle of the small group and shoved Scott against the lockers. "Screw you, Stiles! If he had a problem, why didn't you try to help him, huh?" Toby shouted, turning toward the rest of the group. "What about you, Junkin? I heard you chipped in for him to pick that shit up! Wouldn't go with him though, would ya?"

Reese Junkin, a senior lineman for the team, responded. "Well, I had to—"

"Had to what? Had to make sure if anyone got in trouble, it wasn't you?" Toby turned and gazed at another member of the team. "Jason, didn't you ask him to pick up some Wild Turkey for you? Was that before or after you studied the Sunday School lesson you went over yesterday at church?"

Jason didn't respond; instead, he stared at his feet and shook his head. Toby walked a few steps away, picked up his backpack, and slung one strap over his shoulder.

"You guys make me freaking sick."

Ruby grabbed Toby by the arm. "Come on, baby. It's not their fault. Let it go."

"Let it go? We're supposed to just let it go, is that right?" Toby countered, his voice growing loud again. "We go out there on that field every Friday night. Hell, this whole town shuts down to watch us play. And we tell each other we're brothers! Y'all are standing here talking about Andy having a drinking problem, and not one of you did a damn thing about it. Instead, you sent him with a wad of cash, by himself, to the liquor store. By *himself*!" He stopped, glaring at all of them. "Brothers! You know what? I don't need brothers like this. I'm done. I quit!"

Before anyone could say anything, he spun away from the group and stormed off. Shocked, Ruby chased after him.

"Toby, don't do this," she pleaded.

"Go ahead and quit, Chandler! Quit when we need you. That's okay. You ain't worth it anyway," Blake Barnes shouted, stopping Toby in his tracks. He was a senior and had a reputation for starting trouble. He bragged about the personal fouls and unsportsmanlike penalties he got in games. Trouble seemed to find Blake pretty easily.

Toby turned, dropping his backpack again. "Got something you want to say, Barnes?" he shouted as he stomped back toward him.

Blake stepped toward Toby. "What did you do to help him, church boy? Huh? You're sitting here screaming at us, but I haven't seen you take the bottle out of his hand."

Toby stopped only inches away from Blake. He was shorter than Blake, but that didn't keep him from looking him in the eyes. "Because I don't go around telling his troubles. But if you want to know, yes! Yes, I have tried to stop him. I actually talked to him right before he left and told him he didn't need that crap. So, yeah, I did what I could, and it wasn't enough. Now some girl is clinging to life because it wasn't enough."

Blake moved even closer, taking up almost all the space between them. "But you let him go, didn't you? I heard he asked you to ride with him and you turned him down. Went fishing with your little Special Olympics brother, huh?"

Blake made a gesture with his hands and arms, insinuating an offensive disability. Toby lowered his shoulder and grabbed Blake around the waist, as if making a tackle, and drove him into the metal lockers. The two fell to the tile floor and wrestled in a tangled mess of arms and legs flying everywhere. A crowd gathered as the two exchanged punches, still rolling on the floor.

"Get back! Get back!" screamed Mr. Reynolds, the school principal, as he came running to where the crowd gathered. "Boys! Stop! Get up from there!"

He grabbed Toby and pulled him off of Blake. Blake got in a cheap shot that caught Toby just below his right eye.

"Blake! March yourself to my office and wait for me," Mr. Reynolds exclaimed. "The rest of you—to class!"

"You can say anything you want about me, but if you *ever* say anything about my brother again, there won't be anyone here that can pull me off you," Toby yelled.

He wiped the blood from his lip. Ruby took a scarf from her purse and offered to pat the blood dry. He refused her attempts and stood staring at Blake as he walked away.

"Toby! What was that about?" Mr. Reynolds asked. "I've never seen you like this. You're the one usually breaking this crap up."

Toby licked his busted lip. "Sorry, Mr. Reynolds. This whole Andy-thing has me stressed out, and everyone's saying they couldn't believe Andy did this and Andy did that. Well, he did, and now two lives are hanging on a thread. His, and that girl's."

Mr. Reynolds moved closer. "Son, fighting ain't gonna stop the talk. Andy was our quarterback, and—"

"Is," Toby interrupted. "*Is* our quarterback. See, Mr. Reynolds? Everyone's acting like it's over. Oh, Andy messed up. He ain't coming back. Oh, well, at least it ain't me," Toby mocked, making quotation marks with his fingers. "He's still the same guy he was Friday when they cheered for him. He screwed up! He's still our friend. Our brother! He needs us now more than ever."

"He's a popular guy," Mr. Reynolds continued. "When popular guys do something, people talk. But we can't just punch everyone that talks about Andy."

"He mocked Alec!" Toby said without looking up. "If he talks about my brother, he's gonna get something in return. I'm sorry, Mr. Reynolds, but I'll just have to take the consequences if that happens."

Mr. Reynolds reached out and placed a hand on Toby's shoulder. "Son, I admire how you treat Alec. The way you show love to him is amazing to watch. I think several of these boys on the team have learned a lot about compassion by watching you." He turned and looked down the hall, catching a glimpse of Blake. "Even Blake. I think your example is why you boys are so good at playing together. You care for each other—"

"I quit."

"What? Quit what, son?"

"The team. Football. I'm done!"

"Toby, you don't mean that. You have a lot of emotion built up in you right now. Football is something you love. I see it! And Alec. What about Alec? He loves it, and he loves watching you play. If you quit, he won't be out there. You know that, right?" Mr. Reynolds looked at Ruby, still standing by Toby. "Ruby, run on to class, sweetie. I need to talk to Toby."

Ruby grabbed Toby's hand, pulling it up and kissing it before letting go. Toby watched her walk away as Mr. Reynolds continued.

"Son, I have to talk to Blake, too. I want you to go to Mr. Smith's office and wait there. I'm going to call Coach Woods, and the three of us will talk in a few."

"No! Don't say anything to Coach yet. Please, Mr. Reynolds."

"When you're not at practice today, don't you think he'll wonder why?"

"Please, Mr. Reynolds," Toby pleaded. "Just let me do it."

"Okay," he agreed, "but if word gets to him before you do—well, I just wouldn't wait too long."

A FEW HOURS into the day, word of the fight had spread. Many that gathered to watch the fight also heard Toby announce he quit the team, and that seemed as popular of a topic as Andy's accident.

The lunchroom was already full when Toby came through the lunch line and made his way into the seating area. Ruby was at his side and the two walked toward the table they'd gathered at many trips prior. The table they shared with other members of the team and a few girls from school was what some called the "popular table," but to Toby, it was his friends' place to eat, and nothing more. Regardless, he stopped two tables before that one and set his tray down.

"Babe," Ruby said, her lips pursed and brows drawn together in confusion as she stood holding her tray, "this isn't where we sit."

Toby never looked her way. He sat and began opening one of his three milk cartons. "It is today," he replied.

Ruby shrugged and sat beside him. A younger kid across the table from him gawked at Toby. The kid was small, probably a ninth-grader, someone Toby had never met before. Toby glanced up, making eye contact. The younger kid looked away quickly, dropping his head and hoping Toby didn't notice him staring, but he couldn't help but wonder why he was sitting there.

Toby reached across the table. "I'm Toby. What's your name?"

The kid slouched and slumped in his seat. He quietly muttered, "T-T-Terry. Terry Wilson."

Toby sat a little taller and reached farther. "Well, T-T-Terry Wilson, I'm Toby, and this is my hand." Toby moved his hand as if it were loose from his arm, letting it flop limply. "Terry Wilson, usually when someone extends their hand to you, they want to shake yours." He smiled warmly at Terry and lifted his eyebrows.

"Oh, my bad," Terry replied, obliging the handshake and sitting straighter.

"Mind if I sit here with you, Terry Wilson? And my girlfriend, Ruby?"

Ruby smiled. "Hi."

"No, sir. You can sit here," Terry enthusiastically said, still smiling.

Toby started looking around. First over his left shoulder, then his right. He looked nervous.

Ruby turned to him. "Baby, you okay? What is it?"

"My friend Terry here replied, 'no, sir.' I thought my dad was behind me."

They all laughed. Toby always had a way to break the ice and made everyone feel like a friend. It was probably a side effect of his interactions with Alec. Whatever it was, Ruby was drawn to it. She loved the way younger kids were drawn to him, like a role model, but one they could relate to.

"Toby, hun. What is this all about?" Ruby finally said.

"What?" he replied.

"You know what," she said, throwing her leg over the table bench as if it were a saddle to face him. "Your anger? You quitting the team? New table? All this. Toby, Andy messed up. We still love him, but you can't let *his* mistakes change *you*. Just be there for him and don't change."

"Ruby, we failed him. His team failed him! So many people knew he was drinking more and more, and we just thought that was okay." Toby grabbed a milk carton and drank the last bit from it. "We were like, 'Oh, Andy is going through a phase. Oh, Andy is just having fun.' Well, now look!"

Ruby grabbed his hand. "Stop it! I'm not gonna let you do this. It isn't your fault. You can't fix everything. You can't keep—"

"Hey, guys!" Alec interrupted. His class had just come to lunch and he always sat by Toby. "Why aren't we over there at our table?"

"We just didn't sit there today, buddy," Toby replied, sliding over, taking Alec's tray, and setting it on the table for him. "Sit and eat, bud. Y'all late today, huh?"

"Yeah. Michael dared Franky to moon Heather!" He laughed so hard he had to stop talking. "He did it! He showed her his butt. Mrs. Terry kept us late and talked about not showing butts." Alec looked at Ruby, still giggling. "Ruby Sue, has anyone ever mooned you? That's what it's called when you show your butt to someone."

"Oh, my," Ruby said, giggling. "No. No, I don't think I've been mooned before, Alec. Guess I've been lucky."

Toby giggled as he motioned for Alec to sit. "Now, I don't want to hear about you mooning nobody, you wild man, you."

"Toby?" Alec said, his laugh suddenly ending.

"Yeah, champ? What's up?"

"Who's that?" Alec asked with his arm fully extended and finger-pointing across the table.

Toby smiled at Terry. "Alec, that's my new friend, Terry Wilson. Terry, meet my brother Alec. He's prettier than me, but I run faster."

"Because you cheat!" Alec shouted. "Hi, Terry. What position do you play?"

Terry looked at Toby with a raised brow and then back at Alec. "I...I don't play football."

Alec tilted his head. "Why?"

Toby jumped in. "Alec, my friend Terry here probably has another talent. One that I don't have. Probably does it better than any of us. Ain't that right, Terry?"

Terry was quiet for a second and then quietly said, "Well, um, not really."

"Toby, why is Terry sitting here if he ain't awesome like us?"

Toby had to think quickly. Alec said what was on his mind, and it usually came out unfiltered. "He probably just hasn't found what he's the best at yet. You know, like you. You were so good at so many things, it took you a long time to figure out which was your best thing."

"Like being the team manager?" Alec proudly replied.

"Exactly!" Toby exclaimed. "Like being the team manager. You had been coming to the games all these years and didn't even realize you knew every number, every name, every play, and more than even the quarterba—"

"Even more than Andy," Alec shouted.

Toby sighed. "Yeah, even more than Andy,"

Terry stood. "I gotta go. My class already left, but I was enjoying being here. Thank you for talking to me." He grabbed his tray and raced toward the window to leave his tray in.

"Toby, where were Terry's friends?" Alec asked as they watched him exit the cafeteria.

He looked at Ruby, who was gathering her things. He tightened his lips, and his eyes narrowed. "I—I'm not sure buddy."

"Toby. Does Terry Wilson not have any friends?" Alec asked.

Toby watched as Terry exited the lunchroom. "Not sure, buddy. Maybe they were just out today."

Alec smiled and cheerfully exclaimed, "Terry Wilson has new friends now, huh, big bro?"

Toby returned the smile. "Yeah. Terry Wilson can be our friend. Absolutely."

SCHOOL ENDED A FEW HOURS LATER, and Ruby was hurrying to her car. She worked a few days a week at her mom's flower shop, and today was one of those days. She got to her car and went to open the door when she was startled.

"Slow down, babe! Where's the fire?"

Toby was sitting in his car, parked beside hers.

"Toby!" she gasped. "Why aren't you at practice? Please tell me you're not serious about this quitting nonsense."

Toby got out and walked around to her side of the car, smiling. "Would you leave me if I was?"

Ruby tilted her head and gave a sly grin. "Maybe."

"Well, I guess I'd better head over and take my cussing from Coach then," he replied while shrugging. "Besides, as mad as I was, I thought about it, and I can't do that to Alec. This is his life. I've already been thinking about what happens to him after I graduate."

"You'll figure it out, babe. You always do," Ruby said as she sat in her car. "I gotta run. I told Mom I would head over as soon as school was out. She's doing the homecoming flowers for Riverdale. Call me later?"

Toby smiled as he walked back around and closed his door. "Of course."

He began the trek from the parking lot to the practice field. He could hear the coaches shouting, whistles blowing, and the popping of pads against each other. Not too many times in Toby's life had he been on that side of the fence when those sounds were on the other.

He was dreading the talk with Coach Woods. He knew Principal Reynolds had already talked to him, but he still had to own his actions. Coach Woods was big on that. He always told his guys, "It's okay to mess up or do something wrong, but it is never okay to not own your actions. If you don't own your actions, all you're doing is telling yourself that it's okay to screw up."

That played in Toby's head over and over. He rehearsed his words as he walked, changing them many times. He even contemplated not bringing it up at all and letting Coach Woods initiate the talk. But he knew better. He knew Coach Woods would make it uncomfortable until he did. That was the whole "owning it" thing he was so high on.

Inside the locker room, he took his time getting into his pads and practice gear. He thought about waiting there and talking to Coach after practice. But he knew there would be consequences for that, too. He would just go on out and join in as if nothing had happened. That was his plan. And it worked until about three steps inside the practice field gate.

"Well, well. What do we have here?"

Toby didn't look up. He knew Coach Wood's voice. "Sorry, Coach. I'll run extra, stay late; whatever you want."

Coach Woods blew his whistle. "Everyone, take five. Get some water."

He met Toby halfway onto the field. "Son, you lost your watch?"

"No, sir," Toby replied, stopping just a few feet away. "Coach, I know you already know. I know they told you. I'm not quitting, Coach. I just said that while I was mad. It's not a good excuse, but it's the truth."

Coach Woods squinted, the sun peering down in line with his eyesight. He took his hand and created a visor with it, shielding his vision. He peered at Toby as he spit out sunflower seed hulls. "Yeah, I've heard. And I already knew you didn't mean it."

He positioned the remaining seeds in his mouth and cracked open another with his teeth. He turned and nodded toward the water coolers where the team had gathered, nodding. "That, right there, is why I know you didn't quit."

Toby glanced that way, and Alec caught his eye. Like every day, Alec was filling cups and making sure everyone got water, even if they didn't want any. "Alec? Yeah, I thought about him all day."

Coach spit out another batch of seed hulls. "That goes without saying. But I'm talking about those other guys. The guys you promised to always have their backs. Toby, I've coached many years, and I can tell a quitter from a winner. Son, you're no quitter. I know what all this was about today. We don't have to talk about you, and you ain't gotta run. But what we are gonna do is get this over with right now." Coach blew his whistle. "All right, everybody bring it over here and take a knee."

Everyone hustled to where Coach was and grouped together, as instructed, and knelt to one knee. Toby joined them; all eyes fixed on him. He felt each person staring at him as if he had just shouted a cuss word at full volume. There was chatter among the team as everyone settled in.

Coach blew his whistle again to quiet everyone. "Listen up. Let's get this elephant out of the room. I don't have to tell you what happened this weekend. You already know. It's all over the place. Andy made a mistake, bad judgment; just stupid. Call it what you will." He paused, swishing the sunflower seeds around in his mouth before spitting out a few hulls.

"Now, a young lady is paying the consequences of his stupidity. My understanding is that they now think she may make it. That's good, that's great for her—and Andy. But how many times have we sat right here on this field and had talks about this type of stuff? About how your actions can affect others? I have talked 'til I was blue in the face about not doing stupid crap like that. But as sad as this situation is—and trust me, that girl's family is praying hard—I feel like something could have prevented it." Coach paced back and forth in front of the group. All eyes followed him, attentive to where this was going.

"I've already heard all the rumors, all the talk; hell, I heard about Blake and Toby's fight, which don't think y'all are off the hook, either. Boys, something like this will either make us or break us. I don't break easily, do you?"

A few shuffled around; grunts were made, but no one said anything.

Coach took a few steps to the side of the group. "Y'all sure are quiet. Do I need to ask again?"

"No, sir!" came a few vociferous shouts.

"Okay, let me lay this out," the coach continued. "What we are *not* gonna do is forget this and act like it didn't happen. It did happen, but we can't change it. Now first off, Andy is one of us. What he did was wrong, but there's not one of you that I wouldn't take in as my own, and that includes before and after you screw up. Sometimes the 'after' is when you need love the most. If we show them a little love, that doesn't mean that we support what they've done, but we just show that we still care about them." He stood peering out at the players, pausing to gather his thoughts, and removed his ball cap to wipe the sweat from his brow with his forearm.

"I heard Andy is at home. His dad bailed him out last night, and he isn't leaving the house. If this young lady—well, if things go bad, we all know he's gonna go right back in there. So, I want each one of you to send him a message. All of you! If you don't have his number, get it! Tell him he's still part of this team and this family. He is still a Tiger. We'll worry about the consequences after we let him know we love him. And next thing, after practice, I want each of you to come by my office and pick up a permission form. We're going down to Memorial Hospital to see that young lady. Wear your game day clothes, shirt and tie; look presentable. We may not all get in to see her, but we're all going. All forty-two of you. Next thing is, I've heard the last about pointing fingers. Do I make myself clear?"

"Yes, sir!" came a collective reply.

Coach returned to his original spot. "That really bothered me. Hearing how y'all turned on one another. Blaming each other. Andy is old enough to make his own decisions. Sure, we can persuade him, talk him outta stuff—better yet, lead by example—but in the end, if he wants to do something, he's gonna do it. Now, once we leave this field today, no more of that. Understood?"

Every player shouted. "Yes, sir!"

Coach grabbed a handful of sunflower seeds from his bag. Ready to toss them in his mouth, he muttered, "Okay, let's get back at it."

Toby stood quickly. "Coach, can I say something?"

"Not now, Toby. Let's get back to work."

"Coach, please?" Toby pleaded. "Just real quick."

Coach Woods glared but nodded.

"Thanks, Coach." Toby glanced around at everybody. "Guys, I owe you an apology. I sat out today because I was selfish. Me and Andy were—*are* close. I forgot that every one of you here is a part of his life, too. Me and Andy played ball together since we were like six years old, so it kinda hit hard for me. To think that our playing days may be over got the best of me. Blake, today, can we put that behind us? I mean, I was—"

"Already have, bro," Blake interrupted. "Already have."

Toby looked around at everyone else, pivoting like a needle on a gauge. "Guys, I'll never step out like that again. Coach is right. Let's show Andy that he's still our brother, and let's rally for that girl!

Because of the actions of one of our own, she's paying for it. Now, we play for her!"

The rest of the practice was an enthusiastic one. Coach Woods knew that it would take a moment like they'd had to get over their hump. They'd lost one of their own. Although Andy was still alive and well, his chances of ever seeing playtime on a football field were slim, and it affected the team. Some more than others. If anything was going to crack the armor of the Oak Creek Tigers, this was it. It was only Monday, but if a team came to their turf ready to play on Tuesday, the boys from Oak Creek were hungry, and they were ready!

After practice, Toby walked from the locker room. As he pitched his towel in the laundry, he heard his name called.

"Toby! I was hoping to catch you." He turned, seeing Coach Smith, the offensive coordinator, hastily walking his way.

"Yeah, Coach. What's up?"

Coach Smith stopped as he neared Toby. "How do you feel with Gamble in?" he asked, referring to the second-string quarterback, Mike Gamble, a junior with limited playing time.

"I'm okay with him, Coach," Toby replied, confused why what he thought it would matter.

Coach Smith took a deep breath, raising his eyebrows. "Well, I need you more than okay with him. He's not Andy. You two had a connection. You sensed what the other needed. That's gone. And Andy made things happen when nothing was there. Toby, if we take this thing to state, it's gonna be on your shoulders."

Toby bit his bottom lip and hesitated before answering. "Coach, with all due respect, we have a lot of good players on the team. I think we can all absorb what Andy was for the team. We got this, Coach." Toby smiled and slapped Coach Smith on the shoulder. "But yeah, Coach. You can count on me."

Coach Smith returned the smile. "If we had a dozen more like you, son, we would be hell on wheels."

CHAPTER 4

WHO IS LACY HOLLINGSWORTH?

THE OLD SCHOOL BUS CAME TO A HALT, ITS BRAKES SQUEAKING LIKE A giant hinge opening for the first time in many years. The day was colder than the previous; a cold front pushed across the south, making the comfortable fall temperatures drop enough to require a light jacket. The parking lot at Memorial Hospital was wet from the rain that came in with the front, and puddles showed the disrepair of the lot.

Coach Woods instructed the team to wait on the bus as he went inside to find out the protocols for visitors. A few minutes passed, and he emerged, walking back across the lot. He boarded the bus and stood at the front.

"Okay, boys, we don't get to go past the lobby. Mr. and Mrs. Hollingsworth will meet us there. They're the parents of the young lady we came to see, Lacy. I want you to file off here as if we're at an away game. I want silence and order. When we go in there, I want each of you to shake their hands. Understood?"

"Yes, sir!" came the reply, almost in rehearsed unison.

Each boy filed off the bus. Alec made the trip with the team, as well. He was as much a part of the team as anyone else. They all walked into the hospital lobby and stood in silence, some with their hands in their pockets, swaying nervously. Lacy's parents awaited them just inside.

Mrs. Hollingsworth sat in a chair, her exhaustion apparent in her slouched posture. Her eyes were dark from crying and lack of sleep. Mr. Hollingsworth had been pacing, but as the boys came in, he stopped and watched. His button-up shirt was untucked, his appearance no longer mattering to him. He also appeared fatigued and worried. Mrs. Hollingsworth stood, joining him in front of the team.

One by one, they shook Mr. and Mrs. Hollingsworth's hands, most not saying anything. A few announced their thoughts and prayers. Coach Woods stood beside the parents, and after the last teammate stepped by, he addressed the group.

"Guys, this is Mr. and Mrs. Hollingsworth. Their daughter, Lacy, is the young lady we've been praying for. Now, we all know the circumstances that led to this, so we won't discuss that. But I brought y'all here today for one reason. I've talked to Mr. and Mrs. Hollingsworth, and they agreed to this. I want y'all to see the consequences of poor decisions. The faces of these two show great concern and worry. This is a mother and father that haven't slept much in the last few days. This is what a bad decision looks like. I wish I could let you see Lacy. You would understand then."

Mr. Hollingsworth looked over at the coach. "May I?"

"Of course," Coach replied, extending his arm toward the boys.

"I appreciate y'all coming here," he began. "Lacy has shown improvement overnight, and we know that it's the results of all the prayers, like yours. We thought we had lost her. What we know is that she isn't out of the woods yet. Her back is broken in three places, but by the grace and mercy of God, she isn't paralyzed. She will pretty much have to learn to walk again because of the nerve damage, but not *if*, but *when* she pulls through, she will exceed their expectations. She always does." He put an arm around his wife.

"We know about Andy. We know what happened. Believe it or not, we pray for him on every occasion we pray for Lacy. We don't hate him. We hate the actions that caused this, but from what we understand, Andy is a fine young man that made a bad decision. Now, many of us, including Andy, are suffering from that."

Coach Woods nodded and stepped in front of the parents. "Boys, here's what we'll do. Lacy Hollingsworth is two floors above us. She's seventeen, a senior at Covington High. That's all I'm gonna give you. What I want you to do is learn who Lacy Hollingsworth is. I want to know her favorite color, her favorite food, what her hobbies are. Lacy Hollingsworth is the newest member of our team." He looked over at the Hollingsworths. "All of this, of course, with your approval."

"Coach, we're honored, but really, you don't have to do that," Mr. Hollingsworth replied.

"Mr. Hollingsworth," Coach Woods continued, "these are some fine young men. It will be their honor."

THE TRIP back to Oak Creek was filled with chatter. Many wondered how they would find out so many details about a girl from another school. Some searched social media. Others messaged friends at other schools. The new task had nothing to do with football, but Coach Woods always seemed to find ways to tie everything into the team building that he preached.

When the bus arrived at Oak Creek High, it was time for the team to get ready for practice. As they exited, a familiar sight caught a few eyes.

"Hey! There's Andy!" someone shouted.

Sure enough, Kyle had brought Andy down to see the team. They all rushed over, many of them unsure of what to say. Toby wasn't one of them. He ran right up to Andy—almost ran through him—and hugged him as tightly as he could.

"Dude," Toby exclaimed, "I've been calling you for like three days. You okay, man?"

"I'm good, bro," Andy replied, giving Toby a complex hand grasp, almost choreographed. "I don't have a phone right now. Dad thought it would be better to stay off it a few days."

Doug, Billy, Jake, and a few others joined in as they got caught up with Andy. Coach Woods nodded at Mr. Higgins. "Kyle," he said. "Good to see you."

The guys made way for Coach, giving him room to stand in front of Andy.

"Coach," Andy said, nodding at him.

Coach Woods didn't reply. Instead, he stepped closer and hugged Andy. Placing his hands on his shoulders, he stepped back, extending his arms, and leaving his hands there. "Well, son, we made a mistake, didn't we? You know it, I know it," he turned and looked at the team, "and they all know it. But let's not talk about it. Let's just recognize that it happened, own it, and pray that we all come out a better person."

Andy nodded.

Kyle stepped toward Coach Woods. "Coach, we came to clean out his locker and turn his stuff in. Figured you'd need it. And if he can, Andy would like a word with the team."

Coach wrinkled his brow and stiffened. "Turn in his stuff? He's quitting?'

"Well, no, but he—"

"Well, if he ain't quitting, and we ain't kicking him off the team, I don't need his stuff."

"But, Coach," Andy said, "I'm pretty sure the state won't let me play, at least until after my trial and stuff. Right now, I don't even have a hearing date."

"True," Coach replied, "but you're still part of this team. We're kinda married now." He laughed. "Good and bad, thick and thin. Look, son, I don't condone what you did. I don't think anybody does. You made a bad decision—a very bad one. But here's the deal. When we make a mistake, that's when it's easy for us to judge and point fingers. If you do something bad, does it make me look better? Well, hell no. It just makes you look worse than before you made it. If we support someone, we support them when they need it. It doesn't mean we support their mistake, but we support them as a person.

Ain't that what Preacher John says when he talks to us? Don't he say judge not, that ye be not judged?"

Andy nodded again and noticed the other boys nodding, too. Coach continued.

"Son, you're part of this team, and that won't change. It's time for us to learn from this, not condemn you. Now, you're right. You probably won't play, but until they tell me otherwise, I expect you on that sideline. With all this happening, you need something to keep you thinking straight. You need what you love to do to be a part of your daily walk—"

Kyle interrupted. "Coach, I'd rather not. I know you have good intentions, but we know the backlash that's coming. I know we'll hear all the remarks and everything that comes with it, and—"

"Andy!" The second interruption came as Alec's glee erupted. He ran past everyone and hugged Andy almost without slowing. "I love you."

Andy smiled and hugged Alec. "I love you, too, A-man. Man, I needed that hug."

Coach looked at Kyle. "See what I mean?"

———————

IT WAS THURSDAY, the day before the first game without Andy as quarterback.

Per Coach's instructions, Andy was at practice all week but only observing. Mike Gamble ran the offense at quarterback, and Andy even helped coach him through a few plays as he adjusted to the new role. The day's practice had been a good one, and Coach decided to end it a few minutes early. He blew his whistle and directed everyone to come in around him.

"All right, guys. Tomorrow night, Franklin is gonna come in here thinking they're catching us distracted. I don't believe that'll be the case. Every single one of you has the same job you had last week when you beat the number three team in the state. The only difference is Mike will be under center. Now, if the rest of you do your jobs, just like you did last week, we won't have to worry about distractions. Don't worry about the last play. Don't worry about the next play. But on every down, do what you're supposed to do for that play! You give it your all, on *that* play! With that said, I want to know if there's anyone who doesn't think they can do their job tomorrow."

"No, sir!" came a thunderous reply.

"Good! One last thing. Remember who we play for. We play for ourselves, and we play for Lacy. Who did their homework? Who knows something about Lacy besides what I told you?"

Nobody said anything. A few lowered their heads to not make eye contact with the coach.

"Nobody?" Coach asked. "Not a single one of you found out one thing about Lacy Hollingsworth?"

"I did, Coach," Scott Stiles said as he stood. "I found out that she likes tacos. A lot!"

Coach laughed. "And how'd you find that out, Stiles?"

"Facebook, sir. She goes to the Taco Hut every week for Taco Tuesday."

Laughter erupted across the group.

"Facebook stalking?" Coach continued, shaking his head. "Okay. Well, at least you attempted to find something out. Anybody else?"

A shout rose from another player. "She attended SeaWorld camp last summer, Coach."

"Let me guess, Facebook also?" Coach replied.

"No, sir. Instagram!"

Laughter again rippled through the group.

"Okay, okay, but does anybody else know anything about Lacy Hollingsworth besides what she puts on social media?" he asked.

Hesitation stilled the bunch before a blanket of silence covered them. A long, tense minute passed as the players stole glances at one another, all of them avoiding Coach's stare. Finally, Andy stood.

"I do, Coach."

Coach Woods looked at him with wide eyes. "Son, I didn't even think you knew about this little activity. Whatcha got, Andy?"

"Lacy is only four home runs away from breaking her school's record in softball. She has offers from seven schools to play at the collegiate level but chose Coastal Community College because she loves how the campus looks when the sun rises over the oaks lining the campus. In tenth grade, she won the state 4-H championship for archery. She also volunteers for Big Brothers/Big Sisters, three years now, and spends lots of weekends with kids that don't have role models to look up to. She loves Christian music, and her favorite group is Casting Crowns. She loves the color red. Her favorite dessert is banana pudding, but only the kind that's baked, with meringue on top. And like Stiles said, she does love tacos."

Coach Woods took his cap off and ambled toward Andy. He stopped a few feet away, tilting his head. "How'd you find all that out?"

"Her parents, sir," Andy replied.

"Her parents? But...how?"

"Coach, I had to see her. I asked Dad to take me. He talked to her parents at the hospital, and they agreed. I went Tuesday after I left here. We went back last night, and I'm going tonight. I sat with her mom and dad, and they told me what a wonderful girl she is. Last night, I got to go in and see her. She wasn't awake, but seeing her was tough. I—" Andy's voice cracked, and he stopped to take a deep breath and push back his tears before continuing.

"I stayed until way past the last visiting time. Dad waited for me. Never rushed me. She's waking up more now, and I'm hoping tonight, I get to see her and maybe talk to her so I can apologize. I know it's not enough, but it's all I can do now. Coach, I screwed up. I want her to know that I'm suffering, too. Not like she is. I can't even compare it. But Coach, this has made me different." He started to sit and remembered one last thing.

"Oh, and that SeaWorld camp, she didn't just attend; it was part of her early-college program. She was going to—I mean, she *is* going to be a marine biologist."

Coach stood for a few seconds before saying anything. He put his cap back on and gazed at Andy. "You've been there the last two days?

You found out all that, and you didn't know about my little assignment I told the team to do?"

"Yes, Coach," Andy replied. "I know a lot more about her, too, but I don't want to keep going. Dad's waiting for me out by the gate. We're heading straight there as soon as you tell me it's okay to leave."

"Hell, son. Don't let me keep you waiting. Go!" Coach Woods shouted.

Toby smiled as Andy took off toward the field house to grab his belongings. Coach Woods watched him the entire way, standing in silence. He realized he hadn't a clue what to add to Andy's words. It was unexpected, something that caught him off-guard.

After Andy disappeared into the corridor of the field house, Coach dismissed the team without asking for anyone else's findings on Lacy Hollingsworth.

CHAPTER 5

THINGS ARE DIFFERENT

FRIDAY ARRIVED.

In just a few minutes, the stadium lights would come on. The town had dealt with adversity before, and those lights seemed to always have a way of making people forget about their worries, like in 2003, when a late-season tornado tore through Oak Creek on a Monday night, ravaging much of the farmland and a portion of the town.

Two residents lost their lives during the horrific storm. There were talks of canceling that week's game, but a little normalcy was needed. When that Friday night rolled around, a record crowd showed up and paid tribute to the two lives lost. Oak Creek won that game, one they weren't supposed to.

But things were different this time. There was no tornado, and luckily, no deaths as of yet. But still, there was a different feel to things.

Their starting quarterback—a leader on the team, the town's gridiron hero—had been shown in a different light. No matter how the residents felt about Andy, they knew he'd made a decision that changed the life of a young lady, possibly ripping a scholarship away from her. Even with different circumstances, those lights could still drag out the best in everyone in town. Once the ball was kicked off and pads started colliding, they had something to cheer about.

Coach Woods stood atop the hill overlooking the stadium. He reflected on the games already played and how the one played in a short while would be different; not just the fact that he had a new starting quarterback, but how one of their own had made the decision that led to it.

"Filling up fast, huh, Coach?" Eric Chandler, Toby's dad, said. He had just dropped off Alec and was making his way down to grab a spot alongside the fence.

"Yeah, it is," he responded, turning and extending his hand to shake Eric's. "I hope we're as ready as these fans are."

"You always have them ready. Besides, I know how bad these boys want it, especially now. Good luck, Coach. Give 'em hell."

Eric started down the hill, past Coach Woods, and toward the stadium entrance.

Coach called out to him, "Hey, Eric. You got some good boys. Makes it easy on me. I think Toby is gonna do something special tonight. He's just carrying himself differently, like he has a new purpose."

Eric stopped and looked back at the coach. "He's gonna give you his all, Coach. You can count on that."

Coach Woods walked toward the field house to give his final instructions to the team. He knew nothing would change their mindset moments before kickoff, but he had a reputation for pregame speeches that got the team firing on all cylinders. This week would be different, though. The boys had heard enough talk and inspirational speeches. They needed to play some ball. Coach Woods understood, and he knew when to keep quiet and let them play.

They emerged from the field house and stood atop the hill where Coach Woods stood moments earlier. Slowly, they trotted down to the gate and onto the field, lining up in rows to stretch and warm up. There wasn't much chatter from the bunch. Usually, they made the entrance as if entering a war, their battle cries alerting the enemy of their presence. But tonight, they walked with a purpose, a sense of something bigger.

Andy wasn't dressed out in his full uniform, but instead wore jeans and his jersey. He stood in the end zone and watched as the teams readied themselves for battle.

Someone shouted Andy's name from the sideline area, just over the spectator side of the fence. Andy turned and was surprised to see Lacy's dad. He hesitated at first, only responding with a wave before turning his attention back to his teammates. His thoughts were far from anywhere on that field, though.

What's Mr. Hollingsworth doing here? he wondered.

He snuck a glance back over his shoulder. Lacy's father was still there, leaning on the fence and watching the pregame warmups. Mr. Hollingsworth looked his way again, and Andy quickly turned, hoping he hadn't caught him ogling his way.

In reality, there was nothing to be worried about. Andy had sat with the man for the last three nights. Nothing could be said that hadn't already been said. But this was different, outside of the hospital and the safety of not having the public scrutinize his every move. He wanted to go over and see him, but what about those in the stands?

He already felt hundreds of eyes on him as he walked out with the team. Andy considered what their thoughts were: *alcoholic— senseless—selfish—foolish!* He'd already felt for years that much of the student body felt that he was privileged. His family had done well for themselves, and it showed.

Andy never wanted for anything. When most kids got summer jobs, Andy went on vacations. His first vehicle was a brand-new truck. He enjoyed the perks, but he heard the remarks, too. He knew under the breath of some that he had been called rich and too-good. Now Andy carried a new label, one that toted a much heavier, drearier burden.

But...what if he *did* walk over and talk to the father of the girl he almost killed? Would the people in the stands even know who he was? And what would everyone say? Would it be a good thing if they saw? Or would it be another one of those "the privileged kid got off easy again" moments? He stood and contemplated his options.

"Andy, look over there," Coach Woods said as he neared Andy, pointing toward Mr. Hollingsworth. "Somebody you know came to cheer us on."

"I saw him, Coach. Kinda surprised me."

Coach Woods blew his whistle and shouted instructions. "First team offense, let's run through some plays." He looked back at Andy and added, "I invited him."

Andy didn't respond. He gazed at Mr. Hollingsworth again and wondered why Coach Woods hadn't told him. Lacy's dad made eye contact and waved him over. He clenched his lips and started his way, knowing it was inevitable. He kept a steady pace, only looking up when he was close enough to speak.

"Hey, Mr. Hollingsworth. This is a surprise, seeing you here."

"Your coach invited me. He said that y'all were dedicating the game to Lacy. Thought I'd at least stop by and show my gratitude. Can't stay long. My Lacy-girl is staying awake more now, and I want to be there."

Andy grinned, and his bright eyes showed excitement. "Really? That's great! Mind if I come to see her tomorrow?"

"Sure, that's fine. You have my cell number. Call me first. She has another neurological test in the morning; let's make sure she's up to visits after getting moved around. Her back surgery is Monday *if* she passes her neuro part."

"Yes, sir," Andy replied.

Coach Woods joined them, extending his arm and shaking Mr. Hollingsworth's hand. "Mr. Hollingsworth. Glad you made it."

"Bob; please, call me Bob," Mr. Hollingsworth replied, smiling at Coach.

Coach returned the smile. "Well, I hope we don't disappoint you tonight."

Bob leaned forward onto the fence again. "I'm not going to be able to stay long. Want to get back to my baby girl, but I've read up on you. These Tigers seem to be the real deal according to most of the sportswriters around here. What y'all did to Henderson was...well, that was a beating! Sixty-three to seventeen? Coach, come on!" He winked and gave a little mock huff.

Coach Woods laughed. "Hey! I played everybody I could. I think I even played a guy that didn't dress out for that game."

Andy let his thoughts wander again as the trio stood at the fence and made small talk, allowing his gaze to roam the stands. It may have only been a couple of people looking his way, but it felt like most of the attendees were fixated on him. He saw people he knew, people that had cheered for him just a week prior. Now, he was sure their thoughts and opinions of him were much different.

"Andy! Andy? Son, are you going to respond to Mr. Hollingsworth?" Coach Woods blustered.

"Huh? Oh! Sorry, sir! My mind was running around again," Andy replied, regaining his focus.

Bob grinned. "I can't imagine why. I was saying, I'm going to grab a spot to sit. Looks like this place fills up rather quickly. Andy, call me tomorrow, okay? Good luck, Coach."

Bob turned and found his place near the end of the bleachers so he could exit early in the contest while Coach Woods and Andy focused on the game.

Andy was right. Talks about what had happened went throughout the crowd like ripples from a stone thrown into water. Some stories were factual, while others were far from it. Some rumored that Andy's dad had bought his way out of it, even fixing the toxicology report. Others said that the young lady was still fighting for her life. While she did have a long way to go, her injuries looked far less grave than just a few days prior. Nonetheless, the talks were there, and almost none of them were in favor of Andy—hometown football hero or not.

Midway through the second quarter of the game, Oak Creek was already in commanding control of the game. They led Banks County by a score of twenty-one to zero. Just as asked, Toby picked up the slack of not having Andy in the game. And, as expected, Mike, with his first time at team quarterback, started nervously.

On the opening drive, he threw an interception, but afterward, he settled down and played solidly. It seemed as if Oak Creek was cruising toward another blowout victory. Even with Blake and Toby being adversaries a few days earlier, they were high-fiving and celebratory chest-bumping after every good play.

Toby scored a touchdown, his second of the night, and headed to the sideline. As was the case most of the time, Alec was the first to meet him.

"They can't stop you, Tobe!" he exclaimed. "You da man, big bro!"

Alec was a huge part of Friday nights, not just to the team, but to the crowd. He was a fan favorite of the student section, routinely running to them whenever he thought they weren't loud enough

"Come on, you can get louder!" he shouted to them, and they responded with a thunderous roar every time. He waved his arms frantically to get them on their feet, and if someone didn't, he singled them out. "We are all in this together," he routinely yelled at whoever wasn't doing their part in cheering. And when he had the entire crowd on their feet, it was electrifying.

Oak Creek was about as full of pride as they came. It was apparent, even to those that didn't live there. They loved their football, and they loved their boys that played the game.

Just a few years ago, a big-time newspaper from up north sent one of their reporters down to cover football. He was writing an editorial about how influential the sport was to the south; particularly, to small towns. By accident, Oak Creek was one of his stops. The reporter came to see Grantsville, who was the number one team in the state. Ironically, Grantsville had issues at their stadium due to a late-season storm, so they moved the game to Oak Creek. After the game, he expressed what he'd witnessed, writing:

I came looking to cover a powerhouse team. Grantsville fit the bill, and I was delighted to cover them. The task took me to a small town, one that sat upon a hill.

Oak Creek was a town I had never heard of, with a population

hovering around 1,200; graduating classes numbered on either side of thirty students. Downtown was charming, almost lost in time, but well kept with few vacant buildings. In truth, though, Oak Creek was already slowly dying. The railroad was gone, and the mills were on the way out. There wasn't much left to be prideful about.

But there was football.

I stopped on my way to the stadium to grab a pack of gum from a small convenience store in the middle of town—actually, the only convenience store. As I walked to the door, I noticed the lights were out inside. An older gentleman getting in his pickup nearby called out to me, "They're at the stadium. It's Friday."

I looked around and noticed that most of the other buildings had grown dark as well. Surely, the whole town hadn't shut down for a football game. A high school game, at that. I found out that yes—yes, they had. They'd all ventured to the stadium that sits just to the southwest of town. Not only were they there, but they were also decked out in school colors and had their noisemaker in hand.

Most of the people in the stands cheer for this same team their entire lives. They bleed blue and white. If you played here, they remember when you "caught that touchdown to win the game back in '95" and when "that running back fumbled the ball in the fourth quarter in '88." Fans are invested, hard-core, feverish; which can be challenging sometimes, but it also gave me chills as I drove through the town and saw flags flying on almost every business and signs in the yards of the well-manicured lawns.

I knew I found sacred ground. Small-town football is a religion here. There are heroes made between the goalposts, and if the lights are on at the stadium, you can bet your best hunting dog they'll be out in town...at least in this town.

That article was clipped and hung in almost every place of business in Oak Creek. Many parents and students had a copy in their scrapbooks. It wasn't too often that Oak Creek was mentioned in a national publication. The article in full made Oak Creek sound more like a sports-craved fanatic community with little else to cheer about, but the way that they talked about being fans of their team outweighed any bad terminology used, and that was as good as saying that Oak Creek was the best town in the south with an even better football team.

The clock ticked down to show all zeros on the scoreboard. The Tigers added another score, but Banks County found a crack in the armor and snuck in for a score of their own. But at twenty-eight to seven, Oak Creek felt good going into the locker room at the half.

"Okay, boys, gotta clean up some mistakes," Coach Woods barked as the players filed in and grabbed a squirt bottle of water. "Too many mental errors. Not enough hustle!"

He stomped around as if they were taking the beating of their lives and not ahead by three touchdowns. In true Cecil Woods fashion, he was never satisfied with enough to win, but only when they'd given their best to win.

In a game a few years ago, Oak Creek was physically outmatched. Their opponent was bigger, faster, and had three times as many players to choose from. As expected, they lost that game by a landslide. After the game, Coach Woods told a reporter, "I have never been more proud of these guys. They played their best game all year."

Some looked at that as the old coach had grown soft and accepted the loss as being okay. But, in fact, he knew his boys were outmatched, and they knew it, too. But that didn't stop them from believing they *could* beat them. The grit and hustle shown in that game were what Coach Woods had instilled into every player that ever donned a Tiger jersey. That was his calling card—a never-quit attitude.

Coach Smith joined in on the verbal lashing. "*Where* is my offensive line? Are you guys still here? You let that defense get to Mike all night. Toby is out there fighting for his life!"

The team took the scolding just like they did every Friday night. They were used to it. No matter how hard they played, it wasn't enough, but then, just like clockwork, the clock would strike 0:00, and all the coaches would tell them how proud they were. But that halftime speech was expected.

Andy stood off to the side. Being on the receiving end of the speech was something he'd lived through many times. As bad as he wanted to be playing, it was the first time he was thankful he wasn't in the game. Even when he knew he'd played his best, somehow the coaches made him feel like he had a little something extra to give.

Mike Gamble walked over to Andy. Taking over as the quarterback in Andy's absence had thrown him directly into the spotlight, and everyone was watching to see if he was up to the challenge.

"Little different from practice," Mike said as a sly smile escaped with his words.

Andy's brow wrinkled as he gave Mike the "I-told-you-so" look. "The talks are the same, though. Get used to not doing enough."

"When we get to state, I'm not sure I can handle all that. Think you'll be back?"

Andy leaned back against the lockers and lowered his head. "I doubt it. Dude, I screwed up big time. Hasn't even been a week, and people are slandering me for being out here. I hear the talk, man. I don't even know if I would come back if I could. I mean, y'know, I love this. It's my life. But I went from being Johnny B. Goode to Johnny Gone Wrong all within a week."

"It was an accident, man. Quit beating yourself up over it," Mike pleaded. "Besides, they said that girl would—"

"Lacy! Her name is Lacy. And *that girl* had her whole life planned out—college scholarship playing softball. That was her ticket to school so she could become a marine biologist; her dream. Her family ain't got a way to pay for that. But now," he turned and pounded the locker with his fist, "even if she is gonna make it, she won't be the same. She'll never play ball again. I screwed that up!"

Mike grabbed Andy's shoulder and turned him so that they were facing each other. "Dude! It was an accident!"

"No," Andy insisted. "I'm tired of people telling me it was an accident. Accidents happen for no reason. I was the reason! It wasn't an accident; it was a decision, and a decision that I made."

"Let's go, Mike!" Coach Woods shouted.

Mike looked around to find that he and Andy were the last ones in the room. Their conversation had distracted him from everyone else heading back for the second half. He glanced at Andy without saying anything else and patted him on the shoulder before running out.

Andy stood there momentarily, reflecting on everything that had happened in that room for the past four years. Games won; games lost. Blood and tears had been shed there. Friendships were made that would last a lifetime.

For Andy, football was more than a pastime. It was more than a way to be popular at school. It was the one thing in life that he cherished.

Sure, he had everything he needed. He had grown up in a well-to-do family, taken the best summer vacations, had the trendiest clothing, a nice truck; everything that ninety percent of the rest of the kids in town would love to have. But still, even with all that, he had an emptiness that only the sport seemed to fill.

He excelled in it. His parents loved him and showed him they did, but he got even more satisfaction from the praise he received from the people around town, the school, and the local paper. He found a way to feel needed and wanted in a world that so easily found everyone's faults within themselves. But while he soaked in all the praise, he overlooked one thing—the reality that he tended to see past his faults.

Andy knew that even though he didn't drink every day or even every week, he was starting to enjoy it a little too much. He even remembered Toby telling him that alcohol would control him if he let it. But he thought, *Nah! Not Andy Higgins! I have my whole life together.*

And then, it happened. It controlled him. And because it controlled him, it only took one time to change the life of someone else.

Standing alone in the locker room, Andy felt the pressure of his horrible decision weighing impossibly heavily on him yet again. He prayed that if God would give Lacy her life back, uninterrupted, he would bear her injuries for her. But deep down, he knew that wasn't possible. What was done was irreparably done.

Andy gathered himself and ambled toward the field. The thumping of the bass drum pounded as the band finished their halftime performance and exited the field while playing the beginning notes of the school fight song. He stopped just before the slope carried him down and looked out over the field.

The fight song was playing full force now, a tune that he'd heard at least a hundred times. But it sounded different; not that it *was* any different. The horns were slightly off-key, an occasional stray note escaping the valves. The lone sousaphone hit the low notes that carried above the other wind instruments. Blue and white flags danced in the wind as the color guard synchronized their every move. It was a sight that Andy could get lost in, and he had.

Andy listened to it, realizing he'd never really *listened* to it before. It was part of the pageantry of the game, but not his part. His part was playing the sport he loved. But as he listened, he began to understand that without that familiar fight song played so loosely by the small band, the game would never be complete. With the chance of it all being taken away, every aspect of the game seemed important.

He stood until the last note was played and the last baton was twirled, watching from the top of the hill. He no longer felt every eye on him, instead consumed with his thoughts. *What if this is over for me? What if I've already played my last game?* Despite trying to block them, the thoughts were present, embedded in the vault that held all the memories he cherished.

"Andy? Are you okay, son?"

Andy turned quickly, as if shocked back into reality. "Oh! Umm, yes, sir," he mustered out. "Just watching the band, Mr. Reynolds."

Principal Reynolds had just locked up the field house, as he always did after halftime to keep out unwanted guests. He was on his way back to the stands but paused to take advantage of his first chance to be alone with Andy since the incident. He wanted to give his thoughts and offer support but figured that he'd heard enough in the last few days.

"Looks different from up here, doesn't it?"

Andy nodded. "It does."

"Come on. I'm about to close this gate. You want to be on this side of it, don't ya?"

Andy moved a few feet to the inside of the fence and smiled half-heartedly. "Guess I do, sir."

Mr. Reynolds closed the gate without locking it and hung the loose clasp over the fence post to hold it in place. They began walking down the hill together. Andy paused before reaching the bottom.

"Mr. Reynolds, can I ask you a question?"

"Of course, Andy," he replied, stopping and turning to show Andy that his attention was on him.

Andy took a deep breath and let it out. "You know everything that's happened. I'm pretty sure everybody does. It's weird being here, to be honest. Coach has always told me that I could talk to him about things that bother me, but, umm, I am afraid I've lost his respect, and I'm not sure if he would give me the time now. Mr. Reynolds, I know I messed up, and I know someone is paying the price for it. But I'm here, at my school's football game. Even if I'm not playing, I am still here. That girl I hit, Lacy, doesn't have that opportunity to be at her school's game tonight. I thought being here would help me get my mind off it, but it made it worse. I'm not sure I should be here."

Mr. Reynolds smiled with closed lips. "Sounds to me like you're eaten up with guilt. That's hard to fix. But I'll give you two pieces of advice. First, Coach Woods would give you as much time as you needed. I've been around him for many years, and he would fight an army for any of you boys. He's hard on y'all because he's trying to get your best. He wants to teach you how to tap into that little extra that most people don't ever use. When he says that you can talk to him about anything, he means it." He stepped a little closer. "The second part is more personal. Are you okay with me talking to you about salvation?"

"But I know about all that, and—"

"Then you know about repentance, too, I take it?"

Andy shifted his weight from one foot to the other and then gave him a blank stare and a slight nod.

Mr. Reynolds laughed. "Not so sure, huh? Well, many people aren't. Repentance is when you give it all to God; your worries, your sin, your guilt. Your life!"

Andy squinted and looked puzzled. "I thought that was when you got saved?"

"Well, yeah," Mr. Reynolds continued. "But you can't have salvation without repentance. You see, just by asking Jesus into your heart and acknowledging that He died for your sins is a big step to securing your eternity, but repentance is letting go of all the bad stuff, and you give that to Him, too. He will bear those burdens for you."

"Kinda like the way I feel," Andy said, staring off into space.

Mr. Reynolds tilted his head. "You'd take her pain and injuries, wouldn't ya?"

Tears welled up in Andy's eyes. "I prayed and asked Him to give them to me a few minutes ago."

Mr. Reynolds sensed that Andy felt all the guilt he could possibly bear. Worried the moment might send him even deeper into depression, he thought the best thing to do was revisit it later.

"You'll get through this. There ain't many people as tough as you." He patted Andy on the shoulder and started walking. "Come on. Let's go watch the rest of this game."

THE GAME CONTINUED JUST as the first half had played out. The Tigers dominated their opponent and pushed their record to nine wins and no losses. They were one game away from a perfect regular season. Only once in school history had such a feat been accomplished.

Mike finished his first game as the team's starting quarterback, giving him the confidence he needed. Toby scored four touchdowns in the game, tying his best mark. It seemed Oak Creek was unstoppable.

Toby emerged from the field house just as Andy was getting into the truck with his dad. "Hey, Andy!" he yelled. "Going over to the church for the Fifth Quarter. Gonna have pizza. Wanna come?"

The Fifth Quarter was an event that his church held after every home game. The students of Oak Creek High, including the players, came together to celebrate and pray for anyone injured. It was a tradition for many that had come before the current team.

Andy briefly looked at his dad before turning back to Toby. "Nah. Gotta get home. Thanks, though."

"Okay, bro. Holler at me tomorrow evening after five. Gotta work."

"Sure thing," Andy replied, his voice heavy with an underlying sadness.

CHAPTER 6

THE LETTER

THE SUN ROSE OVER THE TALL PINES STANDING ALONG THE PROPERTY boundaries of Andy's house. A new day had sprung to life outside.

Andy peered through the large picture window of their family room. Just outside, two rabbits feasted on the clover growing in the centipede grass that had fallen victim to the cooler weather and browned. The bunnies left trails in the grass as they disturbed the dew that settled below and glistened on the ground. He watched them for several minutes, thinking about how carefree they were and how little they had to worry about.

The hardwoods far across the property put on a dazzling showcase of color as if God's paintbrush had used as many colors as possible. The reds, yellows, and oranges blended perfectly, and the sun's rays breaking through made them appear as if they were on fire, with the occasional falling leaf getting caught in the wind like embers escaping a campfire.

Andy began wondering why he'd never noticed how beautiful the place was. Had the events of the last week opened a new sense of gratitude within him? Perhaps just slowing down, not rushing off to be with his friends, gave him time to soak it all in.

He glanced at the clock that hung on the wall. It showed 7:37 a.m. *Is it too early to call Mr. Hollingsworth?* he asked himself.

He was anxiously waiting to see Lacy and, hopefully, talk to her. Would she forgive him? Would she scream at him? He'd played out every scenario in his head. He was nervous, and perhaps even a little scared to see her now that she could interact. But after a week of beating himself up, he had to let her know he'd taken full responsibility for his actions.

Andy made his way into the dining room and found his dad sitting at the table, drinking coffee, and reading over some papers. He sat with one hand holding a letter and his chin propped on the other. His face slackened; his brow furrowed and his eyes darted as if in heavy thought. The nervous tapping of his foot under the table and his heavy breaths gave away his inability to hide his worry.

"Dad. What's wrong?" he asked as he peered over his dad's shoulder, trying to read the papers he held.

Kyle sighed before laying the papers down and drug a hand over his face. Scoffing, he said, "Well, just about everything that I need to go right lately. It's the insurance. They're denying the claim—even the liability—until after they conduct an investigation. They're not paying for any of your truck, which I knew they wouldn't, but if they deny the liability, I'm not sure what we'll do."

Andy reached down and grabbed the stack of papers, scanning through them vigorously. "But how, Dad? It was good. I remember looking at the date on it when the cop asked for it."

"The alcohol is the issue," Kyle snapped without looking up. "We're in breach of the agreement due to the violation. It won't pay because alcohol contributed to the accident. You committed an illegal act, which led to the accident."

"So, it's not gonna cover my truck," Andy said, sliding out a chair. "Not even just to fix it?"

Kyle finally locked eyes with Andy and shook his head. "Nope," he responded sharply before taking a sip of his coffee. "And the thing is, when this goes to court, we're probably gonna get hit with replacing *her* car and paying for all the medical bills. And *then*—if we get lucky—the Hollingsworths won't sue us for pain, suffering, and losses. I mean, Mr. Hollingsworth has already stated that this whole mess will cost his girl her scholarship. That will pretty much take everything we have to pay for."

Andy laid his head on the table. "Dad, I'm so sorry. Just when I think we can get through this, something else hits." He stood and started across the room and then up the stairs.

"Hey, where are you going?" Kyle called to him.

"Back to bed! I can't screw anything up there."

"We're not going to see Lacy?"

Andy stopped on the fourth step. "Will they even want to see me once they learn about this insurance thing?"

Kyle took a deep breath and moved from the table to the stairs so that he could face Andy. "Son, running from it won't make it go away. You're going to have to face it—all of it. If they find out through a letter, like I did, it'll be worse. Let's go visit. Maybe you can talk to Lacy and get some closure, and I'll talk to Mr. Hollingsworth. I think we need a lawyer to sort it all out, but we won't just leave them to handle things on their own. That's not who I am. That's not who you are. Yes, you made a bad decision, but now we take responsibility. Go do what you gotta do to get ready. Call Mr. Hollingsworth, make sure it's okay to come, but *do not* say *anything* about this yet, and let's figure it out. Okay?"

Andy clenched his lips, holding in the words that wanted freedom, but nodded and continued up the stairs. Moments later, he was back with the clearance to visit, and he and Kyle were on their way.

After the sixty or so miles had passed under Kyle's truck, they found themselves at Memorial Hospital. The hospital itself was intimidating enough. Standing twelve stories and with more wings to the building than Andy cared to count, it served several counties and handled almost any disaster thrown at it. For a small-town boy, it was quite impressive.

Once inside, it offered quietness, but oddly enough, it was a cheerful, soft sort of quiet. The hospital allowed positive space that others could open up into, a space that was ready to support their needs. Andy noticed how simple things were, but he immediately knew why people brought flowers to hospitals. It needed something to add to the emotional healing, something that broke up the hard corners and bright lights.

The place was clean and inviting, but it did nothing to his emotions. His thoughts turned to the human side of the architectural prose. Andy knew that humans were still animals and that habitat mattered; a person was more prone to relax when they enjoyed their surroundings. Mental and physical health were too intertwined to separate. The hospital's efforts not to offend anyone succeeded only in being uninspiring and failing to lift the spirit. He remembered from the last few days that Lacy's room was much the same. It offered little to appeal to mental healing.

"Dad," he called to Kyle as he noticed a gift shop just off the lobby, "can we grab some flowers? Something to leave in Lacy's room? I've got my own money."

Concerned, Kyle asked, "Can she have them? Those intensive care units are strict."

"Not sure, but I bet the lady in the shop knows," Andy suggested.

To Kyle's surprise, they were allowed. Andy picked out a bouquet with the most colors, a beautiful spring mix with reds and yellows. It came in a vase with a large red and white bow. Flowers in hand, they headed to the seventh floor and followed the signs to the I.C.U. waiting lobby. Andy made his way in first and immediately saw Mr. and Mrs. Hollingsworth.

"Mr. Hollingsworth," Kyle said. "Hey, Mrs. Hollingsworth. How is she?"

Mr. Hollingsworth stood and greeted Kyle and Andy. "She's doing good. She started her soft food diet this morning, and so far, so good. We have a neuro scan at some point this morning, but that could be in five minutes or five hours. Who knows? But the doc says that she's improving faster than his anticipated plan."

Kyle extended his arm and exchanged a handshake with Bob. "That sounds like good news."

"Better than a few days ago, for sure," Ann, her mother, added. "My girl is a fighter. Always has been."

"Can we see her? I brought flowers," Andy exclaimed as he held out the bouquet for Ann to see.

"Those are beautiful, Andy! We still have a few minutes before we can go back, but she's going to love those."

Andy smiled, setting the vase on a table, and then seated himself beside them as if guarding a priceless treasure.

The minutes ticked by slowly as the group made small talk. Kyle pondered how to address the insurance situation. He desperately wanted an opportunity to arise that would allow him to present the topic, but he didn't know when that would happen. As he nervously fidgeted, a nurse finally appeared and opened the double doors, announcing that visitors could come back.

Andy suddenly felt a rush of anxiety come over him. His breaths deepened as he tried to get his feet to cooperate. Kyle placed an assuring hand on Andy's shoulder to help calm him, but Andy felt as though his heart might leap from his chest.

They made their way through the doors and took a right that led them to unit 3A. Lacy's parents went in while Kyle and Andy stood just outside. They could see in, and Lacy could see them. Andy watched her, and he could tell that she was already wondering who they were, her eyes slightly narrowed and her brows drawn together.

As they waited for approval to enter, he couldn't help but stare at Lacy. Her face was still swollen and bandages covered most of her head. Like every other time, he thought, *I caused that*, biting his lower lip in nervous anticipation.

Bob stood straight after leaning over to hug his daughter and motioned toward the door. "Lacy, baby, this is Kyle and Andy Higgins. They came to visit if you're up to visitors."

Lacy glanced again at them and then back to her dad. When he didn't offer any other information, she looked at Andy, who smiled at her. She saw the flowers but still couldn't help but wonder who would bring her such a beautiful gift. Finally, after several tense moments, she said, "Sure, Dad. I guess."

Ann grabbed the only chair in the small cubical and slid it closer to Lacy's bed and took a seat by her, holding her hand. Kyle and Andy stepped a few feet into the room; Kyle stood just inside, with Andy in front of him.

Andy took another step closer, smiling and extending his arm. "I —umm, I brought you these." He realized quickly that her IV lines kept her from reaching and was hit by another wave of guilt.

"Oh, sorry! I'll set them on your table. If that's okay."

Lacy looked confused, her eyes narrow and her bottom lip softly wedged between her teeth. "That's fine," she responded. "Do, um, do I know you? Are you from school? Sorry, I'm just still kinda—well, y'know—shook from all this."

Andy stole a fleeting look at Lacy's dad and then focused on her. He swallowed hard and took in a deep breath. With his hands now free, he jammed them both in his front jeans pockets. "Well, not exactly. I, um, I—"

"Baby, Andy here is the boy that was involved in the wreck. He was the other driver," Mr. Hollingsworth interjected.

Lacy's brow raised high enough to wrinkle the bandages as she struggled to understand how Andy was involved. "But Mom said it was a drunk driver that hit us?"

Ann leaned over further, stroking her daughter's hair. "Yes, hun. It was. Andy is that guy."

The confusion instantly left Lacy's face, replaced with sheer anger and heartbreaking sorrow. "Why are you here?" she screamed as she grabbed the bed rails, fighting to sit up. Tears welled up in her eyes. "Dad, why did you let him come? Why?!" Enraged, she looked back at Andy, who backed up a few steps. As tears rolled down her face, she grimaced in pain and held her ribs with one hand, and sobbed, "*You did this to me? You ruined my life? Get out! Get out now!*"

"I'm so sorry," Andy replied as tears escaped his eyes. "I—umm, I just—"

Kyle grabbed Andy by the arm. "It's okay, son. Come on. Give her some time and space." He looked over at Bob. "Mr. Hollingsworth, I'm sorry. We will be in the lobby."

Andy tried to step backward again, tripping over his own feet as Kyle pulled him. His eyes were fixated on Lacy as she continued yelling at him and weeping. His breathing was heavy and sweat beaded across his forehead. They exited the unit and returned to the waiting room.

"Dad," Andy cried. "I just want this to end. I don't even care anymore if I go to jail. Send me! At least I won't be reminded of this every day."

Kyle hugged him tightly and kept him upright as Andy sobbed and his knees buckled. He knew Andy had made the decision that caused so much pain, but he was still his son, which he loved more than life itself. It ate at Kyle as much as it did Andy, but for different reasons. Kyle hurt for his son.

"Son, we will get through this. We always do," Kyle reminded him. "But you have to realize what Lacy is going through. She's just now comprehending what all happened. It's gonna take some time."

Before Andy could reply, Mr. Hollingsworth joined them in the lobby. He saw the tears rolling off of Andy's cheeks, but what was a man in his position supposed to do? Should he tell the boy that had changed the future of his daughter's life that everything would be okay? He knew it wouldn't. No walking across the stage at graduation. No college softball. A lot had changed, and a lot would never be the same, and sadly, it would never be okay.

Bob moved closer and said, "Andy, Kyle; guys, I'm sorry. I know this didn't go the way you wanted, but Lacy has a lot to take in right now. A lot of emotions are running around inside her. Let's give it a few days, and I'll see if she's up to talking to you. What do ya say?"

Kyle nodded. "Sure. Sounds good. Keep us updated on her condition, and if there's anything we can do, let me know."

He wanted to discuss the insurance situation with him, but after the emotionally charged meeting, he felt it may be best to handle it later. So instead, father and son walked from the lobby and toward the elevators, and within a few minutes, they were on their way back home.

Andy stared out the passenger window. Without turning, he

whispered, "Dad, when is my hearing? When will we find out what my punishment is?"

"Not sure yet. The lawyer told me it could be a couple of weeks, maybe even a month."

"Whatever they choose, it can't be worse than how I feel or what I'm going through now."

"Son, as bad as you think it is, never say it can't be worse. You're still alive. Lacy is still alive."

Andy had no response. He watched the trees pass by in a blur and let his mind go blank. Before long, they pulled into their driveway. Andy was just getting out when his phone alerted him to an incoming call from Toby.

"What's up, dude?" Andy answered.

Toby came through from the other end. "Hey, man! Dobson closed the sawmill today—rain. Was gonna see what you were doing. Wanna throw the ball around?"

Andy let out a sigh. "Nah. Just got back from Memorial. Tried to see Lacy. Just not up to doing anything."

"Oh, yeah! I forgot about that. How is she?"

"She's pissed. Man, she screamed for me to leave. Didn't even get a chance to speak. But I don't blame her. I'm a screw-up! They just need to go ahead and send me to jail. I messed up her whole life. Messed mine up, too. I don't want to even get out and—"

Toby was quick to cut him off. "Dude! Just stop it. I'm not gonna let you drown in a pity party. Sit tight. I'm on the way."

"No," Andy insisted. "I'm gonna go take a nap. I'm good."

"See you in a few."

Refusing to take no for an answer, he hung up before Andy could respond. A few minutes later, Toby arrived and parked just off the drive in a grassy area. He exited his car and walked toward Andy's house.

"Over here!" Andy shouted from just to his left where he was sitting on the fence that bordered the field beside his house.

"Is it okay where I parked? I still gotta get that oil leak fixed and didn't want to spot up your drive," Toby shouted. "I left a spot the last time, and I know your dad had a fit."

"You're good," Andy responded as he stood. His shoulders were slouched and his face slackened.

Toby stopped just a few feet away from Andy. He clenched his lips and shook his head. "Bro! Get your crap together! I will not let this happen. I know what led to this, and I know it was wrong. I'm not going to sugarcoat it, man."

Andy looked surprised. "What are you talking about? I'm living a nightmare. Do you think I want this? What am I supposed to do? Act like nothing happened?"

"No!" Toby said, his voice getting louder. "I *want* you to act like it happened. Like Coach says, own it! But sitting here and pouting isn't gonna help anything. Tell me, what's your plan?"

Andy lowered his head again and hesitated. "Guess the judge will tell me my plan."

"Just like that?" Toby shrugged, turned, and stomped away after Andy didn't say anything. He stopped about twenty feet away and added, "So we're just gonna let the judge be the deciding factor on what we do from here on out?"

Andy threw his hands in the air. "What am I supposed to do? Tell me! Hell, it seems like I can't make a good decision, so tell me!"

Toby stormed back toward him and lowered his voice. "You're like a brother to me, man. There's *so* much you can do. Hiding in your room isn't one of them."

Andy gazed up at Toby, fighting to keep the tears in his eyes from spilling over onto his cheeks. He didn't say anything, standing in silence instead.

Toby adjusted his ball cap and began again. "You said she ran you out. Why?"

"Why do you think? I did that to her," Andy whispered.

Toby shook his head. "You're still thinking about it like you're the victim. Look at her side of things. She has—"

"I have!" Andy shouted. "Everyone is saying that. 'Look at *her* side. Think of what *she's* going through.' Man, that's *all* I think about!"

"I know, but I'm not talking about that. You're responding to how those actions are affecting you. Your actions now, *after* it has happened—brother, that's what will define what others think and what defines how you feel about it."

"Then what do I do, huh? Tell me if you know so much," Andy said, huffing in frustration.

"She doesn't want to see you, right?"

Andy let out a laugh laced with sarcasm. "Yeah, you could say that."

"Well, write her a letter."

"You serious, man?" Andy said as he laughed again. "What is this? The seventies?"

"I'm very serious. It's easier to write it and let her read it than to talk to her face to face. Everything you wanted to tell her, put it on paper and let your dad take it to her parents. Just try it, okay?"

Andy shook his head. "Dude, anyone else, I would've already run them off. But you're right, I guess. At least I can apologize in writing. Better than nothing."

Toby playfully pushed Andy. "Ran me off, huh? Well, you better run with me. Come on. Let's get outta here for a while. Let's go throw the ball around, fish or something—anything. Get your mind right. And besides, I think Gamble can throw better than you. You may need to prove me wrong."

Andy chuckled. "Oh, Gamble? You and him are new besties now. I see!" He started toward his house, adding, "Let me tell Dad I'm going with you for a while. Go ahead and get to starting that rust bucket you drove into my yard."

⸻

AS THE EVENING CAME IN, Andy and Toby found themselves at some old coal ponds on the outskirts of town. With the shorter days, the sun had already settled in behind the tall pine trees. The reflections across the water created an almost endless picture of water to land. The beautiful orange and pink hues shining through the thin clouds made for a picturesque setting. A gentle breeze rippling across the water bent the images, letting them dance as if Mother Nature's band was in concert.

Neither Andy nor Toby was fishing, having simply arrived at the location after endless driving and settling in on a place to skip rocks and finish talking. As they walked the bank and pitched flat rocks across the water's surface, Toby brought up the topic that he'd tiptoed around all day.

Toby took the rock he was holding and with a sidearm motion and flick of his wrist, he sent it skipping across the water before it finally sank below the waterline. He stopped and let out a sigh, loud enough to catch Andy's attention.

"Y'know, Andy, you can find an answer in everything. Even skipping rocks."

Andy's brow furrowed, confused by the out-of-the-blue statement. "I guess so. Like the answer on who's better at skipping rocks? That's easy. Me!"

Toby turned to look at him. "For real, bro. Think about it. That rock is going along, just passing through life, until something happens that makes it lose momentum and it sinks. Its life is over. But what if it had something that kept it afloat?"

Andy shook his head. "No! Don't do it, man."

Toby laughed. "Do what?"

Andy skipped another rock across the lake. "You *know* what. You always want to make a point by using something else to do it—like skipping rocks."

"Think you know me, don't ya?" Toby replied, skipping a rock of his own. "Look, man, just hear me out."

Andy took off, shaking his head again. "All right. Go for it. Let me have it."

Toby hurried his steps, passing Andy and stopping in front of him with a hand on Andy's chest. "Dude! We've helped each other through so much. Remember when my car broke down?'

Andy smiled. "Which time?"

"Any of them. But when my transmission went out, and it took me forever to save the money to fix it, you took me everywhere I needed to go. You even gave me the last hundred dollars I needed to get it fixed. That's what we do! So now, I'm here for you."

"What's that got to do with skipping rocks?" Andy asked as he stepped around Toby and started walking again.

Toby again hurried and caught up. "What happens when that rock loses speed? It sinks, right?"

"Yeah. So, you're telling me I'm sinking, or just slow?"

"Not unless you don't have anything to keep you up. Here's the deal, man. Imagine if that rock had something that made it float. The worry of sinking would be gone. It's the same with us, man. God is our floatation device. We can't sink with him. We just—"

"Whoa! Whoa, man! I know you mean well, but I ain't ready for all this 'God' talk. I'm saved, and I do right. I'm just not gonna go around beating my chest for God. Besides, He could have stopped this wreck. He chose not to."

Toby stopped in his tracks. "Seriously!?"

Andy spun to face him. "Couldn't He? Isn't He in control of everything?"

Toby took a heavy breath and let it out slowly, struggling to control his temper. "Wow! Let's just blame God for this. Coach Woods would be happy that you owned it. Yes, He is in control of everything, but at the same time, He gives us choices to make. It's part of our faith-building and how He provides grace when we make the right choices. Dude! Just listen to me. You may be saved. You gave your heart to Christ in Vacation Bible School when we were ten. I was there. You gave your *heart*, but did you give your *life* to Him? There's a difference. I promise He can help you get through this!"

Andy turned and stomped away, his friend right on heels. "Not today, Toby. I just needed some time out today, not a lecture."

"Okay, man. No worries. You know I love you, brother, and I'm just trying to help. Let's get back. Dad is grilling burgers this evening, and Ruby is coming over. Wanna join us?"

"Nah," Andy replied. "Just gonna hang out at home. But I'll take one of those rain checks you're always giving me. Besides, I think I have a letter to write."

Toby smiled and patted Andy on the back. "Come on, man. I'll take you home."

ANDY STOOD outside as Toby's car drove out of sight. He looked around at all the things that God had blessed him with—many acres of land, a house much larger than a family his size needed, nice cars —but yet, he still felt as if he was living day to day. Andy realized Toby almost always had a smile on his face and seemed to be in a good mood.

He thought of where Toby was going—home to spend time with his family, grilling and enjoying time together—and how those were things he hardly ever did with his family. His dad worked hard, and although he supported Andy in everything he did, he was hardly ever there.

Is it true? Can I be missing the one thing I need to be happy?

But what was that one thing, anyway? Family time? Being proud of something earned or worked for? Or perhaps, maybe the relationship with God that Toby always hyped up really did mean more than just the talk.

Andy, deep in thought, found himself walking to the edge of his yard, overlooking the meadow that had become mostly brown except for the few spots of green that peeked through the cut hay. Several large round bales lay scattered throughout the fields. He could walk all day and most likely never leave footprints on everything they owned. He thought about Toby's modest little home and lot, just big enough to separate the houses in his neighborhood.

The more he thought about it, the more he wanted what Toby had—whatever *that* was.

Andy finally walked inside and went upstairs to his room. The house was quiet, as no one was home. He sat at the desk in his room, the top littered with everything except what he was looking for, and pulled a backpack from underneath the mess. Andy looked inside to retrieve a notebook. He dug around a little more and found a pen.

Andy cleared some room on his desk and opened the notebook to a clean page. He sat and stared at the empty page for several minutes. Lost for words, he thought, *How do I start? What do you say to someone that just lost almost everything they loved, because of me?*

Finally, he began:

Lacy,

You don't know me. If you did, you would probably wish you didn't. I'm the guy that caused your accident. I am

---

He stopped and read the few lines he had written, wondering if Lacy cared who he was.

Will doing this even make a difference? he thought.

Frustrated and already feeling defeated, Andy tore the page out, wadded it up, and tossed it toward the small wastebasket beside his desk. Missing its mark, the paper bounced off the side and rolled a few feet away. Andy got up to retrieve it, deciding he wouldn't write the letter; besides, he didn't know what to say, anyway. He bent to pick it up and noticed another small wad of paper nearby.

He picked it up to toss it in the can with his letter but noticed a word that had been thrown at him a lot lately: God. He uncrumpled the paper and remembered it was an invitation to a student-athlete Christian event. Something within him stirred as he read:

Come and see how God provides us with the knowledge to make great decisions on and off the field.

Andy stared at the wrinkled paper for several seconds. *Decisions,* he thought. *Man, I wish I had a little help with that about a week ago.*

He shook his head and tossed the two papers in the can, but once again, he was off the mark and they bounced to the side. He picked them up again, and this time, placed them in the can before turning to walk out of his room. As he started, he stopped as if his legs refused to take him any further. He went back to the desk, sitting and gazing out the window again.

"Okay, God, if you want me to write this, I need some help," he whispered.

He opened the notebook. Once again, Andy began his letter:

Lacy,

Let me begin by saying that there is nothing I can put in this letter that will change what happened, and I don't expect this to change the way you feel about me.

Since this tragedy, I've done some serious soul searching, and I'm not where I want to be. The actions, MY actions, that caused this is not who I want to be. I prayed to God that He would take your injuries and give them to me. I know that's not possible, but I would do it in a heartbeat. I own my actions. It was my decision that caused this. It was my actions alone that led to a decision that is out of my, or your, hands.

I went to the hospital several days while you healed and rested. I got to know your parents. They are wonderful people. I envy how much they love you. But as you rested, I got to know you, too.

I asked lots of questions, and your parents were gracious enough to fill me in on what a wonderful person you are. Like you, I've always been an athlete. I think this is what hurts me the most. The thought of taking that from you has affected me in a way I didn't know I could feel. I learned how much you love Christ and how you volunteer so much of your time to Him. They said that you were coming home from passing out gifts at a nursing home when I hit you.

Your kindness is known by many. I learned that, too. That love you have for God is something I wish I had. I think out of everything, that's what I'm the most envious of. A good friend, my best friend, just told me today that giving your heart to Christ is different from giving your life to Christ. That second part, I don't think I've ever done. Lacy, I think that's what I've been missing, and I want to learn how to do that.

I could tell you more about me so that you know who I am—the guy that ruined your life—but this letter isn't about me. It is about you, and how I'm so sorry that you even have to read this. I don't really know what to do now. I don't know what to say. I

---

just wish it never happened. As great of a person as you are, I wish that I could have met you sooner and under other circumstances, but that isn't the case.

I will end this by saying that whatever happens to us both, I know two things: I changed your life, and you changed mine. I want to learn to have what's missing in my life. I want what you have. Whatever happens, I am going to make sure that I find out what that is so that I don't make any more stupid decisions.

If you ever change your mind and allow me to tell you, I will probably stumble all over my words, but I promise that I will apologize with everything that's in me, so help me GOD!

Andy Higgins

ANDY CAREFULLY RIPPED the page out and folded it in thirds. He went downstairs and found an envelope in his mom's study. Before stuffing it in the envelope, he read it again. He contemplated tearing it up, but sealed it and placed it on the small table by his dad's recliner. He grabbed a pen, and on the envelope, he wrote:

Please take to Mr. Hollingsworth to give to Lacy.

He stood and stared at the envelope, reflecting on the words he'd written. It had been one week since the accident. Life was totally different. Andy was truly beginning to realize how one decision could change everything.

CHAPTER 7

MEETING LACY

MIDWEEK AT OAK CREEK FOUND THE FOCUS ON GETTING BACK TO football, something that the school—the whole town—took seriously. The talk of Andy had somewhat subsided. With the first game going into the playoffs, the Tigers were ready to move on.

Andy had not yet returned to school. Holly, his mom, picked up his assignments and had him do his work at home. With no trial date set, the Higgins' thought that it would be better to keep him out until the courts decided his fate. With Lacy's improvements, his outcome didn't look as bleak, but driving under the influence resulting in bodily harm was a serious matter, one that he and his family were worried about.

Andy still felt much worse for Lacy than he did himself. He found himself at the practice field every evening to support his teammates, but Coach Woods was careful about his participation so as to not get in trouble with the state's athletic board. Coach knew Andy needed to be where he felt like his family was. Football was a big part of his life, and it would be a big part of healing his soul.

Just atop the hill from where the stadium sat, the team continued their preparation for the opening round of the playoffs against a foe they had met before, Valley High. Even with Valley barely squeaking into the playoffs, Coach Woods knew they'd play tough. Both teams battled several times in the playoffs, making it an unofficial traditional rival even though they were never on a regular schedule.

"Let's go!" Coach screamed. "You guys look more like a herd of stray cats than a football team! Nobody was where they were supposed to be on that last play. Run it again!"

Coach Woods ran every practice as if he were getting graded, like his job depended on it. He expected nothing less from his boys, either. Unlike the regular season, every game forward could be the last for the year—and the last forever for his seniors.

Breathing hard, Toby scanned everyone in the huddle. "Mike, you have to make that fake to me and hold it in there a little longer before rolling out. Make them think you're giving it to me. Stiles, man, you gotta cut that slant off shorter, just behind the linebackers. You're going too deep, and that safety is gonna light you up. Couple steps and then slant toward the middle."

Toby had always been a team leader, but he'd stepped it up a notch in Andy's absence. The team believed in him, too. Toby never had been one to showboat, but he stood out to his team because he never gave less than one hundred percent. That was why his quick decision to quit came as a shock to everyone, even if just a hastened thought.

Andy stood behind the offense, offering advice to Mike as needed. He thought a lot about how much he wanted to be playing. Andy felt he'd waited his entire life to be a senior in the playoffs, and knew his decision alone had led to an act that might strip him of the one thing he loved more than life—football.

Someone shouted his name, pulling him from his thoughts. Andy saw Mr. Hollingsworth waving. He was standing off to the side of the field, near the field house. The shout also caught the attention of Coach Woods. Andy looked toward the coach and a simple nod of approval was all Andy needed to head that way.

"Mr. Hollingsworth," Andy said as he came closer. "What are you doing here? How's Lacy?"

"Much better. Her back surgery on Monday went great. They

fused two vertebrae and removed a bone chip from the other. A lot less nerve damage than expected."

Andy smiled. "I've prayed for her daily. A few times a day, actually."

"She read your letter, and she—"

"My letter! I didn't even know you got it."

"Your dad came by Monday evening, after her surgery, and brought us dinner and your letter." Mr. Hollingsworth looked out toward the players. "Man, Coach is serious, huh?"

"Yeah, very much so. Hey, what did Lacy say about my letter? I've never attempted that before, and I bet she hates me even more now."

Mr. Hollingsworth laughed. "No, son. Not at all. She got a giggle out of it. She said that the last time a boy wrote a letter to her was in third grade, and it got taken up before it got to her and read aloud to the class. It was good to see her smile. That letter was a blessing to me, too. I needed to see that smile."

Andy felt his cheeks heat up and knew he was blushing. "I'm glad, sir. Would you tell her that I'm praying for her?"

"Why don't you tell her yourself?" he said as he let a grin escape.

"But, but she said she didn't want to see me. She said that—"

"That was before," Mr. Hollingsworth continued. "Now, she's had time to comprehend everything, and she wants to see you. She has a lot of anger built up, and she needs to forgive you so that it goes away. You see, she serves Christ so hard that she wants to do everything to please Him, even forgive the ones that she knows hurt her. And besides, she already said that the store should have never sold that stuff to you. It all goes back to a series of bad decisions, not just yours."

"Really, sir? She wants to see me?"

"Yeah, she does. How about tomorrow, after practice?"

"Yes, sir! I'll ask my dad to bring me as soon as practice is over!"

"Sounds good, Andy. I'll see you tomorrow."

Later that evening, Toby dropped Andy off at home. He couldn't wait to ask his dad about visiting Lacy. He needed it as much as anything to help with his emotional process. It had been a rollercoaster ride for the last two weeks, and an acceptance of his apology would be a step in the right direction.

"Mom! Where's Dad?" Andy shouted as he ran into the house.

"Hello to you, too," she responded. "He hasn't made it home yet. Should be here any moment."

"Lacy wants me to come by tomorrow!" he continued, almost shouting as excitement exploded from him.

Holly had been cutting vegetables near the kitchen sink, but she stopped. "Andy, are you sure you want to do this? Are you ready? Baby, you don't know what the outcome of all this will be."

Andy grabbed an apple from a bowl nearby. Taking a bite, he mumbled through his vigorous chewing, "I'm sure, Mom. Hey, by the way, when did Dad take that letter to her?"

"Monday," Holly said as she began cutting again. "He went to talk to Mr. Hollingsworth about the insurance, and—"

"Oh, no! How'd that go? Is the lawsuit filed yet?"

"Actually, that's the one bit of good news we've gotten lately. Kyle met with our agent Monday morning, and they're paying for all of Lacy's costs and replacing her car. We're not so lucky on yours, but we kinda figured that."

Andy smiled, but then his brow wrinkled and his lips tightened, as if his thoughts were trying to burrow through them. "What about her college?"

Holly finished cutting and placed the bowl under a stream of water coming from the faucet. "Well, that's not covered. I don't think any insurance would cover that."

Andy sighed loudly. "But, Mom! I took that away from her, too."

"Well, we may not be out of the woods on that one yet. Even though Mr. Hollingsworth is being so nice about everything, your father seems to think that we'll get hit with a lawsuit. We'll just have to—"

"I'll just have to pay for it. I'll get a job; whatever it takes."

"One hurdle at a time, son."

"Mom, I have to!"

"Have to what?" Kyle asked as he came in. "What are we having to do now?"

Andy met him as he entered the room. "Dad! What can we do to pay for Lacy's college? Is there anything?"

Kyle laid his keys on the kitchen island and leaned across one of the tall stools. "Let's see what happens. Mr. Hollingsworth and I had a good talk about that, and we're going to cross that bridge when we get there. I assured him we wouldn't walk away from this."

Andy tightened his lips as he nodded, knowing the answer everyone had would be the same: wait and see. But Andy was tired of waiting.

He had waited for a decision from the insurance companies. He was waiting for the court to set a trial date. He was waiting to see if his football career was over. Waiting was the hardest thing, but Andy knew that waiting could have been the answer to avoiding all the problems he was facing. He first considered how different things would have been if he had waited to get to the party before he started drinking.

And while waiting was a good choice, he knew deep down that not drinking at all would have been the best choice. But a decision that changed more lives than his own was made, and he had no choice but to be still and continue waiting.

IT WAS THURSDAY, the last practice before the first round of the playoffs.

Fall Thursdays in Oak Creek were important. Some schools and communities rallied on Friday nights, but Oak Creek started the day before. Most of the parents gathered to watch practice as did many of the townsfolk. Spectators outnumbered the players and coaches, their lawn chairs lining the practice field. After practice, a pot-luck dinner was held for everyone. That was who Oak Creek was, a pride-filled town every day, not just Friday nights. They supported their boys, and they let them know it.

Andy stood with the team as they ran through the final few drills. He was physically there, but his mind was already at the hospital, anticipating his meeting with Lacy. He saw his dad arrive an hour earlier and wanted to leave then, but he didn't want his team to feel as if he was abandoning them for his desires.

"All right! Bring it in, boys," Coach Woods yelled.

Andy knew the announcement signaled the end of practice. After a few brief instructions from Coach, the team dispersed to the locker rooms, and Andy rushed over to where his dad was, ready to head to see Lacy.

"Andy!" someone from the crowd yelled. "Hey, Andy! Hold up!"

He was surprised to see Greg Collins, a longtime resident of Oak Creek, and one of their athletic booster club members, waving him over. Greg was a star athlete when he played at Oak Creek. Many people thought he would go on to play in college, but Greg never had a desire to go further. He began working after graduation and had been with the same factory for over thirty years, working his way up into management.

Already in a hurry, Andy wanted to act as if he hadn't heard, but it was too late. The calling of his name caused an automatic reaction to look in that direction.

He kept heading toward his dad as he answered, "Hey, Mr. Collins. How's it going?"

"Andy, hold on a second. Want to talk to you about something. It'll just take a second." He noticed Kyle waiting. "Hey, Kyle. How are ya? Hey, can I borrow Andy for just a couple of minutes, if you have time?"

Kyle shrugged. "Sure, Greg. Anything wrong?"

"Oh, no. Nothing like that. Just want to talk. You can stay and listen," Greg replied, finally catching up to Andy.

"Mr. Collins, I need to hurry," Andy said, slowing his pace. "I promised I would be somewhere as soon as practice was over."

Greg smiled. "No worries. This will be very quick."

"Take as long as you need, Greg," Kyle replied while scrutinizing Andy with raised eyebrows.

Greg glanced at Kyle and nodded before turning his attention back to Andy. "Andy, son, to my knowledge, just about everyone has avoided talking to you about what happened. I don't want you to think we've turned our backs on you. We know the why and whats, and I don't think—"

"Greg," Kyle interrupted. "It's fine, Greg. No need to explain."

Greg looked at Kyle and said, "Kyle, I'll make this quick." He turned his attention back to Andy. "Son, we love you. This town loves you. Hell, three weeks ago, the whole town was shouting your name and looking for you to bring us another title. Now, it would be easy to think that everyone turned their back on you with the way we've acted. That's why I wanted to talk to you. I've talked to several parents here tonight, and we all feel like you're our son. You grew up playing with my Michael before he left for college. You've eaten at the tables of half of those folks over there. We hurt with you. Andy, no matter what caused that accident, we still love you, and we will be there to help you through this. That's what we do in a small town. We're all family. We just didn't know what to say. But we do now. We say that one of our sons needs us, and we're here for you."

Andy reached out to shake Greg's hand. "Thank you, sir. I don't know what to say."

Greg took Andy's hand and hugged him with his other arm. "Family—that's what we do."

Kyle waited until Andy released Greg's hand, and he reached to shake it. "Greg, thank you! We haven't been the best at leaning on you guys either. Honestly, we didn't know how you would respond."

"Well, now you know," Greg replied with a smile.

Andy and Kyle hurried through goodbyes before speeding off toward Memorial Hospital. Along the ride, the sound of the tires on the road was just about the only sound. Neither Kyle nor Andy spoke much about the impending visit. Kyle wanted to talk to Andy, but he could tell Andy was already in deep thought.

Upon arrival, Kyle shut off the truck and almost immediately opened his door. Andy was hesitant and sat staring out the passenger window.

Kyle noticed the pause. "Son, are you sure you're ready for this?"

Andy finally popped his door open. "I am. Sorry. I was rehearsing my words."

Kyle walked around the truck and waited on Andy. "Just relax. Be yourself. Son, if she gets upset with you, at least you've tried."

The two continued inside and down the winding hallways to the elevator. They advanced to the third floor, where the I.C.U. unit was located. As they rounded the corner to the lobby, they noticed several people, but Mr. and Mrs. Hollingsworth weren't there. The double doors leading into the units swung open, and a nurse hastily came out and rushed past them.

"Excuse me! Miss," Kyle shouted, trying to get her attention. The nurse stopped and turned to them. "I'm looking for the Hollingsworth family. Are they inside there? With Lacy?"

"Oh, Lacy! Sweetest girl we've had since I've been here. They moved her. She graduated! She's one floor down, room 216."

They hurried back toward the elevator. Andy took deep breaths, trying to calm his nerves.

"That's a good thing, right, Dad?" he asked. "I mean, they wouldn't move her if she wasn't better, right?"

"I suppose so," Kyle said as he nodded.

The elevator came to a stop, and they stepped off. They looked for the sign that would show them toward her room. A sign with an arrow pointing to the right directed the way to rooms 200 through 220. Off they went.

"Here, Dad. Room 216," Andy said as he came to an abrupt stop.

"You ready, son? Not too late to turn around."

Andy knocked on the door before he had a chance to change his mind or chicken out. A familiar voice came from inside.

"Come in," Mr. Hollingsworth instructed.

Andy looked at his dad. His eyes widened and his breaths deepened. He took another deep breath before slowly opening the door. Tentatively, he took a few steps and followed the swinging door inside.

Mr. Hollingsworth welcomed them as he stood from his chair. "Hello, Andy! Kyle, how are you?"

"Doing well, Mr. Hollingsworth. And you?" Kyle stepped forward to shake Mr. Hollingsworth's hand.

Andy stood positioned with Mr. Hollingsworth between him and Lacy, peeking around to see Lacy and hoping she wasn't looking his way.

"I *can* see you," Lacy responded, leaning to one side.

Andy sighed and stepped to the side, making himself more visible to Lacy. He suddenly wished he would have brought something, anything, to give her to help break the ice.

"Hi," he said with a noticeable quiver in his voice. He cleared his throat and tried again. "I'm Andy."

Lacy shifted and thumbed the buttons on the bedrail, raising the head of the bed. It buzzed softly as it moved her up into a sitting position. The tubes running to the intravenous needles in her arm stretched as she reached for the pole beside her, trying to pull it closer to the bed.

"Not too far, hun," Ann reminded her. "You're not supposed to sit up too much with that back brace on."

"So, this is *the* Andy," Lacy said as she adjusted the pillow under her head.

Andy stepped forward but stopped after only a couple of steps, a nervous tension preventing him from moving any closer. He paused for only a second, but in that second, he noticed Lacy looked like any of the girls at his school. During the first few visits, her face was visibly swollen, and although she still had stitches above her left eye and a noticeable abrasion on her cheek, she looked much better, even pretty, he thought. He noticed her eyes were green, almost an aqua-green color. Her hair was cut where doctors had closed wounds, but she had pulled it back in a ponytail, and it almost hid the injuries.

"Yeah, I guess I'm *the* Andy," he replied as he took another cautious step closer. "The Andy that you wished you'd never seen."

Mr. Hollingsworth grabbed a chair and slid it over to Andy.

"Here, Andy. Take a seat. Lacy has been looking forward to talking to you."

Andy took the chair and slid it a little, positioning it so that it was facing Lacy.

"Thank you, sir," he answered as he sat.

"Kyle, let me buy you a coffee or tea," Bob said. "Ann, why don't you come with us?"

He knew Andy and Lacy needed to talk to get through the awkwardness, and with their parents there, it only made things worse. Ann kissed the top of Lacy's head and squeezed her hand while Andy looked to Kyle for assurance. His father gave him a wink and a little nod, and the adults stepped from the room, letting the door close behind them.

"So, *Andy*. I got your letter," Lacy said, tilting her head toward the nightstand to where the letter lay. "Not too bad for a jock," she added with a sly grin.

Andy softly chuckled and ran a hand through his hair. "I honestly didn't know what to say. I had plenty of words, but nothing made sense. I could have just written, 'I screwed up,' and it would have covered it all, I guess."

Lacy adjusted her bed higher, ignoring her mother's request. "Andy Higgins. The pride of Oak Creek. The quarterback. All-state, two years in a row, and possibly a third this year. Pretty good baseball player, too. Dates Maribeth Jenkins, and—"

"Dated," he interrupted. "We dated, but not anymore."

"You mean, not right *now*," she countered. "Amazing what social media will tell you, ain't it?"

He leaned toward her, resting his arms on his knees. "Look, I wish I could take it back. I really do. My life has been a living hell since this happened, and—well, I know yours has been worse. I mean, I don't want to make this sound like—"

"Like what? Like you're selfish? Like it's your life that was messed up?"

Andy sat up straight, his eyes glossy, and he was reminded that Lacy might never have the same life again.

"Yeah," he whispered. "Selfish. That's probably the best word for it."

Lacy took a deep breath and exhaled, seemingly frustrated. "Tell me, Andy from Oak Creek; would you trade places with me?"

Andy gazed at her, taking in the tubes still hanging from her arms to the complicated brace on her back that he knew she would wear for weeks and the bruises still scattered across her body. He knew his answer, but instead of just a "yes," he struggled to find more meaningful words.

"Well?" she continued. "You said in the letter that you trade places with me. But would you take my injuries? Would you give up possibly ever playing ball again? Would you take my place, Andy Higgins?"

Andy immediately responded with the one word he'd been trying to replace with something more elegant. "YES!" he nearly shouted. "Lacy, I would in a heartbeat. That letter is something I don't think I've ever done before. I'm not talking about writing, but I spoke from my heart. It's like I just started writing and then had to read it myself to see what was there."

Lacy smiled, and they sat without saying anything for a few seconds before she finally broke the silence.

"What about the other part?"

Andy furrowed his brow, and a look of confusion crossed his face. "Other part?"

Lacy adjusted her pillow again, allowing her to lean in Andy's direction. "Giving your life to God."

Andy cupped his chin with one hand, trying to hide the nervous quiver he knew would appear in his voice and the tremble he felt in his lips. It happened every time someone asked about his faith. His words got lost somewhere within his body. He knew what he wanted to say, but didn't know how to explain it to Lacy.

"You mentioned you had given your heart to Christ, but you didn't give your life to Him," she continued. "What did you mean?"

Andy fidgeted, still struggling to find the right words. He had always found it difficult to talk about religion, especially when religion regarded his actions. Finally, he mustered a few words. "I, um, well, I was saved in Vacation Bible School a long time ago. And, I mean, I know what that means, but—"

"But it's hard to give up the things you know aren't in His favor. Is that what you're trying to get out?"

Andy looked up at her, his eyes filled with tears. He swiped his thumbs across his lower lids, hoping to catch them before they escaped and trailed down his cheeks.

"Yeah, that sums it up," he said with a long sigh.

"Andy, I get it. That's called temptation. I have it. My friends deal with it. We *all* deal with it. None of us are perfect, but you know what? Forgiveness is real. Y'know how you said you would take my place? Well, Jesus already has. When He died on that cross, forgiveness became real!"

He nodded wordlessly, trying his best not to look up so that Lacy wouldn't notice the tears he'd failed to stop from falling.

"Andy, your friend was right. Accepting Jesus and giving your life to Him are two different things. But what he didn't tell you is that it's the steps to your relationship and growth in your walk that separate the two. When you admit that you believe in Jesus and you accept Him into your heart, knowingly admitting that He's your Savior, your salvation begins. But it's like school, like being in kindergarten." She stopped and tilted her head. "Let me put it to you another way. When was the first time you ever played football?"

Andy shrugged and stole a glance at her. "I don't know. Like six years old? Maybe seven. It was little league. I think they called it Toy Bowl or something."

"So, let's say you were six," she said with excitement in her voice. "You came out there on that first day, knowing everything about football, right? You knew what zone coverage was. You knew how to spot a corner blitz by how the safety would cheat to one side, correct? You knew that when you rolled to your right, it would pull the linebackers that way and open up a small window for a tight end to be open back on the left about five yards across the line of scrimmage, right? You knew all of that on the first day, didn't you?"

Andy laughed and wiped the last of his tears away. "Heck no! I was scared to death. I couldn't even tell you where a tight end lined up and—wait, how do you know all of that? That's stuff I still have trouble seeing."

Lacy smiled. "I played little league football, too. Yes, a girl played football. I've followed it my whole life, even kept stats a few times. But anyway, that first day of little league, that's like the first day of your salvation. You don't know much about it, don't understand it, don't even know what you got into sometimes. You make a lot of mistakes —a whole lot! But you had a coach and a playbook. You learned and developed yourself into a better ballplayer. You studied the plays and practiced as much as you could because you love it." Lacy paused, noticing Andy's attention.

"Now, imagine that football is your relationship with Christ. You grow in it. You'll still make mistakes, but your coach will help you correct them. Christ is your new coach, and all your Christian friends are your assistant coaches. Your playbook is the Bible. It takes steps. You commit to it just like football and allow yourself to become better. Before you know it, you're an assistant coach yourself."

Andy grinned and shook his head. "Wow. I've never heard it like that before. That's awesome."

Lacy leaned back into her pillow and narrowed her eyes. "Can I ask you something and you be serious about it? I want the truth."

The corners of Andy's mouth turned down as he anticipated the question, not knowing what was coming next. With hesitation, he simply replied, "Sure."

"Are you sure you've accepted Christ?"

He hesitated. Andy sat with his hands clasped, his thumbs circling each other, trying to not make eye contact. But he knew he had to give Lacy an answer, so he began to stammer, "Well, I—"

Suddenly, the door swung open and the Hollingsworths and Kyle walked back in, chattering to each other and overpowering Andy's voice.

"Did you kids get to talk?" Mr. Hollingsworth asked.

"We did," Lacy replied, noticing the look of relief pass across Andy's face.

"Great," he replied, glancing at Kyle over his shoulder. "She's been impatient to ask Andy about the wreck and what he remembers."

"Actually, Dad, we never got to that. We've just been making small talk."

"Well, should we give y'all a little more time? I could go for a sandwich from the cafeteria," Mr. Hollingsworth suggested.

"No, Dad, we can talk more about it on Saturday." Lacy looked at Andy, her brows raised. "I know the playoffs start tomorrow, and you'll be at the game."

"Uh, umm," Andy stuttered. "I had plans, but, I mean—sure! I'll be here."

CHAPTER 8

THE PLAYOFFS BEGIN

It was still an hour before kickoff, and the stands on Oak Creek's side were almost full. The visiting team's fans were also filing in at a steady pace. It was rare that two teams so equally qualified met in the opening game of the playoffs.

While Oak Creek held on to their perfect record, the Valley Bears came to town with two losses, but very important losses. Each came during regional play against ranked opponents, placing them third in their region and having to travel to Oak Creek. Despite Oak Creek's unblemished record, they still weren't at the top of the food chain, holding the number five state ranking.

A sea of blue filled the home side, and the crowd was already getting into the spirit of the game. The band and cheerleaders had held a pregame pep rally that worked the crowd into a frenzy. Cars with more fans continued streaming in, lined up like busy ants bringing food to their queen. It seemed as if the line was never-ending.

For a town that wasn't large enough to fill most major grocery store parking lots, when Oak Creek started the playoffs, they brought back alumni and fans that no longer lived here. Graduates from years past were quick to boast, "Once a Tiger, always a Tiger."

Most stores had closed early, only leaving the convenience store to offer gas and snacks for another hour. Streetlights came on, triggered by the dusk falling over the horizon. Just off to the south of town, a soft glow could be seen rising above the treeline. The stadium lights let it be known that it was almost game time.

The few people left in town didn't let the event go unnoticed; typical chit-chat of the recent cold front and the last batch of garden greens had officially turned to their opinions of how the game should go.

At the old Union Hall, men gathered and perched on the benches out front. A few made their way to the game by kickoff, but some waited it out, listening to the local radio channel broadcasting the game. From there, they could hear the band and sometimes the crowd, making them aware that something had happened seconds before the delayed radio caught up.

"Ol' Mike is better than I thought he'd be," one man stated, referring to Mike Gamble, the starting quarterback in Andy's absence.

"I heard that Valley's running back broke the rushing record last game. He's gonna be tough to stop," added another.

Then there was the inevitable topic, too. "Heard anything about Andy? How's that girl?"

No matter how anticipated the game was, it was linked to Andy, and Andy had been a key reason for the success of the squad. In a small town, even one where news traveled faster than the smell from the nearby chicken houses, events that happened were still big news to everyone. It was discussed daily, along with the rumors that came with them.

Back at the stadium, the crowd grew more excited as kickoff closed in. Both teams finished pregame warmups and were getting final instructions from their coaches before returning to the field. Each team stood at opposite ends, huddled around a coach.

Two long lines of fans stretched from the end zone Oak Creek was gathered at, a longstanding tradition with the Oak Creek faithful. These were the Victory Lines, and the Tigers made their grand entrance by running through the pathway as their fans cheered and shouted their names. Everyone loved it! The fans and especially the players.

Coach Woods finished his pep talk, and the team stood ready to break through a paper mural that the cheerleaders had painted with the team colors and words of encouragement. The cheer squad held tightly to the poles that stretched the banner.

Excitement grew. Fans were on their feet, anticipating the team running onto the field like gladiators making their way to battle in a coliseum. The team inched closer to the banner, some poking holes in the paper to peer through and smile at the support they saw.

Alec was in the middle of the lines of fans, running up and down each side with his arms waving, persuading the crowd into growing louder. As he passed up and down the lines, the crowd responded, like ripples through water. Alec took great pride in prepping the fans, and they loved him. He was a staple at every football event, and his love and enthusiasm for the game were contagious.

Coach Woods enjoyed the enthusiasm as well. He knew it fired up his squad. But he would leave all of that to the players. After his pregame talk, he sauntered over to the sideline and waited for all the glitz and glamour to give way to the game he loved to coach.

The crowd noise swelled. With a few taps from the rim of a snare drum, the entire band came alive as the announcer yelled into the outdated microphone feeding the static-charged loudspeakers.

"Stand and welcome your Oak Creek Tigers!" his crackled, overzealous voice called out.

The fight song played loudly as the band tried its best to keep in tune, but the excitement couldn't escape them either; a few stray notes found their way into the cool night air. It didn't matter, though. Behind the banner, legs were already pumping as heart rates increased. Some jumped with anticipation, and finally, the sound of the paper banner ripping sent the crowd into a craze that not many saw at the high school level. But this was Oak Creek, and this was the playoffs—football was almost as much their religion as what they found in the little church that sat in the middle of town.

The already enthusiastic fan base pushed the decibel limits above that of any musical instrument, drowning out even the bass drums and tubas. The players tore down the Victory Lines like wild animals being released from cages. It was game time!

With both teams finally on their respective sidelines, the focus was back to business, exactly how Coach Woods approached the contest. "Do your job!" he barked at everyone. It was a game; but even in games, everyone had responsibility.

Toby paced the sideline, giving himself last-minute instructions. He took his role as a captain seriously. Every mistake, whether made by him or a teammate, he wanted to correct.

"Yo, Mike," he yelled at his quarterback. "Hey, man, loosen up! You look like you're about to crap yourself."

Mike's first playoff game had his nerves feeling like barbed wire, twisted in all directions and ready to cause harm if touched the wrong way. He gawked at Toby; his eyes were wide and his lips dry. Toby watched Mike's chest rise and fall, knowing he was breathing heavily.

"Dude, I was fine until we ran out here," he explained. "It's like all the plays are running together. I don't want to be the one to screw this up."

"You're overthinking it," Toby assured him. "One play at a time. If you have doubts, I'm here. Just ask me."

Andy hadn't participated in the Victory Lines entrance. Instead, he made his way to the sideline with Coach, ready to observe and help where he was needed. He noticed Mike's anxiety and headed over to Mike and Toby.

"You got this, man. After those first few plays, the butterflies will be gone. Just get through that first series, and this will be just like any other game."

"Toby! Good luck, babe. Love you," Ruby yelled over the crowd as she smiled and blew a kiss.

Alec was nearby and jumped in front of Toby, raising his hand like he'd snatched something from the air. "Hey, Tobe! That's mine," he teased. "Love you, Ruby Sue!"

"Love you, too, A-man," she replied, blowing another kiss.

Another announcement came over the speakers, one that caught the attention of everyone. "Please rise, and with hands over hearts, join us in the presentation of our National Anthem."

Every player from Oak Creek stopped and stood at attention. No matter what they were doing, it came to a halt. They stood tall, right hands over their hearts, left hands behind their backs, their eyes fixed on the flag, not looking at anything else. Standing at attention was as important as any other preparation was for Coach Woods. It showed class and respect, and he had his players practice standing as well, doing it over and over again until they did so perfectly.

As the last notes rang out, the crowd once again erupted, and both teams took the field, ready for the contest.

Oak Creek took the opening kickoff and would start from their twenty-yard line. The teams were set to do battle. From the sideline, Coach Woods screamed instructions. He'd picked up on Mike's anxiety before the game and knew that an easy handoff would be a good play to calm him down and build up his confidence.

Mike looked at him from the huddle as he took the call.

"Okay, guys," he yelled over the crowd noise. His teammates were only inches away, but he had to scream to be heard. "Split right, thirty-two dive, on two. Ready—"

"Thirty-*one* dive. Split right! We run thirty-one, to this side," Toby corrected, motioning to the left side of the huddle.

Mike shook his head and took a deep breath. "Thirty-one dive, on two. Ready? Break!"

The huddle broke, and everyone hustled to the line. Toby stood behind Mike and stepped up close to him before taking his position.

"One play at a time, Mike," he reminded him. "You got this, bro."

The ball was snapped! The first play was underway.

The line blocked perfectly, opening up a seam for Toby to take the handoff. Mike turned and placed the ball into Toby's gut, and he wrapped his arms around it, securing it from escape. He broke through for five yards as a Valley defender met him in a violent collision. Toby spun off the impact, leaving the defender lying on the ground. He continued toward the sideline before cutting the ball back upfield. The crowd, who hadn't yet sat down, erupted in cheers as Toby broke free. He raced for another twenty yards before being forced out of bounds.

Alec had run the entire way with him, down the sideline, and was the first to meet him as he jumped up from the tackle.

"Yeah, bro!" Alec shouted, slapping Toby's helmet and jumping against him. "They can't stop the T-Train tonight." Alec turned to the crowd, waving his hands to signal them to get louder. "Can't stop my brother!"

The team's enthusiasm escalated. In the very first play, Toby had already made a great move that placed them midfield.

"See, bro?" Toby shouted as he made his way back to the huddle. "One play at a time."

Mike smiled as he smacked the side of Toby's helmet. He looked toward the sideline as he took the next call.

"Trips right, rocket screen, on one," he announced to his team.

The passing play was an easy one. Mike would simply take the snap, turn to his right, and make a quick throw to one of the receivers.

The ball was snapped to Mike, and he turned to deliver the pass, but the defensive end had crossed the line. Blake missed his blocking assignment and let the defender come straight at Mike. Toby noticed the missed block and tried to maneuver to pick up the end, but it all happened too fast, and Mike was tackled for a loss on the play.

Momentum can shift quickly and usually does during the first few plays of a game. Oak Creek's crowd became less audible, and the visitors from Valley celebrated the play.

"Blake! That was on you. Shake it off. Let's go," Coach Woods screamed.

Alec joined in on the scolding. "Come on, Blake. You know you gotta pick up that end!"

If a player was ever unsure of their assignment, all they had to do was ask Alec. He knew everyone's assignment on every play. And he was sure to let them know when one was missed.

"Sorry, guys," Mike said once he was back in the huddle. "I

99

couldn't get it off fast enough."

Another play was called, and Toby was determined he'd get back the yards lost. He took a pitch to the left side. The defensive cornerback noticed, pulled off of his receiver, and headed toward Toby. Toby made an adjustment and cut back inside, but was met by another defender before barely making it back to the original line of scrimmage.

The next two plays seemed to fall flat. Oak Creek found themselves in a third down and long situation. Coach Woods told his players he wanted to set the tone on the opening drive, but this wasn't the tone he'd wished for. He knew Mike was placed in a position a young quarterback didn't need to be in.

The play was called, and the team lined up. Mike looked back at Toby. Toby nodded an approval and hopefully some assurance to calm his nerves. Mike took the ball from center and faked the handoff to Toby, then looked left and saw his receiver open. His eyes widened, knowing that it should be an easy first down and save the drive.

He raised the ball to his shoulder, stepped forward, and released. It went straight toward the receiver and looked as if it would be a perfectly executed play. But Toby hadn't seen the linebacker waiting just across the line of scrimmage.

The defender stepped between Toby and the intended target. He snagged the ball out of the air for an interception and raced the opposite way. A host of Oak Creek players gave pursuit, but the head start was too much to recover from, and Valley struck first on the night from an errant mistake. With only a couple of minutes removed from the game, Oak Creek found themselves trailing.

Mike stormed to the sideline, throwing his helmet against the bench. Coach Woods followed.

"Son, pick up that helmet. Regroup. That was a mistake. What do we do with those?"

Mike plopped down on the bench and grabbed his helmet, holding it with one hand. "Own it."

"We *what*?!" Coach shouted.

"We own it, Coach!" Mike shouted.

"We own and learn from it," he barked. "Now get your head in the game and get ready to go back out there and learn from it."

He moved to walk away but turned once more. "And if you *ever* throw a helmet like that again, you'll never wear one for my team again." Coach didn't wait for Mike's response before storming away to ready his kick receiving team.

"Dude, shake it off," Andy said as he sat next to him. "That's the oldest trick by a linebacker. When he recognizes a pass play, he's gonna freeze just out of your sight and hope you don't see him. Always, always check that outside linebacker before throwing a short pass to the flats. Bro, you can't let this shake you. Do what you've been doing in practice. You're ready for this."

Mike shook his head. "I should have checked but I rushed it. I looked, saw Stiles open, and rushed it. Dude, I feel like I'm gonna puke."

Toby knew Coach had already given him a verbal lashing and Andy was giving him refresher instructions. No need for him to add to it. He fist-bumped him as he went by and reminded him, "One play at a time."

After a few back and forths and neither team finding their way to the end zone, the first quarter ended. Both teams had settled in and were playing solidly, but just when it looked like one got the momentum, the other stole it right back. At the end of the first, Oak Creek trailed seven to nothing.

The crowd had also settled in and was a lot less motivated than earlier, with almost everyone seated. However, the student section was still going strong; they never sat from opening kickoff to closing buzzer. They chanted and had choreographed movements as if they were in a contest with the opposing team's student section. To say the least, they were having fun.

Andy had just finished giving Mike a few pointers when he heard his name being called by Greg Collins, the booster club member that had spoken to him after practice just two days earlier. Andy nodded toward him but didn't move that way. He was invested in the game and didn't want to engage in conversation.

"Hey, Andy," Greg insisted. "Andy! Hey! Come over for just a second,"

Andy sighed and trotted toward the fence where Greg was leaning over.

"Hey, Mr. Collins," Andy reluctantly said. "Tough one, huh?"

"Valley is a good team. Hey, look. I've seen you go over and talk to Mike after every series. Others see it, too. I just wanted you to know that it's not going unnoticed how unselfish that is. But I want you to give this to Mike when you talk to him again."

"Sure, Mr. Collins," Andy said, taking a crumpled paper from his hand. "What is it?"

"Just tell him it came from Hank. Someone I'm sitting by wanted him to have it."

Andy examined it, noticing it was folded and taped shut. Confused, he replied, "Umm, okay. I'll give it to him."

They shook hands, and Andy took his place at the sideline as Oak Creek struggled to get any offense going. Another three and out, and the ball was given back to Valley. As Mike came to the sideline, Andy met him to check on him after seeing the tough hit he'd taken.

"Mike, you good? That was a hard lick."

"I'm good," he replied, frustrated with the results. "We can't get anything to work. Even Toby's struggling. Man, I don't get it. We're doing everything as we should."

"Just keep doing what you're doing. Don't force anything. Eventually, it'll happen."

Mike huffed. "I hope so, man. This is frustrating. It would be different if we were screwing up, but we're doing just like we practiced. It's like they know everything we're calling."

He grabbed a water bottle and squirted a stream into his mouth and across his face, shaking the excess from his hair.

"On that rollout," Andy said, "don't forget Reese. He's coming across the middle. If Stiles and Jake are covered at the flats and down the side, Reese should be coming across the middle. He's open almost every time."

"My bad, man," Mike apologized. "I just feel like I'm running for my life and forget to look back across my lane."

"No worries. Just remember he's there."

"Hey, Mike. You're holding your own. We got this, bro. Just keep doing what you're doing," Toby said as he joined them.

Mike fist-bumped him. "Thanks, bro! It's all you. You're keeping us in this."

"Teamwork, my man," Toby said.

Andy walked with Mike as he readied himself to go back onto the field. "Coach is gonna keep calling these short passes. If they're there, toss it. But if not, don't be scared to slang it down the field. You always have someone running that safety off deep. Slang it, man!"

Mike laughed. "Coach ain't gonna let that happen."

"Coach ain't gonna have long to fuss about it if we don't play next week," he said, raising his eyebrows with a smirk.

Mike put his helmet on without offering any reply.

"Oh, I almost forgot!" Andy said, reaching into his pocket for the taped-up message Greg had handed him. "I was told to give you this."

Mike took the paper. "What is it?"

"Not sure, but I'm supposed to tell you it's from Hank."

Mike's eyes widened and his mouth opened as if surprised. "*Who gave this to you?*"

"Greg Collins. Why?"

Mike hastily unfolded the paper and read it:

Mike, I can't tell you how proud I am. I am here tonight watching. You're doing great!

– Hank

His eyes filled with tears and he frantically scanned the stands, up and down each row. For an instant, he forgot about the game.

"Dude. What is it?" Andy asked. "Who's Hank?"

"Mike! Mike," Coach Woods screamed. "Offense, son! Get on the field. Come on. Get in the game!"

"My dad!" Mike shouted to Andy as he took the field, stuffing the message into his armband as he ran.

Andy stood with his arms limp by his side, watching Mike head out on the field. He then turned and looked around the bleachers, searching for Mr. Collins. He finally spotted him, and to his left was a man he'd never seen before. He was medium-built and wore a plaid shirt. On his head was a worn-out ball cap with an Atlanta Braves logo on it.

Is that Hank? he wondered. *Is that Mike's dad?*

But Andy had met Mike's dad. His name was Tim. He had never heard of Hank.

The crowd noise grew loud again. The stagnant production from both teams hadn't garnered such a reaction in several minutes. Andy turned his attention back to the field just as the announcer proclaimed, "Touchdown Tigers!" and he saw Scott Stiles, the senior receiver, raise his arms in the end zone in celebration.

After the extra point, the game was tied at seven points. Mike ran off the field to high-fives and cheers from everyone. Scott was congratulated for his catch and run. The mood was once again in favor of the hometown Tigers.

Coach Woods motioned for Mike to come his way. "What was that call?" he asked.

"Split right, eighty-cross, Coach. Stiles went a little deeper than usual, and that safety cheated up. Andy told me to watch for that, and sure enough, it was there."

Coach Woods glared at Andy, who was standing nearby. He looked back at Mike and narrowed his eyes.

"Good read," he replied, and walked away.

That was about as close to a compliment as Coach gave, and it brought smiles from both Andy and Mike. It was certainly better than the chewing they were expecting.

"Dude, you were right," Mike shouted at Andy. "I've just been taking the easy options and didn't want to go downfield, but I looked, and there he was, wide open!"

Andy punched Mike on the shoulder. "Told you, man! So, Hank? Your dad?"

"Long story, man," Mike replied with a big grin.

"But, what about Tim?"

"He's my dad. Always will be. But Hank is my biological dad."

Andy's forehead creased in confusion and didn't offer any response.

Mike laughed. "Yeah, I know. I'll have to explain later. But in short, I found out that Dad, umm, Tim, isn't my biological dad several years ago. I didn't tell anyone. We thought it would be easier since Hank was never in my life. He left while Mom was pregnant with me and never came back. I found him online about a year ago. He used to live here; went to school here, too, with Mr. Collins, your dad, and several others we know. He promised he would come to a game, but I didn't think he would."

"You're not mad at him for dipping out?" Andy asked.

"Mad? Nah. More hurt than mad, but I'm over it. Hank had a rough life, but in the last few months, we've talked about things, and he's even started going to church and asked Christ into his life. It's not gonna change the fact I was raised by another man, one that I'm thankful for and will always call Dad, but I'm okay with it all. I truly am. Life is about forgiveness and thankfulness, dude."

Andy nodded. "Wow, man. Never knew that. That's great. By the way, scope out the thirty-yard line, up about ten rows. Hank's on his feet, the man with a red plaid shirt."

Mike looked in the direction as instructed. A smile came to him as he raised his hand. Hank returned the wave. Neither could see it from the distance between them, but they both had tears in their eyes.

A couple of possessions later and a few chances at regaining the lead, both teams went into the locker room for the half, still tied.

Coach Woods did what he was famous for, making halftime speeches that changed weary players into new men. He reminded them that coming out in the second half of a game that was tied was like starting over. The pregame jitters were gone, and he instructed them to settle down, do their jobs, and own their decisions on the field.

Whatever the rest of his directions were, they seemed to work like a charm. For the rest of the game, Oak Creek played like a different team. They racked up four more touchdowns while only giving up one. With the final seconds of the game ticking off the clock, the scoreboard read:

TIGERS - 35

VISITORS - 7

Oak Creek was victorious!

The stands started to clear. But, as with most games, the majority of the crowd migrated to a new area and cheered on the team as they came out of the dressing rooms. They stood in small groups, waiting for their victors to come out. Not everyone stayed, but most did. More Tiger fans congregated after the game than the visiting team had brought with them.

Slowly, players started to emerge. *"Way to go Jason." "Good game, Jake."* The congratulatory greetings continued until they were all out.

Andy and Toby walked out together, where they were met by Ruby.

"Great game, babe," she said, greeting Toby with a hug and kiss. "Where's Alec?"

"Thanks, babe," he replied as he placed his arm around her. "He'll be out in a few. He's throwing everything in the laundry room and making sure things are accounted for."

Alec took the manager role seriously. If one piece of equipment was missing or not prepared properly, he felt as if it were his fault. As he put it, "Coach Woods told us to own our jobs, and this job is mine!"

Mike, almost in a jog, hurried past the trio waiting on him. He stopped and scanned the crowd. For Andy, it was clear who he was looking for. Hank!

Toby shouted in his direction, "You lost there, Q.B.?"

Mike replied without turning, "Looking for Hank."

"Who?" Toby responded with confusion in his voice.

"His dad," Andy replied. "His *real* dad."

"What?!" Toby exclaimed, his brow wrinkled. "His dad? But I thought...Tim?"

Andy shook his head and grinned. "Long story, bro. I still don't know all of it."

"Michael! Hey, Michael," came a call from inside a pickup truck parked nearby. It was Hank, waiting to see his son.

"Hank," Mike responded, pressing his body against Hank's truck. "Get out. I want you to meet my friends."

"Wasn't sure if it was a good idea," Hank replied. "Didn't know if your mom was here, and I sure don't want to cause any trouble."

"Mom knows we've been talking. Tim knows, too. They're good with it. Look, she's right over there," he said, pointing toward his mother.

She gave a small wave by lifting her hand from her crossed arms, and Tim, standing beside her, nodded with a smile.

"I'm glad you came," Mike said, stepping back so Hank could exit the truck. "I was surprised. I know you said you would try, but, wow! You're here!"

Hank placed his hands in his pockets and shuffled awkwardly. "Look at you. All grown up. Quarterback. Football star. Man, I've missed out on all this."

Mike laughed. "Not so sure about the star part. I'm out there by default."

"Well, you looked pretty dang good out there to me."

"Come on," Mike said as he placed his arm on Hank's back, gently pushing him to get him moving. "I want you to meet someone."

His mom waved and mouthed the words, "See you at home," and Mike waved his acknowledgment.

"Guys," Mike said as he neared his friends. "This is Hank. My dad. My real dad."

Toby stepped up and extended his arm to shake Hank's hand. "Good to meet you, sir."

Andy followed suit, and Ruby offered a smile and said, "Hi."

"I'll fill you guys in later," Mike said. "Hank—um, Dad—wanna go grab a burger at the Tiger Den? They always open back up after the game."

"I would love that, Michael," Hank said as a huge smile spread across his face.

"What's up, champs?" Alec shouted as he came running out of the locker room. "We are the champions. We are the champions," he began singing.

"Not so fast, lil' bro." Toby laughed as he playfully ruffled Alec's hair. "That was game one. Plenty more to go before we can sing that."

"Who's that?" Alec suddenly asked loudly, eyeing Hank.

Toby hesitated before answering, trying to decide what to say. "That's, umm, that's Mike's—"

"This is my friend, Hank," Mike interrupted, knowing that calling him anything else would confuse Alec.

Alec introduced himself to Hank, who extended his arm to shake Alec's hand, but Alec hugged Hank instead. Hank smiled and placed an arm on Alec's back and grinned at the group.

"Sorry. He likes to hug when he meets new friends," Toby explained.

"All good," Hank replied. "He's good at it. I already feel better."

Alec stepped back and pointed at Mike with his arm fully extended. "He's the quarterback. Mike is my friend, too."

"Well, he is lucky to have you as a friend, Alec," Hank said.

"You ready, Hank?" Mike asked. "I'm hungry."

They said their goodbyes to the group and departed, leaving the four friends behind in a bit of confusion-laced happiness over Mike's new father. Of course, there were still a lot of questions about Hank. Just moments ago, nobody knew Mike had a father he'd never met. There wasn't much they could talk about with Alec listening, but they were happy for Mike nonetheless.

The celebration around them continued for several minutes until finally, one by one, group by group, everyone dispersed. The once-filled parking lot contained a few cars and stragglers, with the streetlights reflecting off of them like spotlights. The epicenter of town had become barren, awaiting the next revival.

CHAPTER 9

I'M JUST NOT READY

THE NIGHT BROUGHT IN A COLD FRONT THAT SETTLED IN ON THE SMALL town. Fog hugged the fields like the clouds had fallen from the heavens, taking up new residence there. The small creeks winding at the base of the hill looked as if smoke was rising from them as dense fog swirled and followed the current. Foliage that had lost most of its summer colors gave way to the wind the front brought. Leaves rained upon the canvas below, covering it like a blanket. It was apparent that the autumn weather was on its way out to make room for Old Man Winter.

Andy was up early. Saturdays usually meant sleeping in, but he anticipated visiting with Lacy. The visit just days prior left him with a different feeling. He had been nervous before, but now he felt excited.

He wanted to know more about her, wanted to know the plans Lacy had. Andy still had plenty to tell her, too. He constantly thought about her question: *Are you sure you've accepted Christ?* Andy questioned his faith and wanted to dig deeper into what it meant to accept Christ. Her analogy of how someone learned about football and became a better player the more they practiced hit home with Andy in a way he could relate to and understand.

Was he more knowledgeable of God's Word now than he was years ago as he sat in a room filled with other ten-year-olds and accepted Christ? The more he thought about it, the more he wasn't so sure.

He sat on their porch swing, his legs touching the ground, but he extended and retracted them, making him gently swing. The clacking of the chain and squeak of the bushings in the swivel were the only sounds that morning. Even the animals had taken refuge with the cooler temperature.

His thoughts were all over the place, from *What will Lacy do about college*, to *How far will Oak Creek go in the playoffs*, and of course, the big one, *Am I a Christian*? Maybe all the talks that Toby had with him about his faith were needed. Maybe he should have listened more.

No matter the missed opportunities, Lacy's words stung the most.

The front door opened, and Kyle emerged with a cup of coffee in his hand and leaned against the porch railing. "Kinda cool out here, ain't it, champ?" he asked.

"Yeah, it is," he replied.

"Still want me to take you to Memorial today? If so, I may have to drop you off and pick you up later. I'm going over to Lineville to look at a camper I found online. I thought we may take it up to the lake a few weekends next summer."

Andy continued swinging, and, almost as if he hadn't heard anything about the camper, asked, "Dad, you're saved, right?"

Kyle took a sip of his coffee and moved to a chair in front of Andy. "That was random. What's on your mind, son?"

"A lot." Andy sighed. He leaned forward in the swing, bringing it to a halt. "Well, are you?"

Kyle knew the question would lead to others. He had never been comfortable talking about his faith or religion. He smiled and nervously chuckled as if trying to buffer the tension. "I suppose so. I did what I was supposed to do, I guess."

Andy hung his head but looked up toward his dad. "Serious, Dad. Are you?"

Kyle took a deep breath and let it out with an audible grunt, his frustration over the question apparent. "What's with this all of a sudden? Yes, I am *saved*," he said, making air-quotation marks with fingers and sitting upright in his chair. "I committed my life to Christ years ago. I know we don't go to church, but I know right from wrong. I do what I'm supposed to do. Am I the perfect example of a Christian man? Hell n—I mean, no. I'm not. But I know I'm saved, and I never—"

"How do you know? Like, how do you know for sure, Dad? 'Cause I'll be honest. I've got serious doubts about my salvation right now."

Kyle sipped his coffee again and shook his head. "I'm not sure I have a good answer, son. I guess if you were sincere when you accept Christ, well, you feel different, or maybe, umm—well, I guess you just know."

Andy leaned back and crossed his arms, sinking into the pillows on the porch swing.

Kyle smiled. "Guess that answer was about as much as you already knew, huh? I can call Ken from the hunting club. He pastors down at First Baptist. You want him to come by and talk with you? Maybe he can answer those questions. With as much as you've been through, it may be good, anyway."

"I'm good, Dad," Andy replied. "When are you leaving to go look at the camper? I need to get ready if you're dropping me off."

"Didn't think you heard that camper part." Kyle laughed. "Give me a few minutes, and we'll head that way. Call Mr. Hollingsworth and make sure it's not too early, though."

"Yes, sir."

BEFORE LONG, they were on their way, riding quietly, for the most part. Kyle brought up the game from the previous night and did his best to avoid religious talk. Andy still had plenty on his mind but kept quiet, mostly engaging in conversation by answering his Dad's questions. His mind raced with the thoughts of whether he had truly accepted Christ.

Finally, Kyle dropped off Andy at the front doors of the hospital with instructions to be ready in about an hour, and Andy made his way up to room 216.

Dang, he thought. *I was going to bring a gift.* He knocked on the door and stepped back.

"Come in," Mrs. Hollingsworth called from inside.

He pushed open the door and peeked into the room. "It's me; Andy," he announced.

"Oh, hey, Andy," she cheerfully replied.

Lacy adjusted herself in her bed and sat up. "Good morning, Andy from Oak Creek," she said with a smile. "Your boys played a good game last night."

"You heard about that? We played a good second half, but that first half was crazy," he said as he found an empty chair and sat.

"I listened to the whole game on the radio," Lacy explained before pausing and tilting her head. "You miss it, don't ya?"

Andy bit his bottom lip and nodded. "Yeah, I do. I think being there makes it worse."

Mrs. Hollingsworth stood. "Well, I think I'm gonna take this opportunity to grab some coffee. Baby, do you want anything from the cafeteria?"

"I'm good, Mom. Thank you."

Lacy sat up on her own, not using the motorized bed to help. She spun, letting her legs hang off the edge. A small but noticeable grimace flashed across her face, but a smile quickly replaced it.

"Wow!" Andy said in amazement, his eyes widening. "You're doing great!"

"They want me sitting in the chair more now," she said as she nodded her head toward a chair placed nearby. "Oh, and I walked down the hall yesterday!"

Andy leaned forward and exclaimed. "No way! For real?"

"They had me using a walker, but, um, yeah," she said, giving a closed-lip smile.

"That's great, Lacy," Andy said, his smile more noticeable than the one Lacy let appear. "I'm so proud!"

"And, guess what? If my neuro test comes back good, I may get to go home in a couple of days and continue therapy from there."

Andy pumped a fist in the air. "Yes!"

Lacy reached for her cup, sipping through her straw. "So, Andy from Oak Creek, why would you want to keep coming to see the girl you put in the hospital?"

Andy tightened his lips and sat in silence, thinking of what the correct answer should be. He knew *his* answer. He felt guilty. But that answer made it about him. He wanted the answer to be about Lacy.

"I think I'm still looking for that answer, Lacy." He sighed. "I felt like I needed to, but not sure why. Kinda like I knew I needed to be somewhere, but not sure what I was supposed to do when I got there. Know what I mean?"

She laughed. "Not at all."

"Me neither," Andy replied, also laughing.

"So, if you don't know why you're here, why am I here? What happened?"

Andy had been worried about that question, worried how he would explain that his decision, a very wrong decision, had led to this. But she already knew. It was apparent from her outburst when she first saw him, but for him to talk to her about it sent a nervous tension all over his body. He thought back to what Coach Woods instilled in him—*always own your decisions.*

"You're here because of me," he stated flatly. His head hung, searching for a spot on the floor to focus on to keep from having to make eye contact with her.

"I know that, but what happened? All I've been told is that you crossed over into our lane, hit us, and that you were drinking."

"Yeah, that's pretty much it. I made a horrible decision. I was going to take a sip, just to taste it. Next thing I knew, I had drunk almost the whole thing. I wanted some water to flush the taste and had a water bottle in the back seat, so I reached to get it and that's when we collided. By the time I looked up, you were there, and I couldn't do anything." He shook his head, disgusted with himself. "I'm so sorry. God, I am so sorry."

Lacy sat silently for a moment. She then softly said, "So, taking your eyes off the road caused this?"

"Yeah, I guess so," Andy replied in a whisper.

"Or was that a bad judgment call because you were under the influence?"

Andy finally looked up at her. "I guess one led to the other."

"A decision to drink alcohol while driving led to this?" she asked, as if coaching him to agree.

"Pretty much," he said, nodding. "A stupid decision. God, what a stupid decision! One that screwed up both of our lives. I don't expect you to ever forgive me, but like I said, I would take all of this if I could. I would swap places. I swear, Lacy! I would."

Andy desperately tried to hide the tears escaping his eyes by quickly knuckling them away, but he knew Lacy had already seen them.

Lacy leaned toward Andy. "Andy, I want to share something with you. Something I'm trying to figure out, too. I was at a nursing home that evening with our student worship team. A little old lady, a precious soul, gave me a bookmarker and said she wanted me to have it. She told me that it had a message on it that she felt God wanted me to have. On it was a verse, Philippians 2:16. I stuck it in my Bible and thought no more of it." Lacy swallowed the lump that had developed in her throat.

"When Mom and Dad retrieved the items from my car, they asked if I wanted anything from the car brought here, like my backpack, phone charger—that stuff. I asked Mom to find my Bible and bring it to me. When she did, that little bookmark fell out. Right after that, Dad brought in the accident report. I asked him if I could see it. Andy, you have a personalized tag, right? What's on it?"

Andy's brow wrinkled, thinking, *What does this have to do with anything*? "My initials and baseball and football numbers, AH-216," he replied.

"216!" she replied. She held her armband up to Andy. "Read my patient number."

Andy looked at it, leaning closer, and read it aloud. "1-0-0-2-1-6."
He tilted his head and shrugged.

"Again, 216!" she shouted. "Then they moved me *here*! My room
number—216!" Lacy grabbed her Bible as she continued. "I saw the
repetition of that number and figured the lady from the nursing home
was right! God was trying to tell me something. I went back and read that
verse from the bookmark, the one that started all of this." She continued
thumbing through her Bible until she came to the right scripture.

"Here! Listen to this: *'As you hold firmly to the word of life. And then I
will be able to boast on the day of Christ that I did not run or labor in
vain.'*"

Andy, still confused, said, "I'm sorry, Lacy. I'm not good at figuring
out what this stuff means."

Lacy laughed and smiled. "Well, at this one, me neither. But I
backed up a few verses. Listen to what I found: *'Do everything without
grumbling or arguing, so that you may become blameless and pure,
children of God without fault in a warped and crooked generation. Then
you will shine among them like stars in the sky.'*"

"I'm sorry, but I, umm—"

"Stop complaining!" she shouted.

"Oh, I'm not complaining, I'm just—"

"Not you, Andy! That's the message God was sending me. Stop
complaining! Be lights among the world! No matter what we labor in,
we should still be a light for others. We should spread God's love and
His Word. I was so consumed with my hectic life, I was complaining
about everything." She shifted a little to ease the tension on her back.

"The day of the wreck, I complained about going to the nursing
home. I was missing a friend's birthday party. But I had already
signed up, so Mom made me go." Lacy spread her arms, her eyes
dancing around the room.

"Look around! Does it suck being in here? Yes! But I'm alive. And
then I think about everyone that doesn't have a place to live. No roof
over their head, no bed. This food? Yuck! But I eat every day, many
times. I had become unthankful, even selfish, for my blessings. God

slowed me down so I could grow in Him. He'll use this for His glory and His good, but only if I let Him."

Andy hung his head again, thinking about what she said. "It was probably me He was trying to reach, and you just happened to be on that road."

"Why do you say that?" Lacy asked.

"That question you asked me a few days ago, am I a Christian—I'm not so sure, to be honest." Andy sat upright. "I thought I was, but I've never been straight up asked if I knew for a fact that I was. I'm not so sure anymore."

Lacy smiled with clenched lips. Her head tilted. In a sweet, soft voice she asked, "What makes you question your faith, Andy?"

Tears welled up in his eyes, and he didn't bother to fight them. "I accepted Christ, or so I thought, in Vacation Bible School when I was, like, maybe nine or ten. I don't think I even knew what it all meant." Andy sniffed and wiped his nose, being careful to explain himself.

"Two of my friends raised their hands when they were asked if they wanted to be saved. I raised mine because they did. I was proud of it, though. Even as long ago as it was, I still remember running home to tell Mom. I couldn't wait! But after that week was over, I never went back to church. I think in the last eight years or so, I've been to church, other than weddings or something, maybe five times."

Lacy quickly added, "But going to church won't make you a Christian. It's what's in your heart. Man, I hate to judge, but there are so many in my church that think they're going to heaven because they sit in a pew every week. Andy, it's about a relationship with Christ. It's about wanting to follow Him and doing His work. It's loving people—everyone, even those, *especially* those—that are different from you. Being a Christian means changing how we live, changing how we look at others, and loving them based on what we've learned through serving Christ. We don't just live for us any longer, we live for Christ and allow Him to live through us. And once that—"

Andy jumped in and said, "*Nothing* changed. I didn't change that day. I'm a good friend, but I'm a horrible person. I've picked on people. I cuss. Not much, but I do. I don't have to tell you I drink. You're here because of that. Lacy, I didn't change anything."

"But Oak Creek loves you. I've seen social media. The whole town brags about you."

He shook his head. "They love Andy the football player. Not Andy the person. I guess I shouldn't have said I'm horrible. I help people around town. I respect everyone and say 'yes, ma'am' and 'yes, sir.' I volunteer for charity and do all that stuff, but what if I wasn't the quarterback? What if I'd never helped win a game? What if I never played at all? Would they still love me?"

"Would they?" Lacy asked.

Andy didn't know how to respond. He raised his hand and rested his chin on it. "I dunno. Maybe. Oak Creek is a small town, and, well, we kinda help everyone out when they need it. Everyone knows everyone. Maybe they would, but probably not as much."

Lacy giggled through her reply. "Boy, you're unsure about a lot of things." Andy smiled and rolled his eyes. "So, Andy, *the person* from Oak Creek, there's only one of those questions you need to make sure you know the answer to. And it sounds like you already know the answer."

Andy nodded, his lips clenched tightly, and didn't reply.

"I can help you make that decision, Andy," Lacy said as she reached for his hand, taking it from where it rested on his knee.

Her touch made Andy nervous. He was unsure whether to tighten his hand or just let her hold his. *What's appropriate?* he wondered.

"Andy, is that what you want?" she asked.

"I don't think I'm ready," he replied, still holding her hand but fidgeting with the fingers of his other hand. "I don't know anything about what to do next. Maybe I should start going to church and learn a few things, or maybe you could teach me, or maybe I—"

Lacy laughed. "Andy, that's not how it works. There's not a test you have to pass to get in, silly. You grow and learn as you build your walk, your relationship. God will show you new things all the time, like that bookmark. A simple little play on numbers was a lesson God showed me. Your decision is the first chapter of a book that God has so masterfully written for you."

Andy was still unsure. *What will it all mean? Will my change be noticeable? Do I have to talk about it?* In just a matter of seconds, dozens of questions raced through his mind.

"Not right now, Lacy," he responded. "I'm sorry. Just let me think about it. I have so much on my mind. I'm worried about you and your recovery, my trial, the playoffs—it's hard to think straight. Please forgive me for not being ready. I just want to make sure that this time, I really do mean it."

"Forgive you? Andy, I'll do better. I'll pray for you. You'll know when you're ready."

He took his free hand and wrapped it around hers. "Thank you," he said. The tension left his body, replaced with...butterflies?

"Hey, guys," Ann announced as she came through the door.

Andy quickly snatched his hands from Lacy's, unsure why, but still worried her mother would be mad at him. Lacy gawked at him, a sly smile on her face and her brow wrinkled.

"I feel more alive now that I have some coffee in me," she continued. "You guys have a good talk?"

"We did, Mom," Lacy replied, "and Andy held my hand."

Andy felt heat burn his cheeks from within, but smiled sheepishly as he blushed.

"Oh, he did? Do tell, what brought that on?"Ann playfully raised her eyebrows.

Andy, morbidly embarrassed, lowered his head before looking up and replying. "Well, umm, I was—"

"It's fine, Andy. I was just teasing. I may not know you that well, but I know my Lacy. Besides, she's already said you're cute."

"Mom!" Lacy shouted.

Ann laughed. "Well, you did! If I remember correctly, you told your dad that at least it was a cute boy that hit you."

"Mom!" she shouted again. "Okay, you can go get more coffee now!"

Andy's pink blush darkened his cheeks to a bright red, but his smile stretched from ear to ear. "It wasn't meant as anything, Mrs. Hollingsworth. Lacy was encouraging me. I've been down on myself lately, and she—well, ma'am, your daughter is an amazing girl. Here she is, laid up in a hospital bed, and she's the one encouraging me."

"That's my Lacy," Ann said as she sat on the bed beside Lacy. "She's always been the shining light for others."

A knock at the door interrupted their conversation. Kyle slowly eased the door open and said, "Hey, guys. Okay to come in?"

"Of course, Mr. Higgins," Lacy said. "Are you here to get Andy, or are you just gonna leave him and make him eat this hospital food?"

Kyle laughed. "I can leave him if you'd like."

"Sorry, Dad," Andy said as he stood. "I lost track of time." He looked at Lacy and explained, "I was supposed to meet him out front about a half-hour ago."

"Mr. Higgins, it was my fault," Lacy said. "I talk too much."

"No worries, dear," Kyle answered. "You can talk your little heart away, and he'll be glad to sit and listen. Right, son?"

Andy smiled. "All day if need be."

Lacy pulled her walker over to her bedside and looked at her mother. "Mom, I want to walk them out."

Ann got up and grabbed the walker, holding it still as Lacy tried to pull herself up. "Baby, without the therapist here?"

"Mom! Please? At least to the end of the hall."

Andy peered at Mrs. Hollingsworth with wide, worried eyes. He didn't know what to say, but he knew that just a few days ago, Lacy couldn't stand. Now, to see her walking would be amazing, but he didn't want her to overdo it and risk hurting herself more than he'd already hurt her.

Ann sighed. "You amaze me. Stubborn, and drive me crazy, but you amaze me. Okay, but just to the end of the hall."

Slowly Lacy began her trek. After a few steps, she stopped just outside her door, glancing up and down the hall.

"What is it, baby?" her mom asked. "Need to rest?"

"Just checking to see if anyone's going to chase me if I take off running," Lacy said with a lighthearted laugh.

CHAPTER 10

JUDGEMENT DAY

MONDAY ARRIVED JUST AS FAST AS THE COOL WEATHER HAD. STUDENTS were roaming the hall before the start of the day, gathering in their usual groups. The topic of discussion around the small town had already changed.

Just weeks earlier, Andy and the accident were the only gossip in the halls. Now, football returned to the top of the list, as the playoffs had everyone in a fever-pitched spirit for the next game. Banners and painted windows had not only shown up in the hallways of Oak Creek High but throughout town as well. Blue and white dominated the scenery.

Round two of the playoffs wasn't uncharted territory. In fact, in the last ten years, there were probably fewer times that the Tigers didn't make it than times they had. But each year brought new excitement. Discussions around town always included phrases such as, "This may be the year" and "These boys have a good shot." This year was no exception, even with Andy's absence. With Mike Gamble doing so well, doubters of his success were growing fewer and fewer.

Andy finally convinced his parents to let him come back to school. Right after the accident, it was probably a good decision to keep him away. But now, while it seemed that the rumors had died off, they agreed it was time to return to some sort of structured schedule.

As he made his way through the halls for the first time in over a month, it was apparent that everyone wanted to catch up and welcome him back. He'd worried that his presence at school would restart the rumor mill, but it seemed as if everyone had moved on from it.

"Andy! It's good to see you back," Principal Reynolds exclaimed as he walked toward Andy, who was gathering things from his locker.

"Hey, Mr. Reynolds. Good to be back, sir."

"If you have any issues getting adjusted, come see me. I know you'll hear things you may not like, but just ignore them. I need you to be a leader. Especially now."

Andy shut his locker and tucked a few books under his arm. "What do you mean? I don't think anyone wants me to lead anything right now, with all due respect, sir."

Mr. Reynolds placed his hand on Andy's shoulder. "Son, the reason it was such a big deal for the kids here was that everyone looked up to you. Not saying that they don't now, but you were the guy that many of these students were inspired by. To see you make a mistake has shown them it only takes one decision to change everything. Take that mistake and do something with it. How you respond will be noticed. Andy, what you do now will make a bigger impact than anything you've ever done on that field."

Andy chuckled. "Wow, Mr. Reynolds. No pressure, huh?"

Mr. Reynolds smiled as he started walking away. "Andy, if I didn't think you were up to it, I wouldn't have mentioned it."

Much of the day went just as the morning had. Andy once again became the subject of many conversations, but the talk didn't involve the accident. Most of the students welcomed him back, and no one mentioned the events that led to his absence. His first day back went much better than he thought it would, and he felt good about everything for the first time since the accident. Life wasn't over, but he realized it may have changed.

He made his way onto the practice field to join his teammates. Coach Woods was already there and saw him coming.

"Andy, go suit up!"

He stopped, confused. Andy hadn't put on his pads since the accident. He wasn't even sure that the state's athletic commission would allow him to.

"Well, go on, son! Can't wait all day," Coach yelled again.

Andy hurried his pace, not toward the locker room, but toward Coach Woods.

"Son, did you leave your ears at home today? I *said* go get dressed," Coach insisted.

"But, Coach. What about the state? Can I? I don't want to mess up our chance at the playoffs."

"Do you want to play football again?"

"Yes, sir! Very much so. But—"

"Then go get dressed," Coach instructed as he turned and stomped away.

Andy followed. "But I—"

Coach Woods stopped and spun to get in Andy's face. "Look, son. I've read the rule book up and down each page. We don't know what will happen in the coming days or weeks, but as of now, there ain't nothing I can find that will keep you out of your pads. Will you play Friday? Probably not, unless I can get somebody down at the central office to tell me you can. But there's nothing in there about practicing. Now, before I change my mind, go get dressed."

"Yes, sir!"

Andy ran toward the locker room. He was still worried his practicing would affect the team's playoff chances. *But Coach checked. He knows the rules, right?* he thought as he changed into his practice uniform. Still, he was as excited as he had ever been to put on a helmet. As he raced back out, he had nervous butterflies in his stomach, much like before a big game. *This is just practice. Why am I so nervous?* he wondered.

Andy took his place in the formed lines where the team was stretching. Normally, Andy was up front, as a leader, but he took a place in the back among many of the underclassmen. He joined in where they were in stretches and continued with them.

After a few minutes of warming up, Coach announced it was time for the first team offense to huddle up. Andy almost took off toward the huddle, but seeing Mike do the same, he quickly remembered that he no longer held that spot. It was a reaction, and being able to follow through with it was one that he longed for again.

As the first team offense gathered, Coach instructed the defense to get ready across from them, and everyone else moved off to the side. Andy started to walk off the field, but Coach Woods yelled to him, "Andy, come over here."

Andy sprinted back, hoping Coach was going to let him and Mike take turns under center.

"Andy, how many practices did you miss?" Coach asked.

"Umm, four weeks, I think, Coach," he replied.

"Four weeks, huh? Damn! It's been that long?" Coach replied, spitting out sunflower seed hulls as he talked. "Four practices a week for four weeks adds up to about sixteen. That seem right to you, Higgins?"

"Yes, sir. That's correct," Andy replied, not sure where Coach's math test was coming from or where it was going.

"All right then, you know my rule about missing practice. Get to it."

Andy's shoulders dropped much like his jaw did.

A huge hill sat to the side of the practice field that carried a grade of about forty-five degrees. Everyone in town, not just the players, simply referred to it as "the hill." It was mostly red mud, and the more it was run on, the heavier a player's shoes became. Just one trip up the hill and back down was enough to make someone bend over and gasp for air. It had been the answer to missed practices for decades. Ruts were dug deep into it from the paths misfortune had taken players. Even former players still talked about "the hill."

Andy hated it! But it wasn't just one trip. Coach required five trips up and down that hill, in full pads and helmet, for each day missed.

Andy continued the math lesson. *That's sixteen days—five trips for each day! That's eighty times up that hill*, he realized.

"Coach, you want me to run eighty hills?" Andy questioned as he followed Coach Woods.

"Only if you want to be on this team. We have rules that everyone follows. We own our decisions."

"But Coach. Eighty?"

"You may not get them all in today, but come see me when you're done. Offense, let's run a few plays," he shouted and then blew his whistle.

Andy's arms hung limp. He let out a deep breath, sighing as he realized what it was going to take to get back in Coach's good graces.

"But—"

Coach didn't turn around, and Andy accepted his defeat.

He trudged toward the hill and thought about all the times he'd seen others run it as punishment. Andy had never found himself in this position. For Coach Woods to hand him such a punishment, even if he had been the star quarterback at one time, was humbling. The one lesson that everyone took from being a Tiger on Coach Wood's team was the one thing that kept slapping Andy in the face: *own your decisions and mistakes.* Andy knew that the only way back on the team was to suck it up and do it.

About halfway through practice, Coach blew his whistle. "Water break!" he shouted.

Andy heard the announcement but wasn't sure if that meant him, too. He looked toward the team as they removed their helmets. Andy wished he could remove his just long enough to catch his breath. His movements were slow and he'd resolved to walk to the top, but the grade coming down almost insisted on a jog.

"Higgins!" Coach Woods shouted. "Gonna join us?"

Standing a few steps up the grade, he removed his helmet and began trekking down and toward the water coolers. Coach was waiting for him.

"How many you got?" Coach inquired.

"Twenty-one, sir," he answered through heavy breaths.

"That's one week of practices," Coach replied. "Go clean your cleats off and get out here with us. I want the same tomorrow and continued daily. You should be caught up by the end of practice Thursday."

Andy was relieved.

Coach knew he was pushing Andy, but he also wanted to make sure the team knew that everyone was treated the same. Andy had been through a lot, and Coach knew it. He was great at pushing kids to be their best, but he was also good at lifting them up. He knew Andy needed football much more than the team needed him. His decision to let Andy practice was one made with dual incentives. Andy would have stability back in his life with something he loved, and the team may find an extra push with him back.

Andy spent the rest of practice watching. He stood behind the offense as he had done the previous weeks; the only difference was that he wore his uniform and pads. He didn't know if Coach would let him take a snap before he finished his hill runs or not, but he remained ready.

As practice ended, Andy trotted off the field with the rest of the team. Many of those that had gathered to watch noticed Andy in uniform, and the talk of his return had already created a buzz among the spectators in lawn chairs gathered nearby.

Kyle leaned on the fence near the field, his forearms resting on the top bar. He had arrived only a few minutes earlier, expecting to pick up Andy, but seeing him in his uniform made him wonder about things.

"Your boy playing this week?" Henry Watkins, an Oak Creek faithful, asked.

"Not to my knowledge," Kyle replied. "I was looking for him. Didn't even know he was in pads out there until practice was over."

"Mike has done a good job for us, but I sure would like for Andy to grab the reins in these playoffs," Henry continued.

Kyle laughed. "Oh, now, Henry. Mike has been super. He's gonna do just fine."

Henry folded his chair. "I know, but your kid has that something extra you can't teach. If it comes down to the wire in a game, Andy has what it takes to get us through it."

A few minutes later, Andy, Toby, and Alec walked out together, and a few of the gathered fans congratulated Andy on being back in pads. "I know that felt good," and "Glad to see you out there" were a few of the remarks made as he passed by.

Andy was thinking, *Nothing feels good after running that hill twenty-one times*, but he held his tongue.

"Mr. Higgins," Alec yelled as soon as he saw Kyle. He gave him his signature hug. "Did you see A-man? He was in his uniform."

"I did, Alec! I sure did," Kyle replied.

"Hey, Mr. Higgins," Toby said, shaking Kyle's hand.

"Toby," Kyle replied, nodding before turning his attention to his son. "So, you went full gear? What was that about?"

Andy smiled and laughed. "Coach tricked me."

"Tricked you, huh?" Kyle said, smirking. "I bet he didn't have to do much to trick you."

"Well, it cost me eighty hills." Andy nodded toward his mentioned punishment.

"Eighty?" Kyle questioned. "You ran eighty hills?"

"Only twenty-one today. But I've got to run the rest before I can fully practice again."

Kyle shook his head. "Coach got you, didn't he?"

Andy shrugged, but couldn't hide his half-smile.

"Well, I do have some good news," Kyle said as they began walking to the truck.

"Please tell me they're giving my license back."

"Not quite, but we're a step closer. We see the judge tomorrow."

"Tomorrow?!" Andy yelled. "So I gotta go to court tomorrow?"

"No court," Kyle explained. "Our attorney was able to get your case looked at by the district attorney. He recommended it to the judge, who accepted, and we see him tomorrow."

"So what does all that mean, Dad?"

"Well, we're hoping to be granted two things. If we get youthful offender status and first-time offender, we'll have fines, but hopefully, that's all. I'm not sure what this does about your license, but we can ask that question then."

"What about Lacy? Will they determine if we pay for her college?"

"No. That's a civil case. But our attorney did request that I invite her parents to the meeting. Seeing that you've taken responsibility would be a huge plus for you, and maybe we could get Mr. Hollingsworth to tell the judge how you've been visiting. He said he would try to make it."

"Yeah, maybe. But still, Dad. We are going to help with her college, right?"

Kyle nodded. "We'll cross that bridge when we have to. I promised them that we would do what we could to help. Let's get past this step first."

"Can I use your phone for a minute, Dad? I want to call Lacy and let her know about the meeting tomorrow. I told her I would as soon as I knew."

Kyle handed his phone to Andy. "I guess it's time for us to get you another one, huh?"

Andy smiled and nodded as he put the phone to his ear, listening for someone to pick up the other end.

"Room 216, please." After a brief pause, Andy continued. "Hey, Mrs. Hollingsworth! May I speak with Lacy, please?" Another pause. "Lacy! Hey! Guess where I'm going tomorrow?"

On the other end, Lacy smiled at the energetic tone in Andy's voice. Her reply followed a slight giggle. "Oh, I don't know. Let's see. My second guess would be on a world tour with a rock band, but that would require more effort than you've shown lately. So, I guess I'll go with the first thing that popped in my head. Hmm? Let's see. I say you're going to talk to the judge about your case. Is that right?"

Andy's mouth dropped. He looked at his dad, who had no clue why Andy looked so surprised.

"What?" he shouted. "How? But—how did you know that? I just found out."

Lacy laughed loudly on the other end. "Dad was in my room when your dad called."

Andy laughed. "Wow! For a minute I thought you had some kind of Christian superpower or something."

"Well, actually, I do," she replied. "It's called prayer, and I've already prayed about this meeting. Everything will be fine."

"I hope you're right," he replied. "Man, I hope you're right."

ANDY COULD HARDLY SLEEP that night. Everything that could possibly happen kept playing through his mind. Even if the judge went easy on him, he knew Lacy would have to face her future on her parents' limited income. The more Andy thought about it, the more and more he tossed and turned.

Midnight came and went, and so did 1:00 A.M. He tried everything from singing songs in his head to humming to get his mind off his situation.

He looked at the clock again: 1:45 A.M. Andy sat up on his bed, swinging his legs over the edge. He looked out the window as the moon cast shadows of the trees against his curtains. They danced like arms swaying in the wind. He got caught up in watching the changing patterns as clouds moved across the moonlight.

Andy's thoughts turned to his conversation with Lacy about religion. *What if I'm not saved?* he wondered. The thought seemed to visit him more and more, as if he'd already placed himself on trial.

He got up and walked to the window and gazed at the night sky. The moon was nearly full. It was a breathtaking sight, overlooking the meadows. *Lord, am I saved? Can you give me a sign?* Andy thought to himself. He remembered how Lacy said she would pray for him. Andy leaned forward, letting his forehead rest on the cool windowpane. He looked up toward the heavens and began talking to God.

It's me again. I know I don't do this much, and You probably think I only do when I need something. But this time's different. I mean, I do need something. I need a lot, really. But if You can do one thing for me, I ask that you put Lacy's needs before mine.

I'm ready to accept whatever my punishment is, but Lord, Lacy didn't have a choice. It's not her fault. I don't know how I'm supposed to do this, but I also want to be saved if I'm not. Well, I'm pretty sure I'm not, and I don't know much about the way I should ask, but can I just ask for help? I want You to show me what You need me to do.

I know there's a lesson in all of this for me, but I can't figure it out on my own. When it comes to all this Bible stuff, Lord, I'm just not that smart. Can you help me?

Well, I guess that's about it, so, good talk, God. Good night. I mean, Amen.

Andy went back to his bed and laid down. For the first time all night, he felt relaxed. Within a few minutes, he was asleep.

MORNING CAME, and the Higgins household was bustling. Holly and Kyle were doing their best to get things in order before leaving for the meeting with the judge. Andy had been up for about an hour and was nervously pacing the yard.

Kyle came out first and shouted, "Let's go, Andy. I want to get there early and hopefully make a good impression."

Andy headed toward the car and opened the passenger door. His mom, Holly, shouted from the front porch as she closed the door and locked it. "Oh, no. Back seat, kiddo! I have to be upfront or I get motion sickness."

"You're going, Mom?" Andy asked as he moved to the back.

"Well, of course," Holly replied as she made it to the car, leaning over and placing her cup in the holder before getting in. "Did you honestly think I wouldn't?"

Andy didn't reply, but the urgency of the day hit a little harder. When both parents went, it usually meant they were worried about how something might go, or because it was a big event they were proud of. A meeting with a judge was not the latter of the two.

The trip to the county courthouse took about forty-five minutes. Most of that trip was silent, except for the occasional small talk to break the apparent tension. Andy was nervous—very nervous. The kind of nervousness he'd never even felt before a big game.

After a brief wait, all three found themselves being led into the judge's chambers by the district attorney.

"Dad, I thought Mr. Hollingsworth was coming," Andy whispered.

"Me, too," Kyle softly replied.

They sat alone in a room with a desk so large it dominated the space.

"Don't worry, son." Holly comforted Andy, placing her hand on his knee as he sat between her and Kyle. "Everything will be okay."

Andy's heart pounded, and his hands felt clammy against his bouncing knees. Just knowing that his fate was on the threshold of the acts that would come next was enough to make him think everything may not be okay—it may not be okay at all.

The door finally opened, and the district attorney entered again, followed by the judge. Andy quickly sat at attention. He wasn't sure if he was supposed to stand. He had only seen court before on television, but even that was in an actual courtroom and not an office.

"Mr. and Mrs. Higgins, this is Judge Thompson," the district attorney announced. "He has been so gracious as to see us this morning."

The judge came around in front of the desk instead of going behind it. Kyle stood to shake his hand.

"Thank you, Your Honor, for seeing us," Kyle said. "I hope we don't take up much of your time."

"No problem, Mr. Higgins," Judge Thompson replied. His voice echoed a thunderous, deep tone across his chambers. "This is kind of my job."

The judge was a large, hulking man, standing much taller than Kyle, who was a good six feet himself. He was broad at the shoulders, and his presence was intimidating. He sat on the front side of the desk, just a couple of feet away from where Andy sat, who was noticeably breathing harder.

"Mr. Gregory here has told me about your case, son," Judge

Thompson said, referencing the district attorney by nodding toward him.

"Yes, sir," Andy was able to muster out. "Thank you for your time, sir."

"Oak Creek, huh," the judge continued. "Folks down that way get serious about some football."

"Yes, sir. They do," Andy said with a slight smile.

"You're their quarterback, I hear."

"Well, I used to be, I guess," Andy replied with a little quiver in his voice. "Before all of this, sir."

"Well, I imagine those folks sure are missing you. Playoff time and all."

"Mike Gamble is the quarterback now. He's doing well, sir."

"Football," Judge Thompson said as he stomped behind his desk and sat, gazing off as if reminiscing. "You know, I almost didn't become a judge because of football."

Andy's eyes widened. He sat up, his back leaving the seat as he eased toward the front of the chair. "Why is that, sir?"

"Injury. Had an offer down in Louisiana. Was gonna play for L.S.U. I planned to play ball and wing it through school. Maybe get a degree in business management or something. Wasn't sure what I wanted to do, to be honest. But God had other plans. I was being stupid; y'know, like kids your age do."

Andy smiled sheepishly and nodded.

"We were down at some old strip mines, swimming. Someone dared me to jump off the high bluffs. Many had gone up there and many had walked back down, scared of the sight once they were looking over the edge. But not ol' Jerry Thompson. Oh, no. I wasn't scared of anything. I didn't know the drought dropped the water level several feet, so ol' tough Jerry Thompson jumped off that bluff, some fifty, maybe sixty feet up. The force of the water kicked my feet out and my backside hit the rock bottom, crushing six of my lower vertebrae. Lucky to not have drowned. Even luckier to walk again."

"Wow, Your Honor," Kyle said, his attention also keen on the story. "Glad you're alive."

"Me, too," he answered. "But nobody wanted a big ol' fat boy with a broken back, and with no scholarship, no ball playing, and not sure what I wanted to do, I had two choices. I could cry myself into a life of self-pity and tell everyone how I was gonna be the next great defensive lineman in the conference if it hadn't happened, or I could refocus, get my crap together, go on to school, and make something out of myself."

Andy stared at him and knew why he'd shared his story.

"You see, son," the judge continued. "I threw it all away because I made a stupid decision. I've asked myself time and time again, what if I hadn't jumped? Where would I be? N.F.L.? Who knows. But *what if* can't change what happened. I could have climbed down those rocks and gotten called a sissy, probably punched some guy in the mouth, and gone on to play college ball. But I didn't. I made a bad decision, and God used it; He used me to make a change. Two years into college, I decided I wanted to go into criminal justice. After that, a couple of years in law school. Thought I wanted to be an attorney, so I did that for a while. All the time, God was preparing me to change lives."

Holly smiled. "Judge Thompson. My boy made a bad decision, and he knows it. I think he's beat himself up over this enough to make this mama's heart ache every night. And we will respect your decision, but as a mother, I have to ask that he get a second chance and not let this go on his permanent record. From your story, I know you're a Godly man. I only ask that you do what you feel is right."

Judge Thompson leaned forward and placed his elbows on his desk. "The decision I made affected me and only me. The one Andy made almost cost two young ladies their lives, and it cost one young lady the life she planned. Drinking and driving is a decision that sometimes leads to consequences that can't be taken back." He looked toward Andy. "Son, what would you have done if you had to visit Ms. Lacy Hollingsworth at the cemetery?"

"I—I don't know, sir," Andy replied, his nervous quiver returning. "I would rather it had been me had that had happened."

"Your Honor," Kyle added, "Andy has been visiting Ms.

Hollingsworth in the hospital. He's taken ownership of what he did. I also, sir, have talked to Mr. Hollingsworth, and I've agreed to help with Lacy's college tuition."

"Yes, yes. I know all that," Judge Thompson replied.

Kyle and Andy looked puzzled as they glanced at each other.

"Mr. Hollingsworth called me this morning," he continued. "Robert—or Bob as he's called now—Lacy's dad, went to the same school I went to. We played ball together. Do you know that man has probably given away more of the money he's made over the years than he's kept? All he ever wanted is for everyone to have what he never had. He didn't have much of anything growing up. Pretty much lived in a shack. His dad did what he could, but it was just tough for them." The judge leaned back in his chair and folded his hands in his lap.

"Robert calls me every Christmas, asks me for some names of kids in the area that won't get much. He brings me a pile of toys for them. Doesn't do it himself because he doesn't want them to know where it comes from. Says to tell them the toys are from Santa. That money he uses comes from scrap metal he collects all year just for that reason. Never asks for help, either. Anyway, he told me how you've been down there. Told me about your offer to help pay for stuff."

He stood and ambled around to the front of his desk again and leaned back against it. "Never in my life have I seen a man ask forgiveness for someone that hurt his daughter, but he did."

Andy looked up at the judge, who seemed to tower over him.

"Young man," the judge said. "I've read all the reports. Mr. Gregory has given me his thoughts. I have heard from the Hollingsworths. I'd like to hear your side. What do you think is fair?"

Andy bit his bottom lip. He fidgeted with his hands and his foot tapped again. "Sir," he finally replied, "may I stand?"

"If that helps you, sure."

Andy stood and walked a few feet to the edge of the room before turning to face them. "Your Honor, you see how easy that was for me to do? Lacy can't do that. I watched just two days ago how hard it was for her to pull herself up on a walker. She grimaced as she took a few steps with it. Lacy will never get to play the sport she loves again, sir. And it's all because of me. I deserve whatever is the harshest punishment you can give, and I—"

"Andy!" Kyle shouted. "Sorry, Your Honor. He's been under a lot of stress."

"No, Dad," Andy said, looking toward Kyle. "Please! Let me finish."

"Go ahead, son," Judge Thompson urged.

"Just yesterday, Mr. Reynolds, our principal, told me how a lot of the younger kids look up to me. Why? Because I do good things around the school? Because I make good grades? Because I make a difference in the community? No! Because I'm good at football. I've thought about that. All day after Mr. Reynolds told me that, I noticed other kids in school." He paused for a second, gathering his thoughts before he continued.

"I passed by Steven Banks. He volunteers over at New Horizons, where the disabled and challenged kids go. I used to pick on Steven. A lot! Why don't people look up to him for what he does? I saw Franky White. Franky works every day after school because his dad is out of the picture. He went to work so his mom could quit her second job. Nobody that I know aspires to be like Franky. My best friend, Toby—" Andy stopped again when his voice broke, tears welling up in his eyes.

"Man! Toby is the one we should look up to. He works every weekend. Volunteers with kids all the time. He makes time for Alec, his little brother who has special needs, and you know what else he does? He tries to talk people out of stupid decisions. The night of my wreck, Toby tried to talk me out of going. Told me nothing good comes from alcohol. Y'know, he was right. He was so right!" Andy wiped a tear rolling down his cheek.

"You see, sir. If younger kids are looking up to me, wanting to be like me, what kind of example am I? Because I can run fast or throw a ball? Sir, if I get off easy, it's not going to show them anything except that the jock got off easy *because* he's a jock. And no matter what I get, it doesn't change the outcome for Lacy. Sir, I own my decision, and I'm ready to take my punishment."

Andy walked back to his seat and sat, crossed his arms, and slumped over in his chair. Holly leaned over, rubbing Andy's back while Kyle patted his son on the head.

"Well, that's a first," Judge Thompson said, breaking the silence. "Never has someone tried to convince me to throw the book at them." The judge returned to his place behind his desk and took a seat. "Andy, I want you to sit up and look at me. I want you to listen to me, and listen well."

Judge Thompson leaned across the desk, his hands folded in front of him, but didn't rest on them. Andy sat up without speaking. He wiped more tears from his eyes as he looked at the judge.

"Son, I hope you're faced with many decisions in your life that affect others. If so, that means you'll be in a position to make a difference. That's what I hope. What I *pray* is that you'll make the right decisions in as many of those that you'll allow God to help you with." He paused to raise an eyebrow at Andy and shoot him a half-grin.

"Andy, it took guts to say what you did. I can't say I would have done that at your age. What it also tells me is that you know how bad that decision was and that you accept ownership of it. Now, I can do what you asked. I could sentence you to jail, fine you for damages, strip you of your license for a few years, and make your life a living hell. But, when I look at you, I see myself at that age. That decision I made was a lesson. I feel like this is a lesson for you." Judge Thompson crossed his arms.

"Son, I'm not going to ruin your life when I think you have the opportunity to use this to change other people's lives. You stood there and told me about all those other people that need recognition. Well, recognize them! If people look up to you, they will recognize them, too. You have a chance to make at least one good thing out of all this, this mess! Son, I'm going to ask you again, and I want you to think hard before answering; what do you think is *fair*?"

Andy blinked several times, trying to contain the tears, but they escaped nonetheless. He wiped his eyes with one hand, his thumb on one side and his fingers on the other, and shook his head, finally ready to speak.

"Sir, I think what's fair is for you to give me what you never got. Another chance. But for this to be fair, I have to have consequences if I don't use my second chance accordingly. If I don't hold up my end of the bargain, I ask you to give me the harshest punishment allowed for my crime. Whatever all that means, sir, I think that's fair."

Judge Thompson puckered out his bottom lip and placed his hand to his chin, resting both elbows on his dark desktop.

"Okay," he said with a nod. "I think we can work from that. Mr. Higgins, Mrs. Higgins—either of you want to add to that or have any remarks?"

"No, Your Honor," Kyle replied, and Holly shook her head.

"Very well. Mr. Gregory, if you don't mind, make notes of this so we can get it typed up and make this show official. Andy, I know you'll need to drive, so let's cover that first. I'm imposing a first offense suspension of ninety days from the date of your arrest. You've served thirty days of that, so you have sixty more days before your license can be reinstated. I'm requiring you to attend and complete a course for driving under the influence, which you'll register for at the state trooper's office. The cost of the class is three hundred dollars. You *must* bring that certificate back to me, so I can send notification to reinstate your license. Understood?"

"Yes, sir," Andy answered.

"Okay; next. I understand that your mom and dad have asked Mr. Gregory for youthful offender and first-time offender status. I'll grant both, under the conditions that all other items in this judgment are taken care of and followed through. If so, this will never be seen on public records."

"Thank you, Your Honor," Kyle said.

"You still have a fine for your actions, Andy. That fine is one thousand dollars. I will *not* strike that. It needs to be paid in ninety days."

Andy nodded and said, "I understand."

"Good. The next thing I want to work on is character building. You seem like a good kid. I did my homework. I called the school, talked to your coach, and even Mr. Hollingsworth agreed that you're a good kid that made a bad decision. To help you get started on making a difference, I'm imposing a sentence of sixty hours of community service to be carried out over one year. I want at least half of those to include time over at New Horizons. You mentioned a young man from your school who already volunteers there. Get to know him. Make this kid one of your best friends."

The judge leaned back in his chair again. Andy peered at him as he nodded, tears still heavy in his eyes.

"Andy, this part is hard for me. I've sat here and instructed some pretty detailed rules for you that will cost you time and money. You asked me for consequences if you slip up. Why is that?"

Andy clasped his hands in front of him, resting his elbow on his knees. "Sir, I'm not very good at keeping promises. Just recently, I've questioned my faith. I thought I'd made God a promise a long time ago, but I didn't. I questioned it for a while, but I know for a fact that I didn't. I want to make sure that when I say I'll do something from now on, I do it."

"You talking about your salvation?" he asked.

"Yes, sir," Andy answered.

"That's bigger than my courtroom, son," the judge replied. "That one I can't enforce, but you better be sure you know the answer before it's too late."

"I'm working on that, sir."

"Let's move on. You want consequences. Well, okay. Another first for me, but here you go. I'm giving you one year of probation. If you slip up in any way, don't make your community service hours, don't complete your D.U.I. course, don't pay your fine, get caught driving before you get your license back, anything *at all* that we discussed that you don't do just right, then, as you asked, you will get the maximum penalty and your youthful offender status will be revoked. Is that understood? Andy, Mr. and Mrs. Higgins? Everyone good with this?"

"Yes, sir. I am," Andy replied.

"Mom? Dad? Y'all good with this?" the judge asked.

Kyle nodded. "I'm good, Your Honor."

"Me, too," Holly added.

The judge stood and stepped around to the side of his desk. "You'll get a call once a probation officer is assigned to you," he told them. "Sometimes that may take a week or so. Just be sure that all of you make that first meeting. They may have a specific way they want to keep in contact." He then walked toward the door. "I hate to rush y'all off, but I have to get ready for the day. It was a pleasure meeting you guys, and I hope this is a lesson learned, young man."

As Kyle stood, he smiled at Andy. "Oh, it will be. I can promise you that. Right, Andy?"

"Already has been," Andy replied.

CHAPTER 11

ANDY'S BACK

THE WEEK FLEW BY. ANDY FINISHED ALL HIS PUNISHMENT TRIPS UP AND down "the hill" and was excited about dressing out and being on the sideline in full gear, even if he didn't get to play. With the extra work he put in at practice, he hadn't had time to visit Lacy, but he had a phone and the two talked every night.

He told her about the judge's decision, and she even looked up opportunities for him to fill the community service hours that weren't filled by New Horizons. She considered it a fair decision, and so did Andy. But still, he felt guilty because Lacy was laid up in a hospital because of his dumb decision.

The pep rally at school ended, signaling the end of the day. The gymnasium had been packed, even with the student body barely filling one side of the bleachers. But this was the playoffs, and many residents of Oak Creek found their way to the rally, some even taking off work early to attend, and the small gymnasium seemed to stretch to hold in everyone.

As the crowd dispersed, talk of the possibility of Andy playing spread. Many had seen him at practice all week, and by Thursday, he had taken a few snaps at quarterback. Mike worked with the starters, but Andy being back in there was exciting, not just for Andy, but for the many townsfolk that still lived their dreams through fall Friday nights.

One of those alumni was Fred Charleston. Fred graduated from Oak Creek almost twenty-five years ago and had dreamed of watching his son play on the same field he had. Fred was nicknamed Bull back in his playing days due to his ability to run over people, and the name stuck. Around town, people simply knew him as Bull Charleston.

Every Friday night, Bull made his way to the stadium an hour and a half early just to make sure he got a perfect spot to see not one of his children on the field, but two. He cheered them on, participated in the crowd cheers, dressed in the team colors, and even helped prepare the before-game meals. But Bull's eyes weren't always trained on the action between the sidelines, but rather to the sides of them as well. Bull was also the father to two girls, and they cheered for the Tigers, one a senior and the other a sophomore. He found that his Tiger spirit was embedded much deeper than he thought.

Like Bull, many others stayed planted in Oak Creek and felt as if roots, very deep roots, were holding them in place. They enjoyed the atmosphere that the small, prideful town produced. They felt committed to the town, and other than the history of the best coal to ever come out of the south, football was the one thing they boasted about. It was Friday evening. It was the playoffs. Where else would they be other than at the pep rally?

A small group of players and supporters were assembled on the gym floor. Andy was in that group.

"Andy," Coach Woods called out. "Let me talk to you in my office."

Andy acknowledged Coach with a nod as he turned to follow. "I guess this is where I get told not to dress out tonight," Andy said with a slight laugh before jogging toward the coach's office.

"Have a seat, Andy. Talked to the folks from the state today."

Andy sat up straight, leaning slightly forward. "Oh, yeah?"

"You can play," Coach responded with a smile.

"Yes!" Andy shouted loud enough to make the people in the gymnasium turn to look. "Thank God!"

"Well, hold on," Coach said. "*They* said you could play. I haven't said that yet."

Andy slouched back in his chair. "Coach, I'll do whatever you ask me to do. Just to have the opportunity to play again is an answered prayer. I never thought I'd get to do this again. Coach, I'll play on the line, hold extra points—anything. Tell me what I need to do to earn it, and I'll do it."

"Well, for starters, you have to show me that this is for the team and not you," Coach explained. "I want to see you being the best teammate those boys could ask for. Andy, you have a gift, son. But sometimes we take for granted what we have. Some of those kids out there work their asses off and will still never be as talented as you. They have the heart and determination, but they don't have instinct. But you know what? I would take those guys every time because I know where their heart is. Andy, I want to see where your heart is."

"Yes, sir. I can do that, sir. I think you're about to see a new Andy. I've thought a lot about all of this, and I need to change a lot of what I do, on and off the field."

Coach stood. "Good. I believe you, Andy. Now go get ready. We're about to board the bus. Folks over at the Tiger Den are feeding us today."

Andy stood and headed out of the office. He stopped in the doorway and turned. "Coach, thank you for the opportunity."

Coach nodded at Andy, knowing he was sincere. He could tell that everything lately had weighed heavily on him. He knew a change was coming, and he knew Andy would make good on his promise.

IT WAS MOMENTS BEFORE KICKOFF, and like most previous Friday nights, the stadium was packed.

Unlike the last few games, the visiting side was filling up just as fast. This week, they were facing Greenbrier, last year's 1-A state champion. Their following rivaled anyone's, including Oak Creek. They arrived early and cheered as the team's bus caravanned into town. The fans were crazed by the success of the team. Even though this year's team had dropped a few games, they finished strong in the season, winning five of their last six games. The Hornets were there to keep that streak alive, and the fans were there to take part in it.

It was almost kickoff time. The coin was flipped, the anthem played, and the bands were in a battle to see who could play the loudest. Andy stood on the sideline, waiting for the game to begin. He looked around at the stands, seeing people he knew and some he didn't. He thought about how it felt and how any given game could be the last.

Memories from the last four years streaked through his mind like an old movie reel. He remembered scores and cheers and after-game victory parties. Suddenly, he was snapped from his daze by the crowd going crazy. As he turned his attention back to the game, he realized he had missed the kickoff. He turned just in time to see Greenbrier take the opening kickoff back for a touchdown. With only seconds run off the game clock, Oak Creek was already on the wrong end of the scoreboard.

Andy met Toby as he came to the sideline. "Dude! What happened? That was down the sideline you line up on!"

"I got suckered inside," Toby snapped, ripping his chin strap loose and removing his helmet. "Looked like they were running a wedge and I bit on it; got trapped inside the wall." He paced back and forth. "Crap!" he shouted.

Alec chased his brother down and attempted to lift his spirits. "Shake it off, big bro. Make up for it! Go show them what you got, Tobe!"

Oak Creek's first possession wasn't as explosive. They took a "beat them down and make them surrender" approach, running the ball nine of the first ten snaps, and found themselves inside the opponent's twenty-yard line, threatening to score. Mike looked to the sideline for the call and got it.

"Mad dog, toss sweep right," he barked off in the huddle. "Scott, line up inside a little tighter and run your man to the middle. That'll give Toby more room."

Toby looked at Scott and nodded.

The ball was snapped, and Mike rolled to his right, faking that he would keep it and turn up just outside the tackle, but at the last minute, he pitched it to Toby. He caught the ball in full stride and sprinted to beat the defender to the sideline. Cutting it upfield, he raced toward the end zone.

Just inside the ten, he cut back inside, spinning. A Greenbrier defender met him in mid-spin and sunk his helmet into Toby's midsection, causing the ball to shoot out of his grasp and bounce across the turf. Players dove after it. There was a mass of tangled arms and legs. From the pile emerged a Greenbrier player, holding the ball above his head in celebration.

Oak Creek's chance to tie the game had literally slipped through their fingers. It was so close, only yards away, but it ended with one unfortunate mishap.

Coach met Toby as he stormed to the sideline, mad at himself and slapping his helmet in anger.

"Toby! Stop trying to score on every play," Coach snapped. "You had the first down! How many times have I told you to stop that spinning crap before you get hurt?"

"My fault, Coach," Toby shouted as Coach moved to yell at another player.

"Dude! You okay?" Andy asked. "This isn't you. You never get shook, bro!"

"I'm good. Just gotta get my head in the game," Toby replied, not stopping to talk.

After Greenbrier's opening game fireworks, they too were struggling. Most of the first half went back and forth with no other scores making their way onto the dimly lit scoreboard. The halftime score showed Oak Creek zero, and the visitors seven.

"Who the hell has on my uniforms?" Coach Woods screamed as he paced the locker room. "It sure as hell ain't the guys I've spent the last four months with! You guys act like you haven't seen a game, let alone played in one."

Nobody in the room said anything while Coach paced and said nothing for a few seconds.

"Scott!" he finally shouted. "What does *rocket* mean?" Scott didn't answer quickly enough and Coach stopped and stared at him. "If Mike calls forty-five rocket right, sweep left, what do you do?"

Clearly intimidated, Scott muttered, "Line up on the right side and run straight and fast as I can, hopefully taking my cover man with me."

"Then why the hell didn't you do that on three of the four times we called that play?" Coach shouted as he started pacing again. "Do you need a ticket to the game, son? Because all you're doing is standing on your side and watching as the ball goes to the other side! Geez, son! Do something! Mike, is your arm sore?"

"No, Coach. It's fine," he replied.

"Then why do you dump the ball off short when we have an open receiver downfield? Not once, but twice! At least one of those was a touchdown if we'd caught the damn thing."

He paced some more before stopping and sitting on a cooler. "Okay, defense," he said as his tone softened. "Not too bad. I think we need to adjust a little, maybe walk-up our safety a little more, but other than that, we're gonna stay the same." He stood again before continuing.

"Look, guys, I don't think you realize it, but this could be some of y'all's last game. I've got six seniors here that may never play again if we don't all do our jobs."

Reality hit hard for those six players. Toby glanced over at Andy as they realized that this may be it, the last game they played together as teammates.

"Now, I don't know about you," Coach continued, "but I ain't ready to call our season over! Are you?"

A murmur filled the room as some became vocal again.

Coach Woods grabbed his clipboard off the floor and stormed out, making one last announcement. "If you don't believe we can win this game, don't come out with my uniform on. The rest of you, let's get out there and let them know that they don't come to our house and go home without a fight!"

The home team Tigers heard all they needed to hear. In the second half, they came out looking and playing like a different team. They had a purpose, drive, and determination that they lacked in the first half. By the end of the third quarter, Oak Creek led Greenbrier twenty-one to fourteen, a score that was still only one strike away from a tie game, but the Tigers had all the momentum, scoring three touchdowns on consecutive drives.

Andy had been coaching Mike the entire quarter. Whenever Mike came to the sideline, Andy met him and went over what he may have missed, but also encouraged him for what he had done right. Andy figured he wouldn't be playing—or so he thought.

"Higgins," Coach Woods shouted. "Higgins! Get over here. I'm sending you in."

Andy couldn't believe what he was hearing. He hustled over to Coach Woods, so excited that he already had his mouthpiece in.

"Go in and call thirty-two rocket, wide left. You take the split, and send Stiles to the sideline," Coach instructed.

"Yes, sir," Andy said as he ran onto the field, repeating the play in his mind. He stopped and looked at Coach. "Coach, did you say get Stiles? You want me to play receiver?"

"You got a problem with that, Higgins?" Coach asked, stepping onto the field.

"No, sir. Just making sure."

Andy played quarterback for the last four years and assumed that if he got in the game, that would be where he played. He ran onto the field, going over the play again in his mind. Someone in the student body saw him and pointed it out to the others. Cheers went up from the student body. Then they grew louder and louder.

"Stiles, you're out," Andy shouted as he neared the huddle.

"What?" Scott replied. "You playing receiver?"

"Apparently, man. Coach said to get you, so I guess so," Andy said as Scott turned and ran off the field. "Thirty-two rocket, wide left," Andy related to Mike.

Mike slapped Andy on the helmet. "Okay, you heard him. Thirty-two rocket. Let's bust their ass on this, guys!"

Andy sprinted to his wide-out spot to the left, which happened to be the home side. That's when he heard it. The student section had started a chant—*Andy! Andy! Andy!* He looked over that way and saw them cheering him on and smiled.

The ball was snapped, and Toby took the handoff from Mike and smashed his way through the line of scrimmage. He then broke it outside to the left. Andy saw him heading his way.

Crap, Andy thought. He had gotten caught up in the moment and did exactly what Scott had gotten yelled at for, watching the play instead of running his guy downfield.

Toby cut back upfield and was tackled after a good gain for a first down. The crowd cheered even louder!

Scott ran back into the huddle for the next play. "Andy, you're out," he shouted over the crowd.

Andy's return was short-lived, and he knew why. He was expecting to get a good chewing out when he got to the sideline, but Coach Woods didn't even look his way. But that was the end of Andy's field time for the game. One play, thirty-seven seconds, and he moved maybe six yards.

The Tigers finished that drive by scoring on a nineteen-yard pass from Mike to Scott, and the team was starting to taste victory. The rest of the game went similarly, with the home team from Oak Creek cruising on to round three of the playoffs.

After the game, the usual crowd of a few dozen that stuck around to congratulate the team seemed to grow to a hundred or so. The players started emerging from the locker room, one by one and some in groups, each receiving praise from the loyal fans.

"Andy," one of the other senior players shouted. "Wanna come by the house? A few of us are getting together to hang out."

"Not sure, man," Andy replied. "No ride and all, y'know."

"I got you if you do, man. You know I'll take you home," he replied.

"Maybe next game," Andy replied.

Toby and Alec walked out and joined Andy, who was waiting for his dad to pull up to the gymnasium.

"A-man," Alec shouted, giving Andy a high five. "You're back, broski. You played tonight!"

"Ha! I'm not sure I would call that playing, dude. More like watching."

"But you were in there!"

Andy smiled at him, playfully ruffled his hair, and then turned to Toby. "Hey, Toby, um, what's that thing you always go to after games? Y'know, at your church."

"You talking about the Fifth Quarter?" Toby asked.

"Yeah, that's it. Mind if I go? And if so, could you run me home?"

"Yeah," Alec shouted. "Yeah, we will take you home!"

Toby threw his bag over his shoulder and smirked. "You know it's *inside* the church, right?"

"You think it might cave in if I'm there?" Andy said with laughter. "What is it exactly, anyway?"

"Sure, man, I'll take you home," Toby said. "We just hang out and eat pizza. Brother Greg is there, and he usually prays for anyone injured on either team and then we go home. That's pretty much it. It's just a chance to fellowship in the Lord's house."

"I always thought that it was like a class or something," Andy continued as they walked together toward Toby's car. "Like Sunday School."

Toby laughed. "Don't get nervous, heathen. We won't make you remember a Bible verse or nothing. At least not on your first time. Hey, there's your dad. Need to tell him?"

"I do! I'll be right back." Andy ran over to his dad's truck, and he explained the plans. Toby watched and was pleased to see Andy turn and start back toward him.

"Can you have me home by midnight?" Andy asked.

"Before then," Toby replied. "I have to work in the morning."

ANDY ENJOYED his time at the Fifth Quarter. When Toby dropped him off at home, his dad was sitting out on the porch, startling Andy as he walked up to the door.

"Dad!" Andy exclaimed. "'Bout caused me to jump out of my skin. What are you doing out here?"

"Thinking, son. I've seen a change in you. Maybe that judge was right. Maybe sometimes God does things to get our attention. Maybe He's tried little subtle things and we ignored them, so maybe, just maybe, sometimes He gets fed up and slams us with something we can't ignore."

"Are you okay, Dad? You don't ever talk about God."

"Maybe I don't. But that doesn't mean God don't talk to me. I've seen how you've changed the way you think about things. Worried how it affects others and all. And I got to thinking, ya know, I better start paying attention to the things God has shown me before He sends me a message, too."

Andy leaned forward, resting his arms on his knees. "Wish I had done that before He sent me one."

"Well, I can take some of that blame," Kyle said as he stood. "I wish I had led you closer to God instead of running from Him myself."

"It's not your fault, Dad," Andy said, standing, too. "I made that decision, and nobody made me do it."

Kyle gave Andy a playful punch on the arm and attempted to change the subject. "So, how was that last quarter thing at the church?"

Andy laughed. "Fifth Quarter, Dad! Fifth Quarter. And it was great. Man, those folks are so happy. I see now why Toby won't miss going. I've missed out on those things."

Kyle put his arm around Andy. "Well, now you know. Come on, let's get in bed. Still wanna go down to Memorial tomorrow, right? To see Lacy?"

"Yes, sir, if that's okay."

"I suppose so, but I think you need to wash my ol' truck first."

"Deal," Andy replied with a smile.

CHAPTER 12

THINGS ARE CHANGING

SATURDAY MORNING DELIVERED RAIN TO THE AREA AGAIN. JUST LIKE IN the spring, the weather patterns shifted back to a wet season in the fall. The area caught most of the storms that formed in the gulf and made their way north, and sometimes even the remnants of a hurricane made its presence known.

Andy was up early, waiting on the digital clock hanging on the porch to show 8:00. He wanted to call Lacy but didn't want to call too early. The clock doubled as a thermometer, and there was a significant change in the weather overnight. Even with the moisture coming up from the gulf, a strong cold front forced the warmer air to the east, leaving a cold wind that dipped the temps into the forties.

"Morning, champ," Kyle announced as he joined Andy on the porch and leaned against one of the railings. His coffee produced a thick stream of steam coming from the cup. "Would it be okay if your mom took you to see Lacy? I need to get a few things done around here today."

"Sure, Dad. I'm about to call her now and see what time is good."

"Great! Thanks, bud." Kyle turned to start down the steps. "I'll be in the shop. Let me know before you guys leave."

"Sure thing, Dad."

He glanced at his phone and saw that it was finally late enough to call Lacy. He quickly entered her number and hit the "call" button.

After only one ring, she answered. "Andy. Good morning!"

"Hey," Andy enthusiastically replied. "I was getting worried. I sent you like three texts after the game last night. How are you?"

"Sorry. I listened to the game on my phone and killed the battery. I'm good. Great, actually. I'm going home today!"

"What? No way! That's awesome news," he shouted with excitement.

"Yep. Dad is getting my stuff together now."

Andy almost interrupted, speaking excitedly as she finished. "I got in the game last night. Like, on the field!"

"I know! The radio guys mentioned you going in."

"Really?" Andy asked, sounding surprised. "I came in and stood in a spot. That was enough to mention?"

Lacy laughed. "Well, apparently Andy Higgins from Oak Creek is a big deal, even if the backup is holding his own."

"I don't know about being a big deal..."

"I don't know, either, but I heard your name being chanted when you came into the game last night."

"You could hear that?"

"Loud and clear!"

"How embarrassing." He sighed. "So, back to you. Are you really going home today? That's so awesome! But I guess that changes my plans. I was about to head toward Memorial to see you."

"Busting out of this joint! Sure am gonna miss this great food, ha! I'll have physical therapy at home for a couple of weeks, and then I'll have to choose a place to go until I'm fully recovered."

"Well, I guess we can text and keep up with one another," Andy suggested. "Unless you want to meet up in town sometime. I mean, when you can and all. Maybe grab a shake or something."

"Well, Andy from Oak Creek, are you asking me on a date?" She laughed.

"No," he answered quickly. "No, Lacy. Not at all. I mean, I just, well, I—"

"Too cool to date a chick like me?"

"No! I would. I mean, I just was talking about maybe getting together and talking, like we have been. I enjoy that."

"Andy from Oak Creek, you have a funny way of meeting girls. Knock 'em off the road and then go see them when they can't run from you."

"Oh, geez. I'm digging a hole here, ain't I?"

Lacy giggled and Andy could feel her positive energy through it. He had accidentally met her, but he was starting to think that maybe it wasn't an accident after all. Maybe all this "God" stuff was meant to happen all along.

"Hey, Andy. Can I call you back later? The nurse just came in to go over my discharge papers. I'm about to be free again."

"Yeah, of course. Call me whenever you can. Talk to you soon."

Andy ended the call and looked out over the yard. He was a little sad he wasn't going to get to see Lacy but was also happy for her to be going home. He wondered if the visits would stop, but he hoped not. Andy had grown fond of them.

Something had happened he'd never intended. He originally wanted to see Lacy because he felt guilty for causing the accident, but she had helped him discover a part of him that hid deep inside. He wasn't sure if it was because of all the times that Toby had chipped away at him, or if perhaps like so many others had said, it was God making His move. He knew that in just the past few weeks he had talked about God more than the last ten years of his life. *Something* was happening, but what? He was still looking for that answer.

Andy walked to the shop where his dad was working.

"You guys leaving?" Kyle asked when he saw Andy enter.

"Not going. Lacy is going home today."

Kyle picked up a towel from the floor and wiped his hands. "Really? That's great."

"Yeah, it is," Andy responded. He picked up a piece of wood from the bench where Kyle was working. "Whatcha making?"

"Gonna be a new gate for the back deck when I get it all put together," Kyle said as he picked up another piece to it. "That's the plan, anyway."

"Say, Dad. Can I ask you something?" Andy said, fidgeting with the piece of wood.

"Sure. What's up?"

"Would it be out of line to ask to visit Lacy at home? Just to talk and stuff. I kinda enjoy visiting her. She's pretty cool."

Kyle smiled as he put down the wood. "Well, that would be up to Mr. and Mrs. Hollingsworth. You're not starting to like Lacy, are you?"

"No, Dad! It's not like that. I mean, she is fun to talk to and all. And she knows everything about football, and—well, Dad, I don't know why I like being around her. I guess it's because after what I did, she still lets me come by, and, y'know, I don't even feel guilty around her anymore. But when I leave, it's back. I think I like being there because I can see that she doesn't hate me. She makes me feel good about what comes next."

"And what comes next?" Kyle asked.

"I wish I knew." Andy sighed. "Man, I wish I knew."

"You will, son. Well, since you're staying here today, I guess I got a helper," Kyle said as he threw a shop towel at Andy.

"Guess so."

THE NEXT MORNING, Andy came rushing down the hall, tucking in his shirt as he kept moving. Kyle and Holly were already up and sitting in the den.

"Where are you heading in such a hurry?" Holly asked.

"Church! Didn't I tell you? Toby should be pulling up any second now."

"I don't think you did, but that's fine," Holly responded, her brows drawn together.

"Sorry, Mom. They asked me to come when I was at the Fifth Quarter Friday night. Thought I told you." He glanced out the window as he grabbed his jacket from a coat rack by the door. "There's Toby! See you guys after church."

Holly glanced at Kyle. "He's like a different kid lately," she said as she watched him run out to Toby's car. "Church? We practically have to force him to go when we have an event or something."

"He's had a lot of questions lately about his faith," Kyle added. "Said he's doubting his salvation. I was gonna get Ken to talk to him. But Andy said he didn't want to talk to anyone." Kyle turned and watched from the window as Toby's car went down the drive. "He's had a lot on him, hun. I think he's just looking for answers to a lot of things, things that are new to him."

"Do you think Lacy is pushing him to go to church? I know she's strong in her faith, and they have been talking a lot."

"Don't know. But if so, I can't say that it's a bad thing."

"Maybe we should start back to church, Kyle. We used to go all the time, and then ball practice and games, and—well, life happened."

Kyle sighed. "I miss it at times. But I just don't want to get caught up in thinking we *have* to go. That's what it came to before we quit going. We didn't go because we wanted to; we went because we didn't want anyone to ask where we were."

"Where do Toby and his parents go? Do you know?" she asked.

"I think down at Crossroads. Little church close to the sawmill. Bill Garrison used to preach there before he passed. They got somebody new now, but not sure who it is."

"Wanna give it a shot next Sunday? I mean, if Andy wants to go, I'd rather he go with us and not have to rely on another family to take him."

"Yeah, I suppose we can give it a try. But that won't fix everything that's happened. I remember what Granddad always told me, 'don't get in a relationship with the church, or you may hurt your relationship with the Lord.' I want us to go for the right reason. If we start going back, I want us there because we want to be, not because we don't want somebody else taking Andy."

"That's not what I meant, babe. You know that," Holly said as she threw a pillow at him. "I enjoyed when we went. I've even been reading that devotional Sarah got me for my birthday. There are days that the lesson touches me, and I sit and think about how good God has been to us. And just think, it only takes a split second for Him to take it all away."

"It's not about the *things*, hun," Kyle reminded her. "What if He had taken Andy?"

"Well, He might as well have taken me, too," she replied. "I wouldn't be able to handle it."

ANDY, Toby, and Alec arrived at Crossroads Baptist Church. Andy was nervous about being there, but also excited. He had talked to Lacy last night, and she had even told him that she was proud of him. But he had those butterflies again—the same ones he felt before a big game.

"Come on, A-man," Alec said as he motioned for Andy to follow him. "I'll introduce you to everyone."

"I'm good, Alec," Andy quickly replied. "Thanks, my man, but I think I'll know most, anyway."

Toby smiled and said, "He's been excited all morning after I told him you were coming with us. Alec loves church. This is his favorite place to be, except maybe for the stadium on game days. But even then, I'm not sure which comes first."

Alec ran off ahead of them, greeting everyone, a few even getting one of his hugs. Andy watched him and noticed how everyone he came in contact with was suddenly filled with joy. Smiles spread across their faces as soon as Alec ran up to them.

"Man, I wish I had that kind of happiness," Andy said. "Your little bro is amazing. I've never seen someone so happy all the time. And he doesn't mind sharing it either."

"Full of love," Toby replied. "God's love is what he calls it. He loves everyone."

Andy watched Alec go from person to person. "Imagine if we all were like that. It would be a better place, huh, bro?"

"No doubt," Toby agreed.

They continued inside and began walking up toward the front, where Toby, Alec, and a few other Oak Creek students usually sat. Andy stopped about midway down the aisle.

"Andy, think we could sit back here?" he asked.

"Wherever you want, man. The students usually sit up front, but we can sit anywhere. You'll know about everyone up there."

"I'd rather just sit here. I mean, if that's cool. You can sit where you usually do, though."

"Nah, man. I'll sit with you. No biggie."

As they found a place near the back, Andy noticed several people from school that he knew. Even a couple from the team. As he gazed around the room, more and more faces were recognizable. Some he had seen in the stands every Friday night. Others he knew from around town. Mrs. Howell, his math teacher, was seated not far in front of him. He was so consumed with everyone there, he hadn't noticed the man that had walked up beside him.

"Good morning, gentlemen," he announced. "Toby, are you guarding the back door for me today?"

"Good morning, Pastor Charles. Gotta keep anyone from slipping out early if you get long-winded," Toby said.

Pastor Charles laughed. "Well, you may have the hardest job in the house today." He extended his hand to shake Andy's. "And you must be Andy. I've watched you play ball but never got around to introducing myself. I'm Charles Tate. I've been the pastor here for about a year now."

"Good to meet you, sir," Andy said, obliging the handshake.

"Pastor Charles moved here from Frankland," Toby said, referring to another small town that they had met a few years prior in the playoffs. "I told him that at least now he can watch *real* football."

"If I recall, wasn't it Frankland that put y'all out of the playoffs?" he joked.

"That's because me and Andy weren't playing!"

155

"Well, I'll let you think that. Andy, it's so nice to have you this morning. Thank you for coming."

"Yes, sir. Thank you," Andy replied.

"And if you boys want to move up front, I promise I won't throw anything at you," Pastor Charles said while smiling. "Even if I do, I'm not a good shot."

Andy smiled back at the pastor but offered no response. It was his first time in a church for worship in over ten years. He was nervous, but eager to learn. So far, he found it much less stressful than he imagined. He had envisioned everyone being straight-faced and serious, carrying Bibles like shields and giving him the stare-down. But it was quite the opposite. Everyone was smiling and having casual conversations. Andy was starting to feel more and more like he belonged.

"Hey, guys," Alec said as he came down the aisle. "Why you back here? Cool kids sit up there," he added, pointing toward the front.

"We're gonna hang out back here today, bud. Wanna join us?" Toby said.

Alec shook his head. "Nah. Jenny asked me to sit by her today. That's Dave's girlfriend, but I think she likes me."

"Heartbreaker! Ouch," Toby teased.

Alec smiled before turning and heading back up front.

"I love that guy," Andy said. "I see why you always choose to spend time with him over any of the guys."

Toby nodded. "I used to think it was more for him. But over the last few years, he's grown up some, and I enjoy it; it's just as much for me. I learn a lot from that kid. I think he's taught me more about compassion than anyone else ever could. He just wants everyone to be happy. He's a great little brother."

"Welcome, everyone, on this fine morning of the Lord's," a gentleman up front announced. The church was small enough that no microphone was needed. His voice carried through the building, echoing from the wooden walls and low ceiling. "If you would, please stand and open your hymnals to page sixty-two, and let's sing three verses."

Andy found himself enjoying the service. He didn't sing along much but enjoyed both the music and the message. His mind wandered some, but he heard enough to know what the pastor was trying to convey. But he was plagued by that one question from Lacy, *are you sure you're saved?* Throughout the service, he kept going back to that question. He recalled that day in Vacation Bible School so many years ago when he'd raised his hand.

What did it mean? Did I do it because my friends did? Did I understand what I was asked? Did I pray the prayer of salvation? I don't remember if I did.

With so many unanswered questions, Andy became more and more convinced that he had the answer all along. He hadn't secured his salvation, and now, he found his thoughts drifting more and more toward wanting it.

Was it the accident that triggered this? Maybe it was Lacy and her willingness to share her salvation story with me. Perhaps it was Toby. Lord knows he's done his part to direct me toward Christ. Thoughts flooded his mind as he fidgeted in the pew.

At the end of the service, Pastor Charles asked the music director to lead them in the invitational hymn. As the music played, the pastor spoke, beseeching lost souls to make that change.

"If any of you hasn't proclaimed Jesus as the Lord of your life, please, come forward. Let's pray together and make it happen today. You know you're hurting. You know that there's an emptiness that needs to be filled. Come," he pleaded.

Andy's heart beat hard in his chest. His feet were restless as he fought the urge to run up the aisle. He had made his decision about what he needed to do; now, he had to find the courage to do so.

"Miss Jill, please continue to play softly on the piano," Pastor Charles asked. "If everyone will, bow your heads and close your eyes. Today could be the day that changes your life. We may not get another chance. Tomorrow is not promised, for we do not know the day nor the hour when we'll be called home. Please, if you need to come, while all heads are bowed, come now."

Andy was fighting it. His emotions ran wild as tears welled up in his eyes. He sniffled and wiped a tear. Toby heard and saw the restlessness. He knew Andy had been through a lot, and he had hoped his friend was ready. Toby reached over and patted him on the arm.

"I'll go up there with you," he whispered.

Andy looked at him with his eyes full, but shook his head and mouthed the words, "I'm good, bro."

Toby nodded, knowing he was battling a big decision. Andy grasped the pew in front of him and continued to stare at the floor.

"Okay! It was so great having everyone today," Pastor Charles finally announced. "Please make your way back here tonight if you can. God bless, and be safe."

And just as quickly as it started, it ended. Andy survived his first church service in over a decade.

Toby kidded with Andy about the church still standing, and of course, Alec joined in the fun. As they walked toward Toby's car, Andy felt his phone vibrate in his pocket. He pulled it out and looked at it, reading a text from Lacy:

How was church? You did go, right? Lol. So, my church youth group is coming over this evening. Pizza party for me being home. Can you come? 5:00. I'll send you my address.

Andy immediately replied:

I don't know any of them. They probably hate me for what I did. Yes, I went. It was good.

Andy looked at Toby and sighed. "Does stress cause you to develop emotional train wrecks?"

Toby shook his head. "That's the spirit moving, my man. The Lord is fighting for you."

"It's not that. I mean, like, feelings for someone."

"Whatcha mean? Hate? Mean thoughts? Whatcha talking about?"

"Lacy. I feel bad for her, I mean, y'know, because it's my fault and all. But I don't know, man. It's crazy. I think I'm starting to like her; I think about her all the time."

His phone went off again. It was another text from Lacy:

They know you. I've told them ALL about you. :) Please come.

"Whoa, bro," Toby said, backing up and gawking at Andy. "Is that you? Andy? Are you in there?"

"Seriously, man. Forget it. It's stupid."

"Wow. Andy Higgins, confessing that he likes a girl. Man, that wreck must have knocked your head somewhere. You *are* acting differently."

Andy texted her back:

I still don't have my license. I'll ask my parents and let you know soon.

Lacy immediately replied:

Great! :)

"Forget it, man," Andy said. "She's just a cool person, and yeah, I do feel bad about the accident. Maybe I'm just trying to make it up to her. Just forget I mentioned it."

"It's cool. Say, wanna come grab lunch with us? Me, Alec, and a couple of guys from our youth group are going down to the diner."

"Nah. Thanks, but I promised Dad I would help him put up a couple of tree stands after church. Do you have time to drop me off before y'all go?"

"Sure, man. It's right on the way."

It wasn't long before Toby had dropped Andy off at his house. He ran inside, looking for Kyle. As soon as he came in, he saw his mom.

"Hey, Mom," he said as he hurried right by her. "Where's Dad?"

"He's in the shop. Why?" she asked.

"Wanna ask him something," Andy said as he turned to go back out.

"Hey! How was church?" Holly shouted.

Andy was already out the door. "It was good," he replied while he leaped from the porch and took off around the house. As he made his way to the shop, he nearly ran into Kyle, who was coming out at the same time as Andy was entering.

"Whoa, there, speedy! Didn't know putting up tree stands would get you so excited."

"Sorry, Dad. How long do you think it's gonna take us today?"

"Couple of hours, three at the most. Why? Need to do something else?"

Andy fidgeted with his hands, a nervous habit. "Well, I was going to see if you could take me to Lacy's. Her friends are giving her a party for getting to come home, and she asked if I could come. She sent her address, and it's closer than the hospital was. It's at five o'clock."

"To her house? Is that okay with her parents?"

"I mean, I guess. She asked me, so..."

"How long you plan on staying? I would have to drive all the way there, come back home, and then come back to get you."

"Please, Dad?"

"You really do care about Lacy, don't you? I know you're taking this whole thing to heart and you feel like it's your fault, but, son, at some point you're gonna have to worry about getting yourself back together."

"Dad, she's become a good friend now. I know, at first, it was just me trying to own my actions, but I've gotten to know her, and even after all of this, she's still trying to help me."

"Help you do what?"

"Help me through all of this. I know it's weird, but seeing how she's handled everything, well, it's made me wanna be a better person."

"Well, I can't argue with that," Kyle said as he turned to go inside. "Yeah, I'll take you. I may just run on into town and look around at the hardware store for a couple of hours. But let's get these stands loaded and get them in the woods first."

"Thanks, Dad!" Andy said.

They spent the next few hours together in the woods, getting things ready for hunting season. Kyle talked to Andy about going back to church as a family, which Andy was excited about. It was time shared that they both needed.

Kyle seemed to open up more about his faith, something he'd always steered away from. But now, with Andy looking for guidance, Kyle felt obligated to grow with him. He also found it was something he wanted. For Andy, faith was something new. Spiritual talks with his father had been few and far between. They each learned a little from each other that day, and their bond was strengthened. They had always been close and had a great father-son relationship, but the uncharted topic opened up an entirely new connection.

The hours passed by quickly, and before long, Andy was on his way to Lacy's. He anticipated getting to see her but was nervous about meeting her friends. The trip took them down a road that had become familiar over the past few weeks, and Andy recalled the first trip to see Lacy at the hospital and how it went.

What a difference a few weeks make, he thought.

"I think it's the next house, Dad," Andy instructed as he watched the navigation app on his phone.

They stopped on the side of the two-lane street that was dotted with small but modest homes.

"You sure this is it?" Kyle asked.

"5521 Dansbury Road," Andy replied. "That's what's on the mailbox."

"Okay. I'll call you when I head back. Probably about two hours. That good?"

"Sure, Dad. Whenever you get ready."

Andy got out of the truck and walked up the sidewalk leading to the front door. Kyle waited before leaving, making sure everything was still as planned. Nervously, Andy rang the doorbell. He stood, waiting, and then suddenly the door opened.

"Andy!" Ann greeted. "Lacy is so excited you could make it. Come in."

"Thank you, Mrs. Hollingsworth," he replied, stepping into their house.

"Lacy and her friends are in the den," she announced.

Andy walked in the direction that Mrs. Hollingsworth had pointed and heard laughter and talking. *Is it too late to back out?* he thought. Again, he became nervous but knew there was no turning back. He turned the corner into the den where everyone was gathered.

"Andy," Lacy shouted. "You made it!"

Andy smiled at her. She was seated on the sofa, wearing her back brace. Then he glanced around the room at everyone. There were boys and girls, all around the same age. A guy, maybe a tad younger than Andy, stood and extended his arm to shake hands.

"Hi! I'm Shawn," he said.

Andy obliged the handshake and introduced himself.

A girl sitting beside Lacy spoke up. "You were right. He is kinda cute."

"Shh!" Lacy hissed as they both laughed.

Andy blushed but acted as if he hadn't heard the exchange. "Hi, everyone," he said as he stepped a little further into the room. "Thanks for the invite."

"Come over here, Andy. Sit by me," Lacy said, directing him to a spot next to her. "Or, you can take a spot on the floor with my crew." Andy took a seat on the arm of the sofa, next to Lacy, and she announced, "These are all my buds from church. My homies!" She gazed up at him and giggled.

"I'm her main homie," another girl announced while stepping over the others on the floor. "Hi, I'm Rebecca."

The greetings continued until everyone introduced themselves. Before long, Andy found himself enjoying being there. His nervousness was gone, and he was just as much a part of the laughter as any of them.

"Pizzas are here," Bob announced as he came into the room. "Andy! I didn't see you slip in."

"Hey, Mr. Hollingsworth," he replied. "Thanks for allowing me over."

He laughed and nodded at Lacy. "Thank my girl. She seems to have grown quite fond of you."

Andy smiled but offered no response other than his expression; his eyes widened and his cheeks reddened once again.

After almost two hours, Andy realized that no one had mentioned the accident. *Surely they know I caused it*, he thought. It was as if they had been friends for a while, and they were all there to enjoy the time —Andy included. He glanced at his phone, reading the incoming text from his father.

"My dad is on the way," he told the others. "He'll be here in about five minutes."

"Wow! Two hours went by fast," Lacy said. "Well, Andy from Oak Creek, I'm glad you came."

"Me, too. You have some nice friends. I was nervous about meeting everyone, but y'all made me feel like part of the gang. I really needed this tonight."

One of the girls spoke up. "That's how we're supposed to treat people, Andy. Can you imagine if we all loved everyone like Christ did?"

"I said the same thing this morning!" Andy exclaimed. "My friend, Alec—you guys have to meet him! He's so happy, and he loves everyone. And he has a disability. You would think that he would have some kind of anger in him when he sees others playing ball and doing things he can't, but not Alec. That dude is amazing."

"I'd love to meet him," Lacy said. "Maybe one day, I'll get to see what it's like over in Oak Creek, and I can meet this friend of yours."

"I've been to Oak Creek. You're not missing much," one of the girls joked.

"See?" Andy laughed. "I knew there had to be one in the group."

He stood and looked around at everyone. No longer was he afraid of what they thought. They had to know what he'd done, but they were there to support Lacy, and that was their focus; nothing else.

"Well, guess I'll go. Dad should be pulling up any second," Andy said with a sigh. "It was great meeting you guys, and I hope I see y'all again."

"I'll walk you out," Lacy said as she reached for two canes that had arm attachments mounted to them.

"No, it's fine," Andy said. "Don't do all that."

"I've got this," she replied, pulling herself upright. "Look! No walker."

Andy smiled and knew he had to accept her offer now that she was standing. As they shuffled to the door, Andy thought of how different things were. He was at the house of a girl he'd almost killed due to a poor decision on his part. And yet, instead of being nervous and scared, they were both having fun.

"I really am glad you came, Andy. Thank you," Lacy said as they neared the door.

"Of course. Thank you for inviting me."

"Are you still struggling with your decision?"

Andy knew exactly what she was asking about; his battle with his salvation. "No, not really. I mean, have I made a decision yet? No, but I know I want to."

"What are you waiting for? Andy, you've seen firsthand how quickly things can change. You came very close to not being able to make that decision."

"I know," he said, lowering his head. "I just, I—"

"Just *what*? Afraid you're not ready again? Afraid it won't be sincere? You were, like, nine years old. Of course, you didn't know everything about it then. Andy, we will never be fully ready if we wait until we're worthy of His forgiveness. That's the great thing about it. He takes us just as we are, and then starts molding us. We can do this right here, right now."

Andy's phone buzzed in his hand. "My dad's here," he said, grateful for the excuse to escape. "I'll call you when I get home, okay? We can talk more about it."

Lacy leaned her walking supports against the wall and stepped toward Andy. She looked at him, focusing her eyes on his. She stayed silent, gazing at him, and hugged him, resting her head on his shoulder.

Andy felt the butterflies return as he took one arm and draped it around her. She squeezed him tighter, sinking her head deeper into his shoulder. He wrapped his other arm around her. His heart raced and he knew she could feel his nervousness as his breathing became more noticeable. She leaned slightly back, tilting her head to look at him once more.

"What are you waiting on, Andy?" she asked again.

Andy wasn't sure if her question was still about his salvation, but as much as he wanted to kiss Lacy, he was scared it wasn't the question she was asking. His phone went off again, and this time, it was a call. Andy released Lacy and stepped back, answering his phone.

"Sorry, Dad. I'll be right out," he said.

Lacy smiled. "Andy from Oak Creek, I guess you better go before you're not allowed back over here—and you've got to come back. I'm not done working on you."

"I hope not," Andy said through a smile. "I'll call you in a few."

CHAPTER 13

RETURNING TO THE GAME

THE NEW WEEK STARTED, AND EVEN THOUGH ANDY WAS BACK AT school and practicing with the team, things just didn't seem the same. He couldn't keep his mind off of Lacy.

He didn't feel the same about Lacy as any girl before. Andy felt a connection to her that made him not only feel good, but he wanted to *do* good. He wanted to do things that impressed her, but unlike the past, it wasn't on the football field. Whenever he understood something Biblical or spiritual, he called or texted her to let her know. She had done something nobody else had been able to do, not even his best friend, Toby. Lacy had him thinking about his salvation.

The last bell sounded, signaling the end of the school day. Andy rushed to change and get out on the field. He wanted Coach Woods to know he was taking his second chance seriously.

"Did you hear about that Harris guy from Lancaster?" Toby asked Andy as they lined up for stretches.

"Nah. What's up with him?"

"He's about two hundred yards from breaking the state record. Told the newspaper that he plans on getting it this week."

Nate Harris was a running back from their opponent's school— the number two team in the state—Lancaster High. He had just committed to Kentucky and came off of a career-best performance in the second round of the playoffs last week.

"It's easy to talk that smack, but coming in here and trying it? That's another thing," Andy replied as he sat on the ground to begin his stretches.

"He doesn't come in here. We go there," Toby reminded him. "We travel this week."

Oak Creek had been fortunate enough to play the first two games of the playoffs at home, but Toby was correct. They'd take the show on the road in a few days and play at Lancaster.

"Still a hundred-yard field with bleachers on each side," Andy said. "Anyplace, anytime—he can bring it and see what happens."

Coach Woods walked around the lines of players, talking to one of his assistant coaches. He was one of the best at getting his boys ready for players such as Harris, but even he knew he had his hands full this week.

"All right, bring it in," he yelled, and he blew his whistle.

The team sprinted up and took a knee around him, creating a half-moon shape.

"Got a tough one this week. Lancaster is bringing one of the best rushing attacks that I've seen in years. So that means we have to play tough, every play. We're not gonna try to start changing stuff now to stop the run. We've held our own all year, and I hope they're looking at our defense like we're looking at their rushing game. But, practice this week will be a little different. Today will be our only day in full pads."

Everyone gawked at each other. Coach Woods was a hard-nosed coach and believed in the old philosophy that they had to practice hard to play hard. His announcement came as a surprise, but a welcomed one.

"We got some guys that are still a little beat up from the last few weeks, so I'm thinking that we'll heal a little so we can offer our best to that bunch from Lancaster."

Coach Woods was a pacer. He couldn't stand still and talk. As he walked back and forth, he spit sunflower seeds between statements.

"This being our only full pad day, I want you to give me what you got," he instructed. "Now let's go! First team offense, let's run some plays."

"This is new," Andy said to Toby as he rushed over with the starters.

Toby laughed. "I almost feel like this is another one of Coach's psychological tricks."

Even though Mike was still the starting quarterback, Andy stayed with the group, mostly watching, but also taking a snap from the quarterback position. The practice was a rough one. Coach Woods demanded near-perfection.

"We'll stay so late we turn the lights on if y'all can't get it right," he barked.

The crowd of spectators had grown over the last few weeks. Folding chairs lined almost one complete side of the practice field. The third round of the playoffs was a big deal in Oak Creek. Even the residents that normally didn't go all out displayed banners in their yards or tied blue and white balloons to their mailboxes. Someone passing through would believe that there was a special occasion that week, such as a fair or festival. But it was much more, at least to them. It was the playoffs, and this was Oak Creek.

"Grab some water! Make it quick," Coach instructed.

Toby yanked his helmet off, and Alec gave him a squirt bottle from the tray he was passing them out from. He walked with Andy toward the sideline.

"We won't be able to practice tomorrow. I see why he said no pads after today," he said to Andy.

"How many times did y'all run that sweep right? Like seven? Eight?"

"No idea. First, Billy wasn't pulling fast enough from his guard position, then I wasn't sprinting fast enough, then Mike wasn't making a good enough pitch. It was too many times, I know that!"

Like their conversation, a dozen more were taking place around the practice field as players expressed frustration over how Coach Woods was pushing them. But for the most part, it was their memory that failed them. Coach always pushed his teams hard, demanding the best from them. But when it came playoff time, he got even more out of them.

He once compared his method to a wet towel. He said, "You can squeeze a wet towel and get most of the water from it, but if you twist it and squeeze again, there's always a little more it can give." Coach was definitely twisting them.

"All right! Let's go," came Coach's instruction, followed by the sound of his whistle. "Gonna run a few more before we switch it over to defense."

Small towns such as Oak Creek were almost always faced with the dilemma of having too few players to have defensive starters and offensive starters. Most played both, so for them to get practice on both sides of the ball, practice was usually split in half.

"Andy, swap out with Mike," Coach yelled. "I want you to take a few snaps under center."

Andy heard the announcement and had to look at Mike to make sure he'd heard right. Mike smiled at him, almost relieved he was getting a break.

"All yours, Andy," Mike said as he patted him on the helmet.

Andy was excited, as he hadn't known when, or even if, he would have an opportunity to play quarterback again. Mike had done such a good job, showing enormous improvement throughout the weeks as they progressed.

"Forty-eight blast, slant right," Coach called to Andy.

Wow! I haven't taken a snap in five weeks, and my first play back, he wants me to throw a difficult pass, Andy thought.

He called the play and lined up. The ball was snapped, and Andy faked the pitch to Toby on his right side. He rolled out to his left and looked for Scott cutting across the field. There he was, just behind the linebackers and in a gap between the safety. He set his feet and fired the ball in his direction. Perfect strike! Scott grabbed the ball in stride and raced by the safety for what would have been a touchdown. The team was exuberant!

There he is! He's back! Get it, Andy! Congratulatory comments were abundant from his teammates.

"Andy! Why did you wait so long? If Jake hadn't been so damn slow reacting to the play, Scott would have been covered," Coach Woods screamed.

Coach Woods was referring to Jake Howard, who was playing the safety position. He should have picked up on Scott crossing and came up sooner, covering him. If Andy made the pass even just two seconds sooner, Jake wouldn't have time to react, even if he'd seen the play developing. But that was the perfection that Coach Woods demanded. Two seconds! It didn't seem like much, but he'd picked up on it, and for him, it wasn't good enough.

Andy, on the other hand, thought the play was perfect. It resulted in a touchdown. But Andy knew that if Coach didn't think it was good enough—well, it wasn't good enough.

"Sorry, Coach," Andy replied. "My first play. I gotta get back into it."

"Andy, you've run that play a hundred times. That ain't a 'getting back into it' thing. That's a 'get your mind in the game' thing. Do I need to put Mike back in until you get ready?"

"No, sir. I got it, Coach."

The next play was called, another passing play. Then another—pass. And another—pass. And another... Six plays had been called since Andy returned to quarterback, all pass plays. Each pass was a great pass. But Coach Woods critiqued every one.

Andy looked at Mike, shaking his head and tightening his lips. He wasn't so sure he wanted the position back. Never before had Coach been so critical of him.

"Thirty-six toss right, rocket left," Coach Woods instructed. "Run it."

Finally, a run play, Andy thought.

He took the snap and rolled to his right, acting as if he was going to keep the ball, turning it up just outside the tackle. At the last minute, he pitched the ball to Toby, who was immediately hit and tackled.

"Andy!" Coach screamed.

He knew it was coming and looked toward Coach without saying anything.

"What are our options on that play?" Coach asked.

"Keep it or pitch it."

"Did you have any running room?"

"Might have gotten a couple of yards."

"Then why the *hell* did you pitch it to *Toby,* who basically already had someone hanging on him?! Trying to get Toby hurt?"

"No, sir," Andy replied quickly.

"Hell! Good thing it was only Cole. Ain't gotta worry about him hurting nobody. I think he hurt himself more than Toby."

A collective laugh came from most of the group—even Cole, a smaller sophomore that knew he had some growing to do. Practice continued, and so did Coach Woods's critiques. It was uncommon for the coach to be so hard on Andy. But Andy stayed focused, trying his best on every play. Finally, to Andy's relief, Coach Woods blew his whistle and announced the switch to defense.

"Man, Coach has your number," Toby said as he and Andy jogged to get to the other side of the field.

"It's all good. I'm just happy to be out here again," Andy replied.

Toby's brow wrinkled as he looked at Andy in disbelief. This was *not* the Andy he knew. Any other time in the past, Andy would have added his thoughts, and most of the time, they wouldn't have been so positive.

The second half of practice went much better. Coach knew defense was their strong point, and he didn't want to change much there. He even joked and had some fun with the team. That was typical of Coach Woods. He started hard on the team and finished praising them. There hadn't been too many times in his career that he'd ended practices on a bad note.

Coach blew his whistle to gather the team and gave a few instructions before dismissing them. As he ended the practice, he asked Andy to stick around for a minute. Andy figured he'd hear more about how he needed to get better and prove he was ready to play again. He dreaded the inevitable talk.

"Son, after many weeks off, I don't think you've missed a beat."

Andy was confused. He had spent most of the practice taking criticism from the coach. "I know I made mistakes, Coach. I guess I was just excited to be back out there."

Coach Woods grabbed a squirt bottle from one of the racks that hadn't been collected yet. After taking a sip, he continued. "Andy, you have a talent that about ninety percent of these kids wished they had. But you don't use it like you should. That's why I was so hard on you today. You let your natural ability take you through the motions, but you don't push to get that extra."

Andy nodded, agreeing with Coach. "My mind hasn't been where it should be, Coach, but I'm working on that."

"I talked to your dad on the phone today. I told him I wanted to work you back into playing this week. Also, I wanted him to know that it may not be at quarterback, and with all you've had on you lately, I wanted to know how you would accept that."

"Mike is doing a great job. Let him take it. I'm good with it."

"He has done a great job. But you can get that ball where it needs to be. You see things that Mike doesn't see yet. He's progressing, and I think he's going to be a fine quarterback, but he doesn't have the talent you do. Yours comes easy. He works his tail off for it."

"Coach, I'll play on the line if you need me to. I just want to play."

"Well, actually, what I talked to your dad about was moving you around a lot. Maybe playing you in the backfield with Toby, leaving Mike under center. May even run you out at receiver some."

"Yes, sir! Wherever you need me."

"But your dad told me about how you've been struggling with your faith lately," Coach Woods said before taking another drink of water.

Andy was taken by surprise. *Why would Dad tell him that? It doesn't have anything to do with football.*

"I thought about this all day, and I think we need you to win state, and I think we need you where you're best able to serve the team. You see, when I say you have a talent, I mean a God-given talent. Now, I was taught at a young age that when God gives you something, you use it to glorify Him. I don't know how you can glorify God through playing football, but He does, and I think He's trying to show you that. Maybe that's why you've had all these questions lately. Maybe He's showing you what He wants you to do."

Andy found himself in a discussion with Coach that he had never been in before, and he didn't know how to respond other than, "Yes, sir."

"Andy, this may not be about football at all. But maybe it's about you having the opportunity to let these guys that look up to you see you respond in a way that glorifies God." Coach Woods stood and started walking toward the field house. "Come on. Your dad is waiting."

"Coach?"

"Yeah?"

"Thank you."

"Andy, I know you think I'm just this mean ol' ball coach that cares about nothing but winning, but there's more to it than that. I care about you boys first, and winning comes after that."

Andy looked at him and nodded with a smile.

"Except in the playoffs," Coach added with a wink.

After a few minutes in the locker room, Andy emerged. He was one of the last few out as a result of his talk with Coach Woods. He walked out by the dark practice field, toward his dad, who was waiting on him while talking to a few other men.

"Got some stains on the uniform today, huh, Andy?" Kyle asked.

"Felt great, Dad," Andy said as he threw his backpack into the rear seat of Kyle's truck.

Kyle laughed. "Even Coach screaming at you?"

"Even that," Andy replied.

William Miller, whose son also played, was there waiting for his son to come out. "So, are you back at quarterback?" he asked Andy.

"Good question," Andy said with a chuckle. "Coach talked to me about it, but never told me anything other than I'll be playing this week; just don't know what position."

"I hope you're back under center. We're gonna need you against Randolph," William added.

"Mike can handle it," Andy was quick to say. "He's done a great job. If Coach puts me there, I'll do what I can, but, hey, Mike hasn't lost a game. Gonna be hard to top that."

"Can't argue with that, Will," Kyle added.

"I'm glad we have Mike," William replied. "He sure surprised me. I think he surprised a lot of folks."

As Andy and Kyle drove off, he saw Coach Woods walking to his truck. "Dad, what did you tell Coach today? He said y'all talked on the phone."

Kyle turned the radio down. "Not much. Just about how he thought you could help them in other places."

"Coach said y'all talked about me going to church and stuff," Andy probed.

"He did, did he? I may have mentioned it."

"Well?"

"Well, what?"

"What did you say about it?"

"I just thought it would be good if Coach knew what all was on your mind," Kyle offered as a filtered reply.

"Like what?" Andy continued.

"Andy, I've known Coach Woods my entire life. That man has y'all's respect. He has the whole town's respect. You think he's just coaching you boys and teaching you football, but he's doing so much more. And you listen to him. Some of these kids probably don't listen to their parents like they do Coach. I've seen him change the lives of some kids that came through here. Some had no plan, no future. He spent time with them, talking and giving advice. And they listened. I just figured that with everything you've been asking me lately about church and getting saved and all, Coach might help you with some of that."

Andy looked over at Kyle, and, as if they hadn't been talking at all, changed the subject. "Toby said he could run me home after practice if you didn't want to come up here every day."

Kyle laughed. "Oh, I guess we're done with that conversation."

"Just thought about it," Andy replied.

"Well, for the last four years, even when you could drive, I may have missed seven or eight practices altogether, so I think I'll be fine."

THE REST of the week seemed to go by quickly, and practices were much easier with the absence of the extra weight of the pads and no pounding on each other. By Friday, school spirit was at an all-time high. There was still an hour before the pep rally, but residents of Oak Creek were already making their way to the gymnasium.

Blue and white team colors dominated the scenery. Cheerleaders, already changed into their uniforms, finished hanging the new signs. "Tame The Lions" and "Tigers Are Really Kings Of The Jungle" were just a few of the catchy phrases they had come up with for their opponent, the Lancaster Lions.

Andy, Toby, and Ruby were walking into the gymnasium together. Ruby was wearing Toby's jersey, as the tradition for couples was at the school, although some wore jerseys of their favorite players in support of them. Andy stopped, alerted by his phone going off in his pocket. He retrieved it and looked at the message. It was from Lacy. Although the two had talked all week, every new message from her brought a smile to his face.

"Lacy?" Toby asked.

"How'd you know?" Andy asked.

"Bro! Your face told me. Admit it. You like her. Nothing wrong with that, man."

"Ask her out, Andy," Ruby added. "She wouldn't be texting and calling you so much if she wasn't interested."

"She's different," Andy replied. "She's a ballplayer type of girl. Nothing like the ones around here."

"Hey!" Ruby shouted.

"Except you, Ruby," he quickly corrected. "But you're different, too. Like my sister, in a way. I would do anything for you."

"Aww!" She blushed, swaying and bumping him with her hip. "Good recovery, Andy. Good one."

"But really. I like her, but I don't know," Andy continued.

"You're scared that you'll do something to hurt her, right?" Ruby asked.

Andy shrugged and raised his brow. "I don't have a good track record."

"Well, you'll never know how it'll turn out if you don't go for it," Ruby suggested.

Andy looked at his phone again. Another smile appeared, this time noticeable.

"See!" Ruby shouted. "You get excited over her texts."

"No! I mean—maybe. And she's coming tonight! To the game! Her dad is bringing her to Lancaster. It's only a forty-five-minute drive from their house."

Toby stepped in front of him, placing a hand on his chest. "Dude, if she's there, do not, and I repeat, *do not* let this affect your focus! Coach is playing you tonight, and this is our toughest game of the year."

"Bro! You know I block out everything when I'm in the game," Andy assured him.

"Yeah, like last week when they shouted your name? You froze and stood there staring at the student section."

Andy laughed. "One time, man. And besides, the play was on the whole other side of the field."

"But still..."

"No worries. I've got this."

They continued into the gymnasium as more and more people filed in.

"Wow," Ruby exclaimed. "I've never seen this many here. Y'know, people from town and stuff."

"They believe this is the year. Just like last year, and the year before that, and every other year. These folks would be here if we were one and nine. It's crazy how they support us. I don't think I'll ever leave," Toby said.

Ruby crossed her arms and a sly grin grew on her face. "Excuse me? And our plans to run away and live at the beach together after graduation was just all talk?"

"Uh-oh. All yours, bro," Andy said as he sprinted toward the locker room.

"Just playing, baby," Toby quickly replied. "But you know we would have to take Alec. He won't let us go anywhere without him."

"I thought so," she said as she leaned over and kissed him. "Better not be getting cold feet on me."

Before long, the gym was overflowing. Both sides of the bleachers were full, and people stood in the corridors. The band struck up the fight song as the team entered from the locker room and took their places in chairs off to one side of the gym floor. Cheerleaders led the students in an array of chants and cheers. After about twenty minutes, Coach Woods stepped out onto the floor.

"Thank you all. And to you," he turned and looked behind him at the crowd of alumni and fans that had gathered, "thank you! We couldn't do half of what we do without your generosity and support. From feeding my boys to packing the stands, you folks are great!"

They applauded in support of Coach Woods. Oak Creek had an elected mayor, but Coach was the leader of the town. Everyone respected him.

"Gonna be a tough one," he continued. "Lancaster is one of the finest teams we've played, and their fans are loud—very loud. Second best in the state, probably; of course, behind our fans. They got a boy over there that promises to break a state record on us tonight. Now, I'm not much on bulletin board material, but I say that's a challenge."

The students went crazy, standing and shouting! Coach Woods raised his hands to signal them to quiet down.

"Now, what they don't know is that we got just as good of ballplayers, just as good of fans, a much better coach," he laughed and a rumble of laughter joined him throughout the gym, "but we got the best student section in the state, and we're gonna get so loud tonight that the lights are gonna shake!"

The students erupted and cheered. Coach Woods had always been great at making sure everyone knew they were important, and at their stage in the playoffs, it was time for him to bring them up a notch.

"What I need you all to do," he said, and then turned to look at the bleachers behind him, "is show up early, pack their stands, and get loud! I know it's over an hour's drive for you folks, but if I can get you there, I promise a good show! These boys haven't popped a pad since Monday, and they're hungry. They're hungry to hit somebody! They're hungry to go to somebody's house, and they're hungry to bring back that 'W!' Tigers, we are hungry, and it's time to eat!"

He raised one hand and strutted off the court as both sides of the gymnasium stood and exploded with cheers. The band cranked back up, and the cheerleaders jumped, flipped, and cheered as if the game had just been won! There was no doubt that Coach Woods had everyone ready for a ballgame.

With almost two hours before their scheduled departure time, the team still had to eat a meal, load the bus, and get ready for a showdown. Everybody was excited, ready, and could hardly wait to get on the bus and head to Lancaster. Most of the guys were going over plays and listening to music through headphones, except Andy.

He spent the time talking on the phone with Lacy while laying on the mats the cheerleaders used for tumbling. She told him about her therapy that day, and that she'd walked with no supports. Andy told her about how Coach planned on playing him more. As far apart as the two subjects were, they each found it just as important, if not more, than their news. In just a few short weeks, they went from strangers to each other's biggest supporters.

Andy couldn't believe how everything had played out. Not long ago, he was worried that he had almost killed someone. Now that "someone" had become important to him. In fact, he began to wonder if his interest went farther than the accident.

"Food is here! Everyone grab a box and a drink," someone announced.

"What are we having?" Mike asked as he headed toward the boxes being stacked on the bleachers.

Toby replied, "Sandwich, chips, and cookies from Papa's Deli. I heard Mom calling it in last night."

"That's the new place inside the truck stop, down by the interstate, isn't it?"

"That's the one. I've had it once. Pretty good Philly steak. Not sure what these are."

Almost as soon as the boys finished eating, they were on their way to Lancaster. The hour drive seemed like two in the old school bus they traveled in. The entire team fit in one bus while the cheerleaders and band traveled in a second. In front was one of the only two police cars in Oak Creek, providing an escort all the way to Lancaster Stadium. Behind the buses was a stream of cars, all with blue and white flags, adorned with tiger paws, writing on the windows, and each packed full of the town's faithful. It must have reached a mile, with dozens of cars in a caravan with the buses.

When they arrived, the boys were glued to the windows, peering out at the early crowd that had already assembled. Flags for the Lions waved in the air, some on poles as high as twenty feet or more. Pop-up-style tents lined the parking areas and smoke from grills could be seen wafting in the air as some tailgated after school. Some of the student groups began waving banners and flags as the buses slowly eased onto campus. "Let's go, Lions!" could be heard inside the bus as they began chanting to the visiting team.

Coach Woods stood as the buses came to a halt outside the field house that would be their gathering place.

"Listen up," he announced. "I want each of you to get off the bus and walk behind me, straight to that locker room. Do not look at anyone. Do not say anything. Don't even think of anything except what you're supposed to do for the next few hours. The coaches and a few volunteers will bring your pads in. I want you to get off and get in that field house. These people are serious about their football, and they will let you know it. We're here on business. Don't let this circus distract you! Understood?"

"Yes, sir!" the team thundered.

"All right! Let's go," he said, and stepped from the bus.

Each player followed. Despite Coach's instructions, it was hard to not look around. It was insane how everyone was already fired up for the game.

A news reporter hurried over and set a camera up just feet from the bus door and filmed as the Tigers unloaded. Third-round playoff games were important. These guys knew it. But they were learning that the rest of the state wasn't immune to the craze that set in every fall, and as the teams battling for the title became fewer and fewer, the craze got more and more uncontrollable.

For many, it was what they waited on all year. A chance to not just cheer on their team, but to brag to coworkers, relatives from other towns; even preachers got to jab at their congregations. It really was a religion. Maybe not on the same scale as the one Andy's decision teetered upon, but one of the rituals, nonetheless.

There were superstitions and lucky shirts. Some had a pregame meal that never changed, and others had to sneak in a flask of some good old southern whiskey to take the edge off. It was high school football, and it was the playoffs. It was generations of players, some going four and five generations deep; grandfathers rooted for their grandsons that wore their old numbers. As some put it, those who didn't take it seriously didn't belong.

The team did as the coach instructed and made it inside the locker room. From there, they could still hear the crowd and the band. It was the atmosphere that made it so special. The pageantry that came from raw emotion built from cheering for players that the townsfolk actually had connections with was electrifying.

Andy was just as excited about the upcoming game as any game he had ever been in. His return to significant playing time was upon him. He checked his phone one last time before placing it in his duffle bag inside a locker. There it was! The text he'd been waiting on:

We are here! WOW! Still trying to park. This is insane. We will be in soon. Good luck Andy! I'm here because of YOU!

Andy smiled and placed his phone in his bag. He no longer had anxiety about the game, but now he had a new purpose. He felt as if he needed to impress Lacy. He knew that she didn't need to see him do well, but she knew a lot about football, and he couldn't make a mistake—not with her watching.

Coach Woods made the announcement to head onto the field and start warmups. It was the biggest game of the year for the Tigers, and if they got past this one, only four teams would remain, including them. As they walked onto the field, the faithful that made the trip let out a thunderous applause. There was standing room only! Both sides were full, and the fence along each side was doing its best to hold back everyone leaning on it.

It was hard to block it all out, as Coach had instructed, but they were doing a pretty good job so far. Many from the stands called individual names, trying to get the attention of their friends. But no player looked in that direction. Game time was approaching, and it was time to focus.

Finally, as the crowd had been worked into a fever pitch, the ball was in the air, the kickoff signaling the start of the battle. Oak Creek won the coin toss but elected to receive the ball in the second half, as Coach Woods wanted to put his hard-nosed defense on the field first to hopefully set the tone.

Three plays in, Nate Harris, Lancaster's star player had already reeled off two great runs, and they were sitting at midfield. Not the start Oak Creek wanted. Coach Woods paced the sideline, screaming instructions to his guys.

Harris again took off around the end after beating the Tiger's front line and looked as if he would have another big gain. Toby saw him cut outside from his linebacker position and raced that way. Harris cut back inside, avoiding an Oak Creek defender. Andy closed ground on him, and just as Harris turned inside, Toby hit him solidly! Harris went down, and the ball shot from his grip and bounced right to Blake Barnes for the Tiger recovery. The Oak

Creek side of the stadium went crazy! The band struck up the fight song, and everything was right again for the blue and white faithful.

Andy stood waiting. Would Coach call his number? He was ready if he did. He moved with Coach Woods' every step, not staying much farther than a few steps away.

"Offense! Let's go," he screamed.

Am I first team? Is Mike going in?

His mind raced as he watched Mike trot onto the field. Coach Woods signaled in the first play, and Mike called it. They lined up and ran the play to perfection, picking up a first down. The crowd was still on their feet!

Andy paced right behind Coach, hoping he would see him and send him in. Two plays later, he still stood there. Then three, and then four. Andy didn't understand. Coach told him that he would use him, even if Mike was at quarterback.

The Tigers marched down the field with ease, making it look simple. After just a few plays, the Tigers jumped out to a seven-point lead, as Toby took a handoff and scampered nineteen yards to the end zone. Andy was ecstatic but also thought his chance of playing may not happen with the offense running like a well-oiled machine down the field.

"Awesome way to start the game," Andy said to Mike as he came off the field.

"Thanks, man. They're giving us that ten-yard cushion on every play—no rush on me at all. I don't get it."

"Just don't get suckered in. That blitz will come from nowhere if you get too comfortable."

On Lancaster's next possession, they moved the ball quickly down the field; this time, the star player kept a firm grip on the ball and rumbled the last ten yards to tie the game at seven each, worrying Coach. He had come into the game thinking it would be a defensive battle. His defense had held strong each week, while their offense struggled at times. If this game suddenly became a shootout, he knew it didn't favor his squad for the victory.

Oak Creek took the ball for the possession at its twenty-yard line. Finally, the time came that Andy had hoped for.

"Andy!" shouted Coach Woods.

Andy stepped into his view. "Yes, sir!"

"Go in and line up in I-formation, behind Toby. Split right, middle screen."

Andy's eyes lit up. That call should get him the ball on a screen pass with Toby blocking for him. He ran onto the field with so much excitement, he started calling the play before he got there. Mike saw him coming and met him.

"Easy! Don't tell them the play," he interrupted. "You getting me?"

"No! You're in. I'm running at halfback."

Mike looked at him and smiled. "That play is coming to you." He slapped Andy's helmet. "Let's do this!"

The offense lined up, and the ball was snapped. Mike faked the handoff, and Andy ran through the line. He turned about ten yards later, and the play worked to perfection. He was open! Mike passed the ball to him; Andy caught it and turned to run. Toby blocked the only defender close to him, and Andy cut outside and raced for forty yards before being chased down.

Oak Creek's crowd roared to life—the Tigers were again in scoring position. Andy heard his name over the loudspeaker for the first time in several weeks. He looked to the sideline, and Coach motioned for him to stay in.

This is great! Andy thought. He was back in the game, contributing, and with his big play, the Tigers were set to reclaim the lead.

Mike called the play, and the team lined up. Upon the snap of the ball, Mike rolled out and looked for Scott on a curl pattern, but he was covered. He turned to run, but a defender was heading straight at him. Andy saw him and threw his body at the defender, knocking him from the play and allowing Mike to race the final twelve yards for another Tiger touchdown!

As they came to the sideline, Mike caught up with Andy. "Hey, great block! Thanks."

"Yeah, man. Good run."

Andy felt good about the game, and being back out on the field was enough to make him forget about the last five weeks and all the turmoil. He was starting to realize that the religion Oak Creek practiced was bigger than Friday night lights. It was part of everything he ever cared about.

He soaked it in. The crowd, the smell of the grass, and the sound of the whistle were a part of him. It was a part of what made Andy who he was. And even if it was a huge part of his life, he realized that everything seemed better. Was it because it was almost taken away from him? Or perhaps, was it like Coach said—maybe God was using it all to draw him closer to Him.

"Andy! Andy," came a call from behind him.

He knew he shouldn't look. Coach had already talked to them about it. But the voice was familiar. It was Mr. Hollingsworth. Andy turned and waved.

"Andy!" he yelled again. "Lacy can't get down here. She's at the end," he said as he pointed toward an end zone. "She wanted me to let you know she's here, and she saw your big play."

He wanted to go over, but he knew that if Coach saw him, it would be the end of his playing time that game. He smiled and yelled, "Thank you!"

The rest of the first half went by quickly, and the Tigers took a fourteen to seven lead before heading into the locker room.

Coach delivered another "we ain't good enough" speech at halftime that left the team wanting to run through a brick wall. When they came out of the locker room to start the second half, the fans would have thought that someone from Lancaster had come in there and slapped every one of them in the face. They were mad! They were rejuvenated! The Tigers were ready to claim the game!

Coach Woods stopped Andy on his way out. "You ready to play a little quarterback?"

"Yes, sir! Wherever you need me, Coach."

"Be ready. May change a few things up."

The news excited Andy even more than he already was. He had waited patiently for the opportunity.

Most of the third quarter wasn't fun to watch; the two teams battled much like what Coach Woods expected—a defensive game. They punted back and forth with neither team gaining the edge. Finally, at the end of the third, Nate Harris found the end zone again for the Lions, knotting the game up in another tie.

Harris was far from the two hundred-plus yards he had promised. He had just broken one hundred yards, still to be considered a good game by most, but the Tigers had done well to hold him in check.

As the Tigers got set to go back out and take the ball following the kickoff after the touchdown, Coach Woods yelled for Mike and Andy. "Mike, I'm going to let Andy take a few snaps. Stay here and get a breather."

Mike smiled at Andy. "Make it happen, man! Go do what you do!"

Andy returned the smile and then looked at Coach Woods. "Thank you, Coach."

"Split right, forty-five slant," Coach called.

Andy turned to run onto the field, and Coach yelled one last instruction. "Andy, if it's not there, tuck and run!"

But the play was there. Andy threw a missile that hit Scott in stride, and he took it another fifteen yards to midfield. Two more consecutive pass plays were called, and Andy hit those, too. It was as if he hadn't missed a game. Andy was feeling it.

From the sixteen-yard line, a simple play was called to pass to Toby in the flats. The corner had been lazy on the previous two plays, and Coach picked up on it. If it held true, it would put Toby in the end zone.

The ball was snapped, and Andy turned to throw to Toby, but Toby had picked up a linebacker that had come in untouched, blitzing, and would have destroyed Andy. He recognized it and kept the ball, racing around the end and slanting toward the end zone pylon.

TOUCHDOWN!

With a great block from Toby, Andy had turned a busted play into points.

Coach met him in a flurry of excitement as he came off the field. "See, Andy? I can't teach that. That's talent, son!"

"That was Toby's touchdown, Coach!" Andy replied. "If he hadn't picked up on that blitz, I would have been smashed!"

"You two have chemistry!" Coach shouted as Andy kept moving.

But the celebration only lasted a few plays; Lancaster found some weak spots in the armor and was moving the ball again. Harris reeled off two impressive runs, and the Lions were again threatening to score.

Toby lined up at his linebacker spot. He had been watching Harris all night. Harris had a habit of leaning with his foot forward in the direction he was headed. Toby noticed it looked like Harris would go left.

"Jake," he called over to the other linebacker, "swap sides with me."

Jake swapped with no hesitation, and sure enough, the ball was snapped and Harris went left on a sweep. Toby fought through a blocker and shot toward Harris. Right before contact, Harris spun back inside and went down untouched. Toby missed completely, but Harris grabbed his knee and screamed in agony.

Toby jumped up and started waving toward the far sideline to Lancaster's coaches, realizing Harris was hurt badly. The injury had happened right where Andy had been standing. He kneeled by Harris, who looked up at him.

"Squeeze my hand, man," Andy told him. "Come on, squeeze it. You're gonna be all right."

Andy knew by looking at the odd way his knee bent that it most likely was a horrible injury, but he felt compassion for him. He had played hard all night and was a great player with a bright future. He was sure all of that was flashing through his mind. Andy could relate.

"Just a sprain, man," Andy told him.

Toby knelt by Harris, too, and said, "You're one tough son of a gun. I hope you're back soon, man. You got my prayers."

"Give us room, guys," the coaches and trainers from the other squad announced as they reached their fallen star.

Several long minutes passed before they tried to move him, and when they did, they carried him off, putting no weight on his injured leg. Coach stood by Mike, Andy, and Toby as they watched him go across the field.

"I heard all that," Coach said. "Great sportsmanship, boys. Proud of you."

A few plays later, the Lions ended up kicking a field goal to bring them within four points, but without their star player, the Tigers were just too much, and Oak Creek ended up winning the game by ten points after Scott Stiles hauled in another touchdown pass from Andy.

The locker room was exuberant as they celebrated the win. Only four teams in their classification remained, and the Oak Creek Tigers were one of them.

After a good talk from the coach and a little more celebration, the team started to emerge from the field house. Almost everyone that made the trip was waiting on the team, and when they came out, cheers were abundant. Congratulatory comments and high-fives were everywhere. Andy took it all in, taking time to talk to everyone that congratulated him. As he neared the bus, he heard a familiar voice.

"Andy!" Lacy shouted. "Got time for an out-of-towner? I mean, with all your fans and all?"

Andy laughed as he jogged over to her and her dad. "We pulled it off," he said.

Lacy stepped toward him and hugged him. Holding his duffle bag with one hand, returned her hug with his free arm.

"So, tell me, Mr. Quarterback," she asked, "why didn't y'all adjust when they pulled the linebacker and went to a nickel defense? That safety cheated to the wide side on every play. All you had to do was slant short to the short side and it was there. Every play! Even the tight end would have been open on a ten and out."

"Hey, I don't call the plays. I just run them."

"And that toss play! They bit every time. You could have kept it for five to ten yards."

"Okay! Okay," he said through his laughter. "Could you just act like you don't know more than me about football?"

Lacy giggled and smiled at Andy. "Probably not."

"Hey, I gotta go. Coach told us to go straight to the bus. I think I'm the last to load up."

"Wanna come over tomorrow?"

"Why don't you come to my place? Let me show you the country."

"Sure, babe," she said before catching herself. "I mean, yeah, if Dad will bring me."

Andy heard the slip-up, and it brought a smile to his face. "Well, Mr. Hollingsworth, I hope you can. And thank you for coming to the game. Two more, and we're state champs!" Andy turned and ran toward the bus. "Talk to you later, Lacy."

CHAPTER 14

I DID IT!

ANDY RODE INTO TOWN WITH KYLE THE NEXT MORNING TO PICK UP A few things from the hardware store. Mr. Harkens, the owner, came out of the back when he saw Andy and Kyle up front.

"Heck of a game last night. We were wondering when Coach was gonna put you back at quarterback," he called to Andy as made his way toward them.

"Thanks, Mr. Harkens. Coach was saving me, I guess."

"Did you hear anything from that kid from Lancaster that went down? They said he accepted an offer from Kentucky. Sure hope that didn't mess that up."

"No, sir. I haven't heard anything. I hope it's just a sprain. That dude is a good back."

"Kyle, you don't work this boy too hard around your place," Mr. Harkens said with a light-hearted chuckle. "He's gonna bring us a title this year."

"Well, today he's gonna bring some posthole diggers, and we are gonna put up a fence," Kyle replied, smiling at him.

Before long, they were headed back home to get started on the list of repairs around the property. Andy looked at his phone and saw a text from Lacy.

"Dad, is it okay if Lacy comes over later today? Her mom can bring her over."

"Yeah, that's fine. But how is she gonna get home? Her mom waiting here on her? That's a good drive."

"I'll ask. If not, I can see if Toby can take us, and I'll buy gas."

"It's fine. We can figure it out. Tell her she can come over."

Just as the northern winds had brought cooler air just days before, the current temps seem to push back, fighting the winter season knocking on Oak Creek's door. But such was southern life. Louisiana, Mississippi, Alabama, Georgia—they all had seasons they called by names, such as football season, tornado season, hunting season, and Christmas. The weather knew no different. Cold mornings in April with frost on the ground often turned into comfortable seventy-degree afternoons.

Andy was reminded of the crazy weather as he worked with his dad; the day had lost its chill, one of those days that summer crept back in for. It was warm; very warm. Sweat dripped from Andy's hair as he tossed his ball cap aside.

He was on hole number seventeen of the thirty that had to be dug for the new fence. His gloves were worn out before he ever started, having been through several jobs around the property. He pulled one off, looking at the blister between his thumb and index finger. With his glove off, he took the opportunity to sneak his phone from his pocket. Lacy said she would text him when they started his way. He didn't see the message yet, so he slipped his phone back into his pocket.

"How many is that?" Kyle asked.

"Seventeen," Andy answered, wiping sweat from his forehead.

"Looks like more rock than dirt," Kyle added as he surveyed Andy's work.

"Tell me about it. Like digging in a gravel road."

"Take a break from digging, and help me stretch this wire," Kyle suggested. He had been tying a broken electric fence along the pasture while Andy dug the holes for the new section.

"Yes, sir," Andy replied, more than happy to drop the posthole diggers.

Kyle could have easily hired someone to do the work, having done so many times before. But with his son going through so many ups and downs, he wanted an opportunity for Andy to talk to him about anything he was dealing with. Andy seemed to find his way through it all with a newfound sense of life, regardless.

A new purpose was driving Andy, and for once, it wasn't all sports-related. He still had that longing for the happiness that he saw in others—the ones that had a personal relationship with Christ. He knew he wanted that, but still, he was hesitant. Andy knew that a major change had come in his life, and he didn't want to screw it up.

After another hour or so, all holes were dug, fence mended, and the water that Kyle had put in the cooler had been drunk. They knew that if they ran out of water on a day as hot as the one they were laboring in, they were done! Andy pulled his phone from his pocket again.

"Dad, Lacy's on the way. Need me to do anything else, or can I go get a shower?"

"You're good. May need to use soap this time."

Before long, Mrs. Hollingsworth's car made its way down the drive. Andy's excitement was apparent as he went to meet them before the car stopped. His eagerness to see Lacy matched his eagerness to play football, which, to Andy, was saying a lot.

"Hello, Mrs. Hollingsworth. Thanks for bringing Lacy today," he greeted her mom.

"Well, that's all I've heard from her. Guess it was either this or deal with a meltdown."

"Mom!" Lacy exclaimed. "I asked twice. It wasn't that bad."

Andy laughed as he went over and took Lacy's hand to help her out. "Hey! Where are your walking braces? The cane things?"

"Don't need them. As long as I'm wearing my back brace and have my boot on my ankle, I'm good."

"But you need to stay off of it as much as you can," her mom instructed. "Andy, I'm leaving it up to you to make her stay off of it."

"Yes, ma'am. I'll do the best I can."

"Hello, ladies," Kyle said as he and Holly walked down to greet them. "Hope you found us easily."

"Yes. The directions brought us straight here," Ann said. "Thanks for having Lacy over. Are you sure you don't mind bringing her back home later?"

"No problem at all. Just tell us what time she needs to be home," Holly said.

Kyle laughed. "Plus I worked Andy today to make up for it."

"Well, again, thank you. You can bring her anytime as long as it isn't too late," Ann said. "Ten or so, I guess. We have church in the morning, and it's our turn to bring breakfast to our class."

"I'll have her there by ten," Kyle agreed.

Soon, Andy was showing Lacy around the property on the family golf cart. He was careful to avoid any bumps or holes, as he noticed her grimace when they first started riding. He sat atop one of the hills that had a pretty view of the meadows below.

"Sometimes, you can see the deer feeding on clover down there," he told her. "I was hoping they were there, but I guess they know it's getting close to hunting season."

"Aww." She sighed. "You don't shoot them, do you?"

"Well, not here. But we have a hunting club, and we go there."

"Just don't tell me if you get one, okay?"

"Deal."

They sat and looked at the scenery for a few minutes, creating small talk, and Andy pointed out the many different animals that he had seen there.

"How far do you feel like walking?" he asked.

"Not sure. What do you have in mind?" Lacy replied, wondering what his plans were.

"Well, I have a place that I go to think, to get things off my mind. But I can only get so far on the cart. We would have to walk about fifty feet or so. If you're up to it, I'd like to show it to you."

"Yeah, I'd like that."

After a brief drive over a small hill and down into the lower areas of the property, Andy stopped the cart.

"Just through that little path," he said, pointing toward a small opening in the tree line.

He helped her step off the cart and walked beside her, assuring her steps. Even as warm as the day was, the early winter's presence was known by the fallen leaves that canvased the ground. They walked just a few feet into the path, and the forest began to open up, revealing a beautiful scene.

With most of the foliage now brown, it appeared that the greens of summer had held on longer here. The air was clean and even had a smell to it that reminded Lacy of honeysuckles, although they were long gone. A rustling creek produced an ambiance of sound that couldn't be heard on the other side of the path they had just been on. A squirrel hurried across the ground and up a tree, escaping the view of its new visitors. The gentle breeze dropped a few more leaves, some making their way onto the water and getting carried away by the current, like a rafter experiencing rapids.

"Well, here it is," Andy said, stopping and looking around. "This is my getaway when the world seems angry at me."

Lacy gasped as she stepped further into the clearing. "Andy, it's beautiful! So peaceful. I can see why you come here to think. It's so pure and calming."

Andy pointed off to a large flat rock that hung over the creek's edge. "That's my thinking rock. I've sat there and got lost in my thoughts. Lately, I've done a little praying there."

"So, it's your praying rock, too," she said as she smiled at him.

"Yeah, it is. I hope so, anyway. I'm not too good at praying, so I just start talking and hope that God hears me."

"Well, silly, that's all that praying is," she said as she hobbled closer to the creek. "We don't need any fancy words or have to do anything special to get God to hear our prayers. We just call His name and talk. He knows our words before they're formed. We pray from our heart, and our mouth is the last thing to know what our prayer is about."

"Here, want to sit for a while?" he asked. "Try out my rock."

He helped her step up on the rock and followed her, sitting next to her with his legs bent and his arms wrapped around his knees.

"You should see this place in the summer. Wildflowers grow along the opposite side over there. Honeysuckles hang from the vines on the trees. The smell is amazing. Birds—so many birds come here, looking for food and water. Everything is so full of life. I guess that's what brings me here. When I feel like the life is being sucked out of me, I come here to recharge."

"I can see why," Lacy replied, looking up into the trees. "I wish I had a place like this to come to. In the neighborhood I live in, we hardly have any place to get away from the troubles of life."

"You seem so happy all the time, though. What could you possibly have to make you want to hide from it all?"

"Andy, everyone has their battles. I have battles daily. It's not so easy being 'the good little Christian girl,'" she said while making quotation marks with her fingers. "Everyone expects so much from me. 'Be the example,' they tell me. Well, I get tired of being the example. Don't get me wrong. I want to live my life for God, but sometimes it seems like everything I do is under a microscope. Why can't I just live for Christ without having to make sure others get a good vibe from me?"

"I feel the same lately," Andy said, looking at her. "I mean, not being 'the Christian guy' or nothing. Lord knows everyone doesn't look to me for that. But because I can run and pass a football a little better than others, I have to be the example. Coach just told me a few days ago that a lot of people look up to me and I need to make good choices. Our principal said the same thing on my first day back to school—first freaking day! Why can't I just be me and not have to worry about an image or how I'm viewed by others?"

Lacy leaned back, letting her hands support her on each of her sides as she laid them on the rock. She looked at Andy and smiled. "Ain't easy being us, is it?" she said and laughed.

"Nope, not at all," he replied as he leaned back as well.

In placing his hands down, he accidentally placed his hand by

Lacy's, letting them touch. At first, he almost removed his hand from hers, but he didn't. He left it there, the sides of their hands touching.

Lacy sighed. "Oh, how I need a place like this."

"Well, I know it's not close by, but you can use this one anytime you want. Matter of fact, having you here makes this place even better."

Lacy smiled at him, letting her hand slide over his. He opened his fingers, and hers clasped inside his. Andy picked up his hand, still locked with hers, and placed it on his knee, sliding closer to her. Lacy laid her head on his shoulder and they sat without saying anything for several minutes.

Finally, Lacy broke the silence. "Andy, why do you want me around? Why do you talk to me every night?"

Andy was lost for words. He felt his hand become sweaty in hers.

Why do I do these things? he thought.

He knew the answer. That was easy. He liked her. He genuinely liked her. Not in a "thank you for helping me" way, but in a "she could be my girlfriend" way. But he couldn't say that. That would make things awkward. He shifted his weight, uncomfortable with the question.

"Well?" she asked again, raising her head from his shoulder and gazing at him.

Andy looked at her, clinching his lips tightly as if the words that wanted to come out needed to be contained. He wasn't sure what to say, but he knew the word "girlfriend" did not belong in his next sentence.

Andy took a deep breath and exhaled. "Because I like who I've gotten to know, and I've wished every night that you were my girlfriend."

What! What had he said?

Oh, no. I just screwed that up. He quickly tried to recover. "I mean, well, not that I want to, like, well—"

"Really? You wish that?'

Andy sat upright, releasing her hand. "I mean—"

Before he could finish, Lacy leaned over and kissed him. It was a quick kiss on the lips, surprising Andy.

"Well, I guess that solves that," he said, laughing.

"Solves what?"

"I didn't know what you would do if I told you how I felt. Y'know, would you run away, hit me, or what?"

"And?"

"I am glad it was the 'what,'" he said, leaning over to kiss her again.

Andy placed his arm around Lacy's shoulders as they sat and took in their moment. Neither said a word, but both were smiling. Finally, Andy spoke up.

"Why is He so good to me after all I've done?"

"Who?" Lacy asked.

"God! I have screwed up so many times. I've rejected Him. I refused to give my life to Him, and still, He gives me all this. I have a second chance at life. A second chance at football. He sent an amazing girl to me, and I still avoid Him like the plague."

"Seriously?" she asked.

"Yes! Serious. He keeps blessing me."

"No, dummy. You think I'm amazing?"

Andy laughed and squeezed her tighter. "Beyond amazing!"

"So what's next?" Lacy asked.

"Well, I could show you the horses over on my uncle's land. It's just over those next few hills," he said.

"No! What's next with *you*?"

"Like what? Like what do I do now that I poured my heart out?" He grinned at her as he slid forward on the rock.

"That too, but where are you with God?"

"I know I need to ask Him to forgive me all that other stuff, but how do I know when I'm ready?"

"Well, what do you need to be ready? Is it a certain thing you're looking for?"

"I'm not sure. I guess if I had to make a list, I would want to make sure my heart was ready. I want to make sure I'm ready to make a change. I want somebody to help me, somebody that knows what they're doing. But I want it to be someone I have a connection to, someone special. Someone that won't judge me and wants to help me grow in Him."

"How's your heart? Is it ready? You know what it means. I've told you that."

"My heart is ready. Sometimes it feels like it's going to pound out of my chest," he admitted.

"Are you sincere this time?" she asked. "Do you want this, and do you think you're ready to change?"

"More than ever before."

"Then I guess we just need to find that someone special that you have a connection to."

"No. I found that. That was the first thing I found. They helped me make all these other things happen—the sincerity, the change— and it took me until today to admit it. Lacy, all of this started happening when God sent you to change me."

Lacy had tears well up in her eyes, and she leaned forward and hugged Andy, who had moved to sit in front of her. "You really mean that?"

"More than you know."

"Then let's do it! Let's punch your salvation ticket today, Andy," she said, sliding up beside him. "I'll help you! This will be the most amazing thing we do today!"

Andy bit his bottom lip and stared at her, not saying anything.

"Andy? You're not backing out again, are you? Please, Andy! You know you want this, and it's going to change so much!"

"Oh, no. I'm not backing out. I'm just looking at you and thanking God for sending you."

Tears came to his eyes as Lacy hugged him again.

"Okay, let's do this before you back out on me again," she said with a giggle.

Andy smiled and turned to face her completely, taking both of her hands in his. "So, is there where I tell Him everything I've ever done wrong?"

"He already knows. Just speak from your heart. Ask him to forgive you for your past and lead you to live closer to Him. Make Him the Lord of your life. Andy, there's no handbook on how to do this, but God knows when you're sincere."

Andy sat for a moment. He looked at Lacy and started laughing. "It's embarrassing. I don't know why, but with you here, I just feel weird."

"Want me to leave? I can wait in the golf cart."

"No! You're part of this. Okay, I've got it," Andy said. He took a deep breath. "Okay, here goes."

Andy smiled at Lacy again and peered up at the sky. He bowed his head and began praying.

"Lord, You're going to have to find my words. I promise they're in here, but I'm not good at getting them to come out right. God, thank You for not giving up on me, and thank You for continuing to work on me. I know I haven't been the best at listening, but You sent someone that finally got my attention. It took us both almost losing our lives, but I finally figured it out. God, I am a sinner. I admit that, and I ask Your forgiveness. I proclaim You as my Savior, my King, and my only God. I give you my life and ask that you use me however you see fit. God, I don't know what else I'm supposed to ask or do, but I'm one hundred percent sure this time that I want my life to change and for it to be centered around You. I hope I did this right, God. If not, please teach me. Well, I guess that's it. Amen."

Andy opened his eyes to Lacy crying. Tears rolled down her face and dripped onto her thighs.

"Did I do it right?" he asked.

"Yes!" she shouted and leaned forward, hugging him.

"What now? Is there anything else I need to do?'

"Well, if you want to make a public confession of your faith, you can do that."

"Like, post about it on social media?"

"Well, if you want. Last week when you went to church with Toby, you said the pastor held an invitation and you felt a calling to go up. Well, tomorrow, you can go up and tell the pastor in front of the congregation that you accepted Christ. That's making it public. That's an act of faith that tells others you're not ashamed of your salvation."

"Oh, okay. Wow! I feel like I want to tell everyone! I feel so good about this."

"About what?" someone shouted. "I figured I'd find you here."

They turned to see Toby and Alec walking toward them. Toby was one of only a handful of people that knew of Andy's secret spot.

"Hey, bro! What are you guys doing here?" Andy shouted.

"Came to get you, remember? Your mom said you were out on the golf cart and I knew where to look. We have that youth party at church tonight. You said you would go. Still want to?"

"Oh, man!" Andy sighed. "Totally forgot about that."

"Hey, guys," Lacy announced. "You must be the Toby I've heard so much about." She looked over at Alec. "And you must be his better-looking little brother. Andy told me about you, too."

"Oh! Sorry," Andy said as he stood. "Guys, this is Lacy. I know you know everything about her because I won't quit talking about her, but now you can finally meet her."

Lacy smiled. "Tell them what you just did, Andy!"

Andy blushed. "I asked Lacy to be my girlfriend."

"That, too, but the other thing."

"Oh!" he said and laughed. "I finally did what you've been after me to do, Toby. I asked Jesus into my life. I finally got saved!"

"My brother!" Toby shouted as he ran to the rock to hug Andy.

Alec came ran also, joining in on the hug. "Yeah, Andy! We're brothers for real now!" Alec released his hug and turned to Lacy, who had managed to stand. "Hi, Lacy," he said and hugged her.

Lacy, caught off guard, hugged him back while smiling at Andy. "You're so sweet," she said.

"Toby's girlfriend is Ruby Sue," he told her. He leaned closer and whispered, "But she likes me more."

"I can see why," Lacy said with a wink.

"So, guess the party at church is a no-go, huh?" Toby asked.

"Yeah. Sorry, bro. Lacy came over, and we're—"

"We can go," Lacy interrupted. "If that's okay with everyone. "I'd like to go. Andy? Can we?"

"Well, yeah, I guess so. If Toby can give us a ride there and back. This whole no-license thing kinda puts a strain on making plans."

Toby replied, "That's why I came, bro. Lacy, you'll love it. We have a band coming, and the lead singer is giving his testimony tonight."

"Sounds great," Lacy said.

"Let's get to going then!" Andy shouted. "Gotta run the cart back up to the house and tell Mom. Wanna pick us up there?"

"See you guys back at your house," Toby replied as they all went back toward the trail.

It wasn't much longer before they found themselves at the church Toby attended. The youth activity area had been converted to a stage, and bright, multicolor lights rotated around as recorded Christian pop music played through the large speakers. The church catered burgers and pizza for the event and most mingled around, chatting while eating.

Lacy found a chair to sit in. The eventful day was starting to wear on her back, but she was enjoying every moment. Andy sat next to her as Toby and Alec found their way into the crowd.

"Lacy? Lacy Hollingsworth," someone said as they came closer.

"Yes? Oh, my God! Sarah! I haven't seen you since summer camp, like three, maybe four years ago." Lacy stood, grimacing as she did.

Sarah noticed the back brace. "Oh, my! What happened? Are you okay?"

"I'm good. Had an accident a few weeks ago and I'm still recovering."

"Wow! I can't believe that I ran into you!" Sarah shouted. "Do you go to church here?"

"No, I was invited by my friend—well, my boyfriend," Lacy replied as she looked over at Andy and smiled.

"I was invited, too! My friend I met in college goes here. Wow! I still can't believe it. We have to talk later, okay?"

"Absolutely. I'll see you before we leave."

As Sarah walked away, Lacy turned to Andy. "What are the chances of that?"

"Running into an old friend? Around here, not too odd."

"No," she answered. "You won't believe this, but Sarah was the one that was with me when I prayed my salvation prayer! She led me to Christ. That girl talked to me for weeks about what all it meant, and finally, we sat alone in our cabin and I accepted Christ!"

Andy gawked at her with wide eyes. "Wow! That's wild. I mean, of all days, on the day that you do the same for someone else. For me!"

"I know! Andy, God is working on us both. I just know it!"

"I hope so. He knows I need a lot of work."

The night ended with almost everyone in tears as the band's lead singer finished with his testimony. He spoke of how he had lived a life of sin and watched several friends die and go to prison. He was broken and felt hopeless, and had even contemplated suicide. But through friends and the power of faith, grace saved him, and he devoted his life to Christ, going all over the southern states, telling his story to youth groups and congregations.

It was just what Andy needed to hear. He knew he wasn't as far into sin as the speaker had been, but hearing how God changed him gave him even more hope. Andy thought about how the coach and principal had spoken to him about being an example. He now understood.

Sometimes it takes someone stumbling up out of despair and making a change, a change so obvious that others notice so that they'll want that change in their life, too.

That night, there in that small country church, Andy made a commitment to himself. He wanted to be that guy. He wanted to be the example, and he wanted to start right away!

CHAPTER 15

IS IT REALLY OVER?

A HEIGHTENED EXCITEMENT WAS APPARENT AT SCHOOL ON MONDAY. Semi-finals! Unlike the finals that resulted in test scores, these finals brought an environment that towns like Oak Creek thrived on. Four teams remained, and they all had a chance to claim the title as state champs.

Oak Creek had a rich tradition of football and was expected to make the playoffs each year, but the semi-finals had only been reached a handful of times and none in the recent decade. Newspapers and local television stations were abuzz about the Tigers. It was a fun time to wear the blue and white of the Oak Creek Tigers!

Friday's win against Lancaster gave the Tigers home-field advantage, and the number three team in the state, the Rockport Raiders, would come calling.

Rockport was no stranger to the Tigers; they had met two of the last three years in the playoffs. Last year, the Raiders were the demise of Oak Creek, defeating them and ending the season. But three years ago, Rockport was dealt defeat at the hand of the Tigers. Oak Creek felt as if a little revenge was at hand, with last year's hopes being crushed early in the playoffs. This week would be a fever-pitched one

—school and community alike were ready to welcome the Raiders back to town.

Andy walked with new energy in his step. Just weeks before, he had been in a situation that could have ended his playing career and possibly sent him to jail. He was so far from where he was now. Andy moved through the halls with confidence, not about his playing credibility but with the confidence that he was following what had been tugging at him all along, his walk of faith. He could tell he was more aware of those he hadn't been so friendly to before, and he went out of his way to make sure he was kind to everyone.

As he came out of his last class of the day, he passed by a group of band members congregated in the hall and nodded. After a few feet, he stopped, turned, and went back to them.

"Hey, guys," he said. "Y'all sounded great last week. Thanks for keeping us pumped up! Y'all do it again this week. Bring it with all you have with those big horn thingies and drums. Man, I like the drums. Anyway, thanks again."

A couple in the group chuckled as he walked off. "Big horn thingies," they laughed. "What's up with Andy?" another asked.

By the end of the day, several had experienced "the new Andy."

"Andy," Toby yelled as he ran to catch up. "Dude! Everyone's talking about your change to being Mr. Rogers," he said, referring to the television icon known for his nice and positive words. "I know you let Christ take over, but you may want to pull back a notch so you don't come across as fake."

"Whatcha mean? I'm trying to be nicer to everyone. Be an example. Y'know, like everyone has been telling me to be."

Toby laughed and patted him on the back. "People think you're up to something. Even Principal Reynolds asked me about you."

Andy smirked. "Well, they better get used to it. I've only got a few more months before I graduate from this place, and I've got some ground to make up."

Toby shook his head. "Man, when you do something, you do it big. I'll give you that."

Andy winked at Toby as they exited the school and headed toward the field house for practice.

After changing, Andy, Toby, and the rest of the Tiger team went out on the practice field. The enthusiasm of the entire team was elevated. Making the playoffs was fun, and even the atmosphere of the entire town showed it, but being deep into them had taken on a new meaning.

For Andy, a new purpose had already found him. His thoughts were filled with making things right with anyone he may have crossed. Sure, football was still fun, and of course, it was important to him, but he wanted football to be his tool to use to tell others about his new way of living.

"All right, boys," Coach Woods yelled as he traipsed through the lines of players readying for warmups. "I don't have to tell you what this week means. There are four teams left, and we're fortunate enough to be one of them. After Friday night, there will be two teams. I expect us to be one of them. This week will depend on what you give me. If you give me a good, hard practice today, it'll be the only one in pads. You get lazy on me, and you'll be wearing full pads to class all week."

Coach pulled one of his old tricks out to get a good practice in. He was good at getting the team to practice hard, but he could always rely on threatening them with a rough week of practice when he had doubts. But he had seen a week like this before, many times. His team was good, and everyone told them how good they were. Sometimes that got to their heads and they started thinking they were better than they were, that they could show up and win the game.

Andy wondered how things would go, now that he had regained some playing time at quarterback. Mike had done well, but Coach had let Andy play most of the second half under center. *Will this be the week that I get my starting job back?* he wondered.

"All right! Starting offense," the coach instructed. "Mike, you're under center."

Well, I guess that answers that, Andy thought.

"Show me something!" Coach barked.

And they did! They had one of the most spirited practices of the year. Everyone worked hard, and the enthusiasm was unmatched. Andy and Mike split time at quarterback almost equally, and each was praised by Coach Woods. Andy even played some at running back and receiver while Mike was under center.

At the end of practice, Coach Woods announced that they had met his expectations and they'd practice in shorts and helmets only. "But if you don't give me this energy tomorrow, Wednesday will be full pads again," he was quick to announce.

After changing, Andy, Toby, and Alec walked to the parking lot where they were met by Ruby.

"Good practice, guys," she said as she grabbed Toby by the arm. "Seems like Coach is getting soft on you guys, though. Two weeks in a row he lets y'all go shorts and helmets on Tuesday? Never seen that before."

"He knows he has me back now," Andy said with a smirk. "Can't get much better than I am."

Toby laughed. "Please! Especially as good as you did when you ran the wrong route on two plays last week."

"Three plays," Alec added. "On forty-five rocket when you lined up in the slot, you were supposed to go five yards and then hard slant to the middle. You went ten yards and curled."

Andy chuckled. "Okay, you got me on that one, Alec. But when I'm at quarterback, watch out!"

Toby stopped and looked over to where the spectators had been sitting. "Hey, guys, hold up. I want you to meet someone."

The group followed Toby over to one skinny, shy-looking kid who was folding his chair. He had on a baseball cap and when he saw them coming, he pulled it down further, trying to disguise who he was.

"Hey, I remember you," Alec shouted.

The young kid looked up and gave a slight grin before looking back down.

"Terry, how ya been, bud?" Andy asked.

Terry Wilson—the underclassman he had shared time with at

lunch on the day he almost quit—was sure not to make eye contact as he whispered, "I'm good."

"Hey, Terry! Remember me?" Alec asked.

"Hi, Alec," Terry said, risking a glance up.

"Whatcha doing out here, Terry?" Toby asked.

"I was watching practice. My mom doesn't get home until late, and, well, it's just us two, so..." he explained. "I, um, really think you guys will win it all."

"Well, I hope so," Toby said.

"Wait! I know you," Andy said as he came closer. "You get to school really early, right? You wait down by the side entrance until the bell rings."

Terry peered up at Andy, nervously nodding his head. "Mom has to drop me off on her way to work."

"Yeah, I've seen you. You were—oh, man!" Andy stopped and bit his lip while shaking his head. "I pitched your backpack in the trash. Me and Stiles were coming in that door and you were there. I grabbed it, and—man. I'm sorry, dude."

Toby glared at Andy. "Why would you even do that, Andy? What good comes from that?"

"It's fine," Terry said. "I dug it out and cleaned it off. It was no big deal."

"Yeah, it was a big deal," Andy continued. "I was a jerk!"

"No, really. It was the day of the homecoming game, and you were just playing," Terry said.

"That was my best game of the year, but that was still a jerk move," Andy replied.

"You passed for two hundred and eighty-three yards and four touchdowns that night. And ran for another hundred and four yards," Terry said.

"I did? How do you remember all that? That was, like, the middle of the season."

"I'm at every game. I don't have a lot of friends, so I sit way up top and keep stats just for fun. I have stats for everyone in my notebook. I think you're one of the best quarterbacks in the state this year. I don't know why there aren't more people recruiting you."

Andy sighed. "Here you are, one of our biggest fans, and I treated you like crap."

"Really, it's no big deal," Terry said.

"Yes, it *is*," Ruby added as she shot daggers from her eyes at Andy.

"I'm so sorry, Terry. Will you forgive me?" Andy said as he extended his arm to shake his hand.

Terry shook his hand. "I already have. That same day. You didn't have to ask. I had already forgiven you."

"Wow," Andy replied. "I'm a fan of yours now, Terry. A big fan."

Terry laughed as he picked up his chair. "Well, I gotta hurry home. Mom told me to be there when she gets home. See you guys later."

As Terry started walking away, Toby stopped him. "Terry, how far do you live?"

"Not far. Two, three miles. Just through town, over in the projects."

"Let me give you a ride. I'm going right by there."

In reality, Terry's house was out of the way for Toby, but he offered kindness during a moment it seemed Terry needed it.

"Are you sure?" Terry asked.

"Positive," Toby assured him.

"I've gotta run, guys," Andy said. "My dad is waiting. See you guys tomorrow." He turned to head toward his dad's truck but stopped. "Hey, Terry, wanna sit with us tomorrow at lunch?"

"Seriously?! Sure! I mean, if it's okay with everyone."

"Well, if it ain't, we'll let Alec handle them," Andy replied with a smile.

As everyone went their own ways, Andy was reminded of how many other younger kids had looked up to him, only to be ignored or treated badly. He knew that with his newfound faith and determination to live for Christ, he had to make that one of the top priorities to work on. But instead of regretting his recent decision, he embraced the opportunity.

He looked forward to showing a kinder, more compassionate Andy, and to letting God use him.

THE NEXT FEW days went by quickly as the team prepared for Rockport. The school planned special events for every day leading up to game day.

As much as Andy was enjoying the activities, it was his new attitude that he enjoyed the most. It was apparent to everyone that there had been a change in Andy. The last several weeks had been life-changing for him, and could have changed in another direction had he let it keep dragging him down. He could have given in, never went to visit Lacy, and never seen how salvation looked through his own eyes, but instead, he didn't. He owned his decision. He decided not only to do what was right for Lacy, but what was right for him, and in the process, he found what had been missing.

It was two hours before the pep rally. No schoolwork was taking place; everyone was too excited about the match-up. Andy, along with Toby, Mike, and Coach Woods, had just finished talking with the local radio station for an interview they would play before the game. As he left the school's office, he felt his phone go off. He stepped back into the office and pulled his phone from his jean's front pocket. It was Lacy.

"Hey, sunshine," he answered.

"Hey! So, I got your text. Interviews, huh? You're becoming a celebrity now. My girlfriend status may be short-lived," she joked.

"No way, babe. You're stuck with me."

"Good. So, me, Mom, and Dad are about to head that way for the pep rally. Mom wanted me to ask, do we need to check in at the office or just go straight to the gym?"

"Straight to the gym. Call me when you get close, and I'll meet y'all outside."

"Awesome," she replied. "See you soon, superstar!"

"See ya, sunshine," Andy said, smiling as he ended the call.

Out on the grounds just below the football field, residents started popping up tents and readying for the game. They had seen how Lancaster tailgated, and now the home campus resembled a tent city, with dozens of tents and folding chairs occupying grassy spots just steps from the stadium. Most set up, staking claim to their area before heading off to the gym to get a prime spot for the pep rally.

Win or lose, this would be Oak Creek's last home game of the year. Of course, a loss would end it for them, but a win and they traveled to the winner of Johnson High and Harrisburg, who were meeting as the number one and number four teams, respectively. To say that this week was huge and their fans were excited would be an understatement.

"Can you believe it, Andy?" Toby asked as he looked down the hill from the gym at the stadium. "This is it. This will be the last time we'll ever play on that field."

Andy hadn't let that thought creep in on him yet. Whether it was the excitement of playing again, his new walk in faith, or just all the things that happened lately, the thought had not crossed his mind.

"Wow. It is, isn't it?" Andy walked a few steps in front of Toby and gazed down at the field below. "Man, what memories," he said, talking as much to himself as he was Toby.

"Remember our sophomore year against Franklin County? Your first game at quarterback. We were up by like four touchdowns; Coach put you in and you got ejected on the second play."

Andy laughed. "Yeah, but remember why? You got blindsided by the linebacker on the first play I was in, so on the second play, I nailed him in the gut with the ball."

"But it was *after* the play. Coach was so mad!"

"What about that crazy ending last year against Thomasville? What was it—like, four, five laterals on the last play?"

"Oh, yeah! Something like that. You finally ran it in to win that game. Crazy," Toby replied.

They had walked to the fence, looking down at the field. Like a movie reel, highlights played through their memories. They talked, laughed, and reminisced about several of their favorite moments. As much as it meant to the town of Oak Creek, it meant even more to the ones that still held onto a few remaining minutes before they walked off the field one last time.

They had won games and they had lost games, and above all, they'd created bonds they would carry for the rest of their lives. It was more than a game. It was a part of their lives, a part that they knew would one day end, but neither realized it would be so soon.

People were filing in fast. The school parking lot was already stretched at the seams and cars started lining the road below the school's entrance—just for the pep rally! Much of the team was amazed as they stood outside and watched as fans kept arriving. Sure, they always packed out the stadium for games, and even the last few pep rallies, but an hour before the cheer session started, the campus was already at capacity.

Andy was walking back to the gymnasium when Lacy called.

"Hey! We're here. Dad's dropping me off and then going to park the car. You said gymnasium, right? The big building at the top of the hill?"

"That's right. Just tell him to pull up close to the front doors. I've got to run inside and grab something, and I'll be right back."

"Okay. We are coming up the hill now. See you in a sec," Lacy said before ending the call.

Andy raced into the gym and to the locker room, retrieving something from his locker. He rushed out just in time to see Lacy and her parents pull up. He hurried over to her door and opened it before she could.

"Hey, Lacy. This makes my day! I'm so glad you get to be here for this."

He leaned in, and she grabbed his arms as he pulled, helping her stand. The back brace that went from just below her shoulders to her waist made standing a struggle for her, but Andy accommodated whenever he was close by.

"You kids don't mind if this old lady stands with you do you?" Ann asked as she got out.

"No, ma'am, you're more than welcome to, Mrs. Hollingsworth," Andy replied.

"Looks like I may have to park in town and walk back," Bob joked.

"Right over there," Andy pointed toward the school, "is a little break in between the buildings. Pull through there, and there are a few places. Some of the teachers park back there."

"You sure it's okay?" he asked.

"Yes, sir. Nobody will be back there. The whole town will be in that gym in a few minutes."

As Bob drove away, Andy reached behind him and pulled something from under his shirt that was tucked in his belt. Unfolding it, he handed it to Lacy.

"If you're going to attend the pep rally, you're gonna need this," he said, smiling.

"Your jersey? Wow! Well, wouldn't that pretty much make it known that we're a couple?"

"I hope so. Here, let me help you."

Andy held it above her head as Lacy put her arms through the openings. He pulled it down over her head and around her back brace.

"Look! Now you can't even tell you're wearing that brace," he said, stepping back to admire her.

Lacy smiled and gave Andy a tight hug. She then turned and looked at her mom, who was smiling back. "Andy," she said, "somehow, out of all of this, you have made my Lacy a happy girl."

"Well, Mrs. Hollingsworth, your girl has made me happy, too. She gave me something that I've been missing my whole life. I found happiness in her, but I found salvation through her, and I'll always be thankful for that."

Ann beamed with pride, knowing that leading someone to Christ was one of the biggest achievements someone could reach.

As Bob rejoined them, Andy showed them all into the gym. It was already packed, and he knew that Lacy wouldn't be able to sit long on the bleachers, anyway. He retrieved some chairs for them from an office and placed them to the side of the bleachers, just in front of and facing where the team would sit. Andy stayed and chatted with them for several minutes before he had to retreat to the locker room until they were told to come out.

The Hollingsworths sat amazed at the energy created by the students and fans. Even the sporting events they had been to with Lacy didn't come close to the enthusiasm shown by the Oak Creek faithful. The students were having a great time and it was expected for them to be loud and excited, but what most surprised them was the folks from town and the surrounding community were just as energetic.

They came in work clothes, overalls, and professional attire. They were young, just a few years into alumni status themselves, and others were fourth-generation alumni. Most of the men wore blue ball caps with the signature white tiger paw on front. They cheered, chanted, and knew the choreographed moves the cheerleaders led them in.

Mr. Reynolds, the principal, who also served as the announcer for the events, grabbed a microphone and stepped just to the side of the basketball court.

"And here are your county champs, your region champs—and soon-to-be state champs—let's get loud for your Oak Creek Tigers!" he yelled into the mic.

The band echoed the fight song off of the gym's cinder block walls. Both sides of the stands stood and clapped for the team as they entered single file and sat in their seats.

Lacy sat directly in front of Andy, with only about twenty feet separating them. She smiled and raised her hand to wave, trying not to be too noticeable. Andy smiled back and winked at her.

The cheerleaders led the crowd in several cheers and songs and the teachers even put together a skit that brought everyone in the gymnasium to laughter. Lacy was having a blast! Andy was too, even though most of the time was spent watching Lacy and laughing at her attempts to follow the arm motions of the cheer squad.

As the rally began to close, Coach Woods walked out after all the numerous accolades were announced. He stood at midcourt and glanced at his players before looking back at the students.

"I know I've already spoken and said I was done," he laughed, "but I lied!"

The students and alumni laughed as he turned to look at both sides.

"I want to take a moment to let these seniors know how much we love them. Can we do that?" he asked.

The applause came immediately and lasted for a few seconds. Then, it started on the alumni side. A few stood. Then more. The applause continued as more and more stood, and finally, everyone in the building was giving the seniors a standing ovation.

"Thank you," he continued. "I know I say every year that each group is my favorite, and, well, I'm gonna say it again. I believe time is the best investment you can give. After this group leaves, my next group of seniors becomes my favorite. After they leave, there's not much I can do about what they do and how they do it. But while they're here, while I've got them, I feel like I have a little say about what they do and who they become." He turned to the side where the alumni sat.

"I can look back over here and see several of my boys from years ago and smile about what they've become. Well, a few of them, but not them on the end down there," he laughed as he referred to two recent graduates who were in college, drawing laughter from the crowd as well. "Nah, I'm proud of them all." He paced back and forth slowly as he spoke.

"Most of these current boys would tell you that I'm hard on them, that I push them too hard. Some might even say I'm mean. But a few years from now a few of them may come back and thank me for demanding their best. That's all I ever ask, and these boys right here have given it this year. Now we have six seniors," he said as he walked their way. "Six fine young men that I expect to see great things from. Reese Junkin, Blake Barnes, Toby Chandler, Andy Higgins, Jake Howard, and Billy Wright," he continued as he went down the line.

"After I spoke a few minutes ago, it hit me. Win or lose—well, we gonna win—but either way, tonight will be the last time these six play down there on that field. When those lights go off tonight, it's over. No more home games. Now, I usually don't do this, but this bunch has proven to me that they're special. They've proven that this school is special to them. I want to offer each of my seniors a chance to get up here in front of you and say anything they want." He smiled and shook his head. "Just saying that scares me."

The six seniors nervously looked at each other, but nobody offered to speak.

"Jake?" Coach asked. "What about you Toby?"

Toby slowly stood and walked to the floor by Coach.

"Well, I didn't know we were doing this, but, man, it's been fun. Hard to believe tonight is it. Last time on that field is gonna be tough. I just want to say thank you to all of you for packing those stands. Come out tonight and let's do it one more time!"

The crowd applauded for Toby as he sat.

"Billy?" Coach asked again.

Billy smiled and shook his head. "I'm good, Coach."

"What about you, Blake? All you do at practice is talk."

He laughed and stood. Without leaving where he sat, he spoke. "Thank y'all for your support," he said before sitting.

"Andy? Reese? Either of you?" Coach asked.

Andy and Reese looked at each other. Reese shook his head, somewhat embarrassed. Andy took a deep breath and stood.

"I'll go. Coach," he said as he walked to the center of the court. "I'll start with what Toby said. Man, I appreciate y'all packing those stands. Trust me, we hear you! But it didn't hit me until today, like Coach said. It happened before I realized it. I missed a lot of games this year. I'm gonna own that reason. I made a dumb decision, and—"

"Andy, you don't have to go into that," Coach interrupted.

"I feel like I do, Coach. If that's okay?"

Coach nodded and waved his hands for him to continue.

"Like I said, I missed games because I made a bad decision. Missing those games made me realize how important this game is to me. And how important this school is to me. But I'm answering for my actions. I'm paying for it through the things the court set. But Coach gave me a second chance. He showed me I was in a position to set an example. Well, over the last few years, I haven't set a good example for many of you, and I am sorry. I want to apologize to my school—to all of you because I took this for granted. My best friend over there, Toby, supported me no matter what, though, and he talked to me some nights until the sun came up. I finally see what it takes to be a good friend, son, student, and football player. Coach will tell you it takes hard work and determination, and while that's true, it also takes believing in something."

He looked over at Lacy.

"I met this amazing girl; don't ask me how we met," he laughed, "but she showed me how to forgive and how to be a light when the world is dark. Even when it's your world that's dark. I may get in trouble for saying this, but I'm gonna say it, anyway. She's the reason I gave my life to Christ, and I stand here today and tell you that He is my Savior, and I live for Him. She didn't give up on me even when I gave up on myself. She is the most amazing girl I've ever met."

Lacy sniffled as tears rolled down her face, and her mom leaned over and hugged her, rubbing her shoulders.

"Sorry, Coach," Andy said as he looked around. "I got off subject. Just one last thing. This is a special place to me. Always will be. This whole town will be. You guys loved me when I needed it the most. I just want to say that I will leave it all on that field tonight! These guys over here are my brothers. I love them as much as myself, and tonight, we're gonna put a whoopin' on somebody! Let's go beat the snot out of those Raiders!"

Applause erupted again. The football team stood, and the few on the front row hugged Andy as he walked back over to them. A few more in the audience stood. Then a few teachers. After a few seconds, the entire gymnasium was again on its feet. Coach Woods returned to the center of the court and raised his arm to signal everyone to hold their applause.

"I need to check his I.D.," Coach said. "Just a few weeks ago, I couldn't get him to read a paragraph in my history class."

A burst of low laughter echoed throughout the gym.

"Folks, I hope you pack that stadium and get loud! See you down the hill in a couple of hours. Go big blue," he shouted.

Lacy got up much quicker than she had before. She hobbled toward Andy as he met her. He went to hug her and she not only returned the hug, but she kissed him—not a little peck. She placed her hand on the back of his head and gave him a big kiss that surprised Andy, and everyone else that was there.

"Lacy!" Ann shouted.

"Sorry, Mom," she said as she turned from Andy, grabbing his hand in the process. "I couldn't help it."

Ann couldn't help but smile. Seeing how full of joy her girl was and the happy tears that ran down her face were enough to overlook the public affection. Andy glanced at Mr. Hollingsworth and was relieved to see that he too was smiling.

"I've got to go with the team." Andy sighed. "They're bussing us over to the diner for the pregame meal and then we have to stay in the gym until game time. We aren't allowed to have anyone in there. You guys still staying for the game? Will I see you after?"

"I think so," she replied, looking up at her dad. "Dad, can we stay?"

"Well, after that speech, I can't run away now, can I? And we can stay for a little while after too, I guess."

"Great! I'll see you after the game." Andy gave Lacy a quick kiss before running to where the team had gathered.

THE TIGERS HAD BEEN FED, speeches given, and the warmups were over. Kickoff was moments away. As expected, the visiting Rockport Raiders had brought a massive crowd and the small stadium probably housed its largest crowd ever. The atmosphere was unmatched, even at Oak Creek, where pride ran strong and deep.

Even though it was against what Coach Woods allowed, Andy spotted Lacy as they awaited the kickoff and went over to the fence to get one last good luck kiss. If it was his last time to play on his field, he would make it a memorable one.

"Andy, Coach wants you," Blake shouted as Andy jogged away from the fence.

Dang! Did he catch me? he thought. Mike Gamble was standing beside Coach Woods. *Maybe this is about us swapping out in the second half again.*

"Andy, you're starting," Coach said.

"What?" Andy asked, surprised. "Really? I thought—"

"It was Mike's idea. He came to me and suggested it."

"I've got another year to play," Mike said. "This is your last time on this field. This is yours, bro! I can't take that away."

"Dud! Thank you!"

"Andy, you got to make something from this," Coach Woods instructed him. "We need to make a statement right off the bat. We're gonna come out slanging the ball, so be ready."

"Yes, sir," Andy replied.

Finally! It was game time! Rockport won the coin toss but elected to give the ball to Oak Creek to start the game.

The stadium was electrifying! There was so much noise that the announcer could hardly be heard over the speakers. The bands were playing, the crowd cheering, and even the paramedics' station in the ambulance at the south end of the field periodically sounded their siren.

Oak Creek took the ball on the kickoff and advanced to the thirty-yard line. Andy ran out on the field to many people's surprise. Even his dad, Kyle, pointed and announced to those around him that Andy was starting at quarterback. As more people noticed, chatter spread through the crowd.

Andy took the first snap of the game, and just as Coach said they would do, they came out passing! He looked downfield to where Scott Stiles was crossing, but he was covered, so Andy looked to his second option, as the slot receiver had crossed about ten yards downfield. He was open, and Andy fired it to him for a first down.

Andy looked over to the coach for another call. He lined up and again dropped back to pass. This time, he hit a streaking receiver down the far sideline for a huge gain! Two plays in, and Andy had passed for almost sixty yards and the Tigers were on the move.

Another passing play was called. Andy took the snap and rolled to his right and looked for his intended target, but he was covered. Andy was already rolling out, so he tucked the ball and ran it around the end where he had an easy ten yards of open field. He stiff-armed a defender and side-stepped another and was inside the ten-yard line. First and goal!

Three plays in, and the Tigers were making it look easy!

Andy looked at Coach for the call. He lined up, took the snap, and dropped back. Stiles was open in the end zone, but Andy's adrenaline was too much to handle; the ball sailed over the head of the intended receiver and through the end zone for his first incompletion.

It was second down from the seven-yard line. They had run four plays, and all had been passing plays. It was time to change it up. Andy lined up under center. He took the snap and took a quick step to his right before pitching a short toss to Toby, who turned the ball up just outside the tackle, and he went untouched for a Tiger touchdown!

Five plays in and barely four minutes off the clock, and the blue and white team was up by seven points! Things could not have started better for Oak Creek, and Coach Woods was looking like a genius for starting Andy, although he was just the recipient of a great offer of sportsmanship.

If the stadium could have gained any decibels, the last play run was enough to push it up a notch. Students, some shirtless in the cool night air, with painted chests, ran across the end zone with large flags, celebrating the touchdown. A sea of blue and white jumped and waved their arms, cheering for their hometown guys. It looked as if the bleachers were one entity, moving together with connected motions. Alec ran up and down the sideline, encouraging the fans to get louder, a feat that was probably unreachable. Everything was picture perfect and was all going the way of the Tigers.

Andy ran off the field. "Whew! We're about to show these folks what it's like to visit Oak Creek," he shouted to anyone within earshot.

A few plays later, Rockport was trying to match Oak Creek's impressive first drive. They started strong, crossing midfield in just four plays. The Tiger defense had seen enough, and like a stone wall, they held back the offensive attack and took over the ball after the Raiders failed to pick up a first down.

Andy, Toby, and the gang picked up right where they left off. Andy was tossing the football like a guided rocket, hitting almost every strike just where intended, while Toby ran like someone fleeing a lost tribe of headhunters on a late-night cable show. Everything was clicking for them, and just as the first quarter came to an end, Andy threw an arrow to a receiver for another Tiger touchdown, pushing the lead to fourteen to zero!

Across the packed stadium, the Oak Creek faithful were already chattering about the trip to next week's game and how they were one game away from playing for the state title. The confidence that they'd already won the game was at a high.

The second quarter seemed to settle down. Neither team was able to put points up. On the old scoreboard, the only lights that changed were the time as it clicked down. With the half coming to a close, it ended just as the first quarter had. Oak Creek held on to the two-touchdown lead, their fans still proclaiming a victory.

Coach Woods delivered the expected fiery halftime speech, reminding his seniors that this could be it if they didn't get it together. He knew two touchdowns could happen for Rockport just as quickly as they had for his bunch. It was hard for the guys to not be excited and all smiles, though. They were one and a half games from playing in the biggest game in the state, and they held a commanding lead. Like most of the crowd, a few of them even hinted about next week's game.

As the Tigers made their way back out, the band came alive. They had just gotten back to their seats after delivering a halftime performance that intensified the crowd. Even the small band, only twenty or so members, did an outstanding job and even recognized the four senior members of the band on the field. Even halftimes at Oak Creek were supported by many.

"Andy!" came a shout as he entered the gate to the field. He looked over and saw Mr. Hollingsworth.

Andy looked to the field where he saw Coach Woods already halfway to the sideline but risked running over to the fence, anyway.

"Good game so far," Bob said. "It's too crowded for Lacy to try to make it down this way, but she wanted me to give you this."

Andy took the small piece of paper that had been torn from the back of the game program.

When you roll right and the left receiver runs a fly pattern, that cornerback cheats to the middle of the field every time. Shorten your rollout and look back left and he will be wide open. You're doing great!

It was signed *"Lacy,"* and she had drawn a little heart by her name.

"Thanks, Mr. Hollingsworth. Tell Lacy thanks, too," Andy said as he ran to catch his team before Coach noticed him talking at the fence.

The second half began with Rockport taking the kickoff across midfield for what might have been their biggest play of the night. With their first play of the second half starting in good field position, the visiting crowd awakened! Cheers came from a different compass point to start the half, as Rockport's traveling crew had been silenced for most of the first half.

The Raiders halftime speech delivered by their coach must have been one for the records. Rockport came out looking like a different team. Two passes and a few runs later, they found paydirt, finally able to change the lights on their side of the scoreboard, which showed fourteen to seven.

A momentum swing was apparent. Members of the Tiger squad paced the sideline in silence as their opponents across the field came alive in celebration. But Coach Woods was alive, too, in a new way as he barked and stomped directions to his team like a drill sergeant that had just been given an assignment he didn't want.

The offense trotted back out, Andy still under center. The first play of the half looked promising. Toby took a handoff and raced for twenty-five yards. The crowd noise shifted again to the home side. The very next play, Andy rolled out to his right. His receiver was covered, but he remembered what Lacy had pointed out.

He looked back to his left. Coach had always told him not to throw across the field from a rollout, but there was Stiles, just like Lacy said, wide open. He launched the ball to Stiles, who caught it in stride and carried it inside the twenty-yard line.

It looked like momentum had found them again! It was short-lived; on the very next play, a short pass from Andy to Scott was caught but fumbled and recovered by Rockport.

That seemed to set the trend for the rest of the second half. Rockport found the answers to all of their first-half woes. Oak Creek did all of their scoring in the first five minutes and never found the end zone again, whereas Rockport was able to break the plane three more times and took the lead.

With the clock reading 0:38 seconds and Rockport up by a two-touchdown lead, defeat was starting to sink into the six seniors wearing blue and white. Underclassmen consoled their older teammates and cheerleaders cried as they watched the seconds tick away.

Andy's eyes held back the tears that he wanted to let flow, but he contained himself as much as possible. He trotted to the twenty-yard line, near the fence, and peered up at the home crowd. He saw faces that had watched him grow up.

Andy curled the four fingers of each hand over the tops of his extended thumbs and brought them together, forming a heart. He kissed the heart and then extended it toward the crowd as a tribute of his affection. He began a slow jog down the entire sideline, continuing the gesture until he reached the far end. Toby caught up with him and they embraced. Both boys gazed at the crowd, each of them with tears rolling down their faces, and did the same to the student section.

The final buzzer sounded, and it was over. No more games. No more grass stains. No more halftime speeches. It was over.

Both teams met at midfield and exchanged a show of sportsmanship, each squad congratulating the other. The players from Rockport were more energetic, but the Tigers held their heads high as they gathered in front of the student section to sing the alma mater one last time. With arms around each other and some embraced in hugs, they sang loud and took in the moment.

Andy looked to the fence at the fifty-yard line and spotted Lacy before the crowd became too thick. As he searched for a way to get to her, he realized that hardly anyone had left. Almost the entire home side remained, singing the alma mater with them. They applauded as the team walked back out on the field, saluting the faithful. It was as if each side—players, and spectators—were congratulating and thanking the other.

But that's what small towns do. They win together, and they lose together.

Finger-pointing was left to the ones that chose not to be a part of either side. But when the points didn't stack up right on their side of the board, they clung to one another and supported each other. That's when they needed it most. That's when they knew if it was still in their blood, or perhaps found out it never was.

Andy leaned over the fence and Lacy grabbed him, pulling him close. Their embrace was one not only of consolation but thankfulness. Lacy had brought Andy back to a good place in his life and for that, he was thankful. She had found Andy most peculiarly, but she felt he was a Godsend, and she felt the weight of the world come off her when he was around. Together, they found love in a way that they didn't expect—through a mutual sharing of their faith, one strong and one growing.

"Baby, I tried," Andy said as they released their embrace.

"You did a great job," she replied as she wiped a tear from his eye. "Don't ever think you didn't."

"I have to go to our team meeting. Can I meet you by the gym in about ten or fifteen minutes?"

"I'll wait as long as I need to."

Andy joined the rest of the team that had made their way up to the field house. Coach Woods stood in the doorway, motioning for the last few to come in.

"Come on in here, Andy," Coach said. "Can't make it last forever."

Andy continued into the locker room, where more hugs and consoling words took place. Coach came in and, as he always did, he found a way to pick the guys up. After all, the accomplishment was still a huge feat. But for some, seeing the prize so close at hand just to watch it slip away made the pain deeper.

As Coach wrapped up his talk, Andy walked outside, still in his uniform. He looked down at the field and the nearly empty stadium, with only a few remaining spectators slow to leave. He saw Lacy near the parking lot that separated the locker rooms and the field and headed that way.

"Gonna wear that uniform forever, superstar?" she said, trying to garner a smile.

"Maybe. What about you?" he replied, referring to his jersey.

"I hope so," she said.

Andy continued gazing down at the field. "Hard to believe it's over."

"Wanna go back down there? I'll go with you."

"Yeah, I do."

The two moved down the ramp to the field and out onto the grass. He walked to midfield and stood, gazing around and smiling. Lacy rubbed his back as he took it all in.

"Lots of blood, sweat, and tears were left out here," he said as a tear fell.

"But look at the memories you made. Not just for you, but for those that watched you. Folks will talk about Andy from Oak Creek for a long time."

"Yeah, about how he lost the game that they should have won."

"Babe, it wasn't just you on that field. It was a team effort," she reminded him. "You got to do what you love, and now God has new plans. Something bigger, I'm sure."

Andy smiled. "I guess so," he said. He took Lacy's hand and looked at her as more tears fell. "I've done many things out here, but there's one thing I've never done." Still holding her hand, he knelt on one knee. "Lacy, pray with me, please."

Lacy slowly kneeled, grimacing as her back brace kept her from bending. She nodded to let him know she was okay, and that he could begin his prayer whenever he was ready.

"You may have to help me. I'm still not great at this."

"Just talk, babe. That's all you do. Speak from your heart."

Andy bowed his head and started.

"God, thank You. Thank You for allowing me to play a sport that I probably wasn't grateful for. But You allowed me to, anyway. I didn't know how much I loved this, and I'm gonna miss it a lot. But You sent Lacy to get me in line for what You have in store for me. I need to ask you something now. Help me find a new passion. Something that drives me as much as football did. And let it be something that glorifies You through it. And Lord, please don't let me mess it up. Thank You. Amen!"

Andy stood and helped Lacy to her feet, gazing at her again.

"So, what now?" she asked.

"I'm not sure. I've learned a lot from Coach Woods. I think I can use some of that. But honestly, I'm excited about where God leads me now that I'm on a new team."

"I'm glad to have a new teammate," Lacy said, squeezing his hand tighter.

The two walked hand in hand to the edge of the playing surface. They stopped, and Andy looked around one more time. They were the only ones there. With a sigh of content, he turned again. Andy and Lacy stepped off the field together and suddenly, the lights in the stadium went out ... for the final time.

EPILOGUE

"For I know the plans I have for you," declares the LORD, "plans to prosper you and not to harm you, plans to give you hope and a future." (Jeremiah 29:11 NIV)

HAVE YOU EVER WONDERED, "WHAT IS GOD'S PLAN FOR ME?"

That scripture is a familiar phrase scribbled in many high school yearbooks, and you may even hear it spoken in commencement speeches. It is used in personal notes from friends when someone needs a little encouragement. Nothing encourages a heart quite like Jeremiah 29:11. But then there are those unwelcome circumstances, where hope feels like a distant dream.

We question God, "How can this be happening?"

Some push this verse aside and look for a different answer. Dread finds its way into our thoughts, and we feel like we're constantly fighting against it. We know God is with us in the midst of fear, but we still wonder. Could this trial really be part of His plan for us?

If you've ever struggled to trust God through life's hardest times, take heart. People throughout history have walked this road and discovered what it truly means to trust our Heavenly Father. It is then that we grow even more closer to our Savior.

When things happen that we can't control, we feel powerless. We long to follow God's plan, but how can we when all we see is vastness surrounding us? There's no paved road pointing the way, and no one there to offer a helpful word of advice.

Emptiness can be scary. It reveals our insecurities, tells us we are alone, and validates our fears. But with God, emptiness doesn't equal loneliness.

During those times when we don't have a clue which direction to go, we can let the stillness push away all distractions, so we sense God's presence more than ever. He will calm our anxious thoughts and give us the direction we seek.

"Your own ears will hear him. Right behind you a voice will say, 'This is the way you should go,' whether to the right or to the left." (Isaiah 30:21).

As a Christian, of course, you want to make decisions according to God's will. But what happens when you just don't know which way God wants you to go?

Sooner or later in life, everybody has to make some decisions. "Which college should I go to? Whom should I marry? Should I take this job offer? Should I move here or there?" The list goes on and on, and as the questions grow bigger and more life-changing, shouldn't God's answers and plan for our lives be clearer as well? If I want to do His will, shouldn't it be easier to see God's plan for me?

It can be difficult to see God's plan and know which road to take. You pray and ask for help, but there are often no prophetic dreams, visions, or strong feelings leading you one way or another. It can seem like God isn't answering you at all.

Many Christians struggle with this because we expect a loud voice from heaven when we talk to God, complete with trumpets and a burst of sunlight. But God doesn't necessarily work that way. Often, He works in whispers instead of shouts. And the way we practice listening is to go in faith and do everything before His face.

And then there are those times the answer is very clear, but we don't act on it. It isn't always so important what we do, but why and how we do it. Are you doing it wholeheartedly because you want to please the Lord? Or are there a few selfish reasons behind your decision?

God is more than willing to show us His will and plan for our lives, but He also wants us to show that we want to know it and follow it. He wants us to make an effort—to seek His will. Then He promises that we will find it. So if you're asking and seeking and knocking and doing everything as to the Lord, then you can rest assured that He will show you His will for your life. His will may not always be what we expect, and it can be revealed to us in unexpected ways, but if we're truly interested, we will find it.

So how do you make your decision? Ask yourself, "Is it good? Is it acceptable? Is it in favor of God?" If the answer seems to be yes, then do it! Prove what is God's will. Test it. He who seeks will find.

Whatever the outcome, when looking back, you may find that what you did was actually tainted with a bit of self-seeking, some demands on others, and so on. This was not according to God's will, and yet you made your decision in faith and with a desire to serve God. That's why God can now show you how you could have done it better, where you should have given up your own will.

Go back and fix things, ask for forgiveness, set things right. It is this that is God's will for us and His plan for our lives: that we learn humility, that we learn how to live as a disciple. The revelation comes unexpectedly—by showing you your mistakes—but because you're seeking to do God's will, you use it to be transformed. This is the renewing of your mind.

No matter where we go, we'll find opportunities to hear God's voice and do His will. We will find our anger, our pride, our stubbornness, and self-seeking, and by putting these things to death, we are transformed more and more into Jesus's image. In this way, we are doing God's will!

Ultimately, this is God's perfect plan for both you and me: that we become free from the way that we are and be transformed into Jesus's image. When we look in the right place for help with life's most stressful decisions, we can always find the answer, and then we can look back and be proud of what we did when the lights go out—possibly, for the last time.

9 780578 955346